YASMIN RAHMAN

ALL THE THINGS WE NEVER SAID

HOT KEY BOOKS

First published in Great Britain in 2019 by
HOT KEY BOOKS
80–81 Wimpole St, London W1G 9RE
www.hotkeybooks.com

A CIP catalogue record for this book is available
from the British Library.

ISBN: 978-1-4714-0829-8
also available as an ebook

1

Typeset by Palimpsest Book Production Ltd, Falkirk, Stirlingshire

Printed and bound in Great Britain by Clays Ltd, Elcograf S.p.A.

Hot Key Books is an imprint of Bonnier Books UK
www.bonnierbooks.co.uk

To Mum,
for just letting me get on with it.

1. MEHREEN

4th April

Bismillah hir-Rahman nir-Rahim . . .
In the name of Allah, the most gracious, the most merciful . . .

I take a deep breath and step onto the prayer mat, ready to
start the dawn prayers. As I mutter verses from the Quran
under my breath, I lose myself in the rhythm, letting the
Arabic flow through me, cleansing me from head to toe. Mum
is kneeling on the mat next to mine. As she turns her head
to the left, I see she's got a slight smile on her face, a visual
expression of the serenity that encapsulates her when she
prays. The same sense of serenity I yearn for every time I
pray.

My religion has always meant a lot to me. People make
fun of how much it dictates my life, but it's the only thing
that's kept me going so far. Sometimes, when the Chaos in
my brain is so loud that it feels like my head is about to crack
open, I *have* actually found some comfort in prayer. Not like
a ray of sunshine floating down or anything, but it . . . it
soothes me, drowns out the incessant voices in my head – for
a while, anyway. I can't really explain it. I guess I'm just a

1

no-questions-asked believer. I believe in God, I believe in heaven, I believe that the afterlife is what we should be preparing for, that it's the only place I'll find true peace.

Mum finishes her prayers and leaves the room, but I stay kneeling on the mat. It's said that dawn is the best time to ask for things, so I start a little personal prayer.

Allah,

I feel like there's something wrong with me: something completely and utterly unfixable. I just want to live a life where I don't keep being overwhelmed by sadness. Where I don't suddenly feel like someone has punched me in the gut and I can't breathe, can't think, can't see – when my head is so crammed with worry that I can't even focus on what I'm doing, who I'm with, or even whether I'm breathing. I'm fed up of feeling like this, of being continuously battered by what I call 'the Chaos'. I want my brain to slow down, to just . . . be normal. I need something to live for, Allah, because right now the only thing keeping me here is you. And I'm starting to feel like that's not enough.

As usual, I find myself so overcome with tears that I can't continue. I curl up on the prayer mat in the foetal position, squeezing my eyes shut, clenching all my muscles, trying to push away the darkness.

'Mehreen! Come down and eat!' My mother's voice is at the pitch that tells me this isn't the first time she's called. When I stand up, my body is stiff and the sun is blazing through the curtains. I wipe my face and compose myself before making my way downstairs.

In the kitchen, Mum is at her position by the sink, furiously scrubbing a pan and talking about some drama involving her family back in Bangladesh, while Dad sits at the head of the table, tapping away on his phone, paying no attention to her whatsoever. The Angry Birds theme tune hums quietly around the room. Imran is leaning against the counter near the toaster, also on his phone. I slip into the room, fix myself some cereal and sit down at the other end of the table.

No one looks up.

No one says anything.

They don't even notice when you're in the room.
THEY'RE BETTER OFF WITHOUT YOU.
They don't care about you.

I spoon some Shreddies into my mouth, feeling the hard ridges of the cereal poke and prod my cheeks and gums. I chew extra hard, trying to cover up the Chaos that's starting to seep through. The Angry Birds theme changes to the melody of having lost a life; Dad grunts, then lets the phone clatter to the table. Imran laughs as he butters his toast. I watch from the far end of the room as Mum dries her hands and touches Imran on the back to squeeze past him to the cupboard. She pulls out a plate and silently hands it to him. He sighs and drops the toast onto the plate before taking a seat next to Dad, who's picked up his phone again.

'Want me to do it?' Imran asks with his mouth full.

'Almost got it,' Dad mumbles. The lost-a-life tune plays a few seconds later. 'Dammit!'

Imran laughs, snatches the phone and starts tapping away.

Watching the three of them is like watching a totally normal family interacting. It's nothing momentous, what they're doing, but it's the little things that make a family a *proper* family.

Look how happy they are on their own.
THEY'RE BETTER OFF WITHOUT YOU.
No one would even notice if you were dead.

Mum's started chopping some vegetables on the counter. I drop my bowl in the sink, roll up my sleeves and grab the sponge.

'What're those marks on your wrist?' she asks, turning her head to look at me, the knife poised mid-slice. Her eyes are firmly fixed on my wrist.

There's a jolt in my chest. The heart I thought had become stagnant starts up again. Jumps straight into my throat.

This is it.

The moment I've been both dreading and hoping for.

I shake my arm to loosen my sleeve so that it rolls down and covers the scars, but it only slips down a little. My heart is thudding so hard I can feel it against my top.

I stare at her intently, hoping that she'll finally *see* me, that this pressure, this pain, will finally go. When I was a kid, Mum used to be able to fix everything with a few words and

4

a kiss; I've been secretly longing for her to do the same with whatever's happening in my head. But when she does finally make eye contact, nothing happens. There's no love on her face, no concern. Her brow is creased, her posture stiff.

'Did you get them from your bangles?' she asks, her eyes only lingering on my face for a second before returning to her chore. 'I told you to stop wearing such cheap jewellery.'

Of course she doesn't see. She doesn't realise because things like this don't exist for her. In her world, there's only sunshine and butterflies. No one ever hurts. No one ever feels the need to not exist. Everything is *perfect*.

'It wasn't a bangle,' I whisper, shaking the excess water off my bowl before placing it on the drying rack. I shove my sleeves down.

'Bangle, bracelet, same thing,' she says, chopping in Morse code. 'Why don't you use all that time you spend in your room to find a job instead? That way you could afford things that don't ruin your body.'

I stare at the knife as it moves up and down between her fingers, willing it to slip, wishing it were my skin beneath it.

'Who'd want to hire her?' Imran laughs from the table, his eyes still glued to Dad's phone. 'It's not like she's actually good at anything. Besides being a loser.'

He's right; you're such a loser.
No one will ever love you.
LOSER. LOSER. LOSER. LOSER.
They're better off without you.

5

I get that urge rushing through my body, that tight constriction in the middle of my chest, my wrists beginning to itch. There's already an image in my head of the trail of red, the sense of relief I'll achieve. I wrap my fingers around my wrist and squeeze.

Dad's phone lets out an upbeat melody and he whoops, patting Imran on the shoulder as he takes his phone to start the next level. Imran sits back in his chair, looking smug. His gaze moves to me, but before he can even start his next insult, I'm out of the room, up the stairs, slamming my bedroom door.

None of them care about you.
CUT. CUT. CUT. CUT.
YOU'LL FEEL BETTER.
They don't want you around.
CUT. CUT. CUT. CUT. CUT. CUT. CUT. CUT. CUT.

The need to cut is a physical thing. My wrists pulse, my heart races, my nails dig into my palms to try to quell the rage within me. But that's never enough. I'm not strong enough to resist. Weak and pathetic, that's me all over. Every time I do it, I hate myself, literally *hate* myself for doing that to my body. But once the thought enters my mind, there's no other way to get rid of it. So I kneel on the floor and take out the craft knife that's hiding under my mattress, like the loser I am.

You're so stupid. **WORTHLESS.**
No one would even realise if you weren't here.
LOSER. *CUT. CUT. CUT. CUT. CUT. CUT. CUT.* **JUST END IT ALL.**

When I'm done and have tidied everything up, I log on to my laptop, feeling completely spent. Cutting usually makes the Chaos quieten down for a bit; it's one of the only times I can actually think clearly.

I load up the website I haven't been able to get out of my head since I stumbled across it a few weeks ago. MementoMori.com – a website with a simple message on the homepage.

Fill out a questionnaire to be matched with a suicide partner and have a pact tailored to your needs.

It's like something clicked into place when I found this site. As if it had appeared to me as a sign. I've been thinking about suicide a *lot* recently, but I've also always felt that it was out of my reach. I may not be the best Muslim, but I know that suicide is a sin, that I'll regret it in the afterlife. The thing I crave most goes against my core beliefs. And as much as I try, I can't change my stance on that. But when I found MementoMori, I realised maybe there was a way out. What I needed was someone else to take away the guilt, take the blame. If I were to join MementoMori, then I wouldn't be the one responsible.

I've been visiting the website on a daily basis ever since. I downloaded the information pack, and have read through the questionnaire hundreds of times. I have my answers written, ready to be uploaded and submitted, ready for me to get this process started, to make it inevitable.

1. Full name
2. Age
3. Location
4. *Why do you want to die?*

It seems simple enough. Everyone should have a reason for wanting to die – otherwise why do it? But I haven't just got divorced, or lost a kid. I'm not being bullied and I'm definitely not pregnant. So why? Why do I feel like this? I've tried to answer the question so many times, but I can't get it to come out right. My words always sound whiny; I fear the matchmakers will read it and decide that I should just stick it out and wait for life to get better. And there's no way I can do that. So instead I delete the story I'd written about how I feel like I don't belong, how I feel invisible and inconsequential. I jab the backspace button on my laptop as hard as I can until the slate is blank once more. I decide that a shorter answer is probably better, and realise that my problems can be summed up in one simple sentence:

I can't handle the pain of being alive any more.

My wrist is pulsing again, my vision blurry from my tears. I hear Mum's laughter float up the stairs and think about her detached reaction to my scars. Without even rereading the rest of my answers, I upload my questionnaire to the website, click the box to accept their terms and conditions and press the submit button before the doubts can creep back in.

2. CARA

You'd think Mum would just go shopping without me, or leave me outside with the dogs on their leads. (I told her I could make a sign that says 'Hungry Disabled Orphan' and make a few quid, but she just rolled her eyes.) For some reason though, she forces me to go in every time, which means I have to be around other people. And I fucking hate other people.

I feel like a bloke being dragged clothes shopping by his girlfriend, having to wait outside the dressing room in that little space saved for men. Unfortunately there's no space reserved for people in wheelchairs. Most of the time there's barely enough room for me to go up the aisles. More than once I've knocked over a whole bunch of clothes, the fabric becoming trapped in my chair as I tried to escape.

'I need to grab that biology textbook for you,' Mum says as we leave yet another shop. 'We're starting digestion after the Easter hols, and I need to brush up on it myself before trying to teach you it.'

I say nothing.

'I saw this experiment idea on one of those home-schooling forums. We just need to get some baking soda and . . .'

I stop listening. Her yapping gets really fucking annoying

after a while. She thinks that by talking to me all the time she'll make me . . . not depressed or something. It's why she's always dragging me out, as if misery is stuck inside our house.

The sky is so dark it looks like it's about to start pissing it down again. I'm surprised Mum isn't already holding an umbrella over me. I keep my eyes straight ahead as I move towards the crossing. I can tell everyone who passes by is eyeballing me, whether it's a quick maybe-she-didn't-notice-me look or the braver I'll-stare-as-long-and-hard-as-I-want-to look that mostly comes from old women or little kids too young to be embarrassed. At the traffic lights, I reach out to push the button for the crossing, but a chubby woman with a dog gets there first.

'I'll get that for ya, darlin',' she says, practically shoving me out of the way.

She looks right at me as she presses the button, her eyes skimming over my face, over my wheelchair, settling on my body as she tries to diagnose me, tries to piece together my story.

I turn away, wishing she'd disappear, that her yappy fluff-ball would eat her up or at least bite her on the ankle so she'll stop giving me the pity face. She stands silently and I know she's waiting for me to thank her. For me to act like the damsel in distress I so obviously am.

I've mostly learned to tune people out. Learned not to bother putting up a fight. Stopped trying to make them see that while I might not be able to use my legs any more, I still have a functioning brain. That I'm still a person.

Or maybe I'm not. Maybe I'm only half a human now. (Paraplegic humour, get it?)

I ignore the woman and look straight ahead, wishing I had the courage to move forward right now, straight into the middle of the busy road.

But that wouldn't work; what kind of monster doesn't do an emergency stop for a cripple?

The woman's hovering so close I can smell the vinegar-laden chips she just ate. Her dog sniffs at my ankle, then the right wheel. He lifts his leg.

'Michael, no!' She tugs on the lead and jerks the dog back before he actually manages to piss. He whimpers. 'I'm so sorry!' she says. To Mum, not me. 'He's just a bit . . . over-friendly sometimes.'

'Oh, it's no problem,' Mum says. 'He's a cutie. What breed?'

Vinegar Lady launches into a full-blown conversation about her rat of a dog who's now sniffing at my feet again. I zone out, just listening to the slosh of the tyres on the wet road, the clatter as they go over grates. Wondering what it'd sound like if a car rammed into my chair.

Then Vinegar Lady is whispering, and I know she's talking about me. My disability. You'd think she'd be more subtle, especially since I'm right in fucking front of her. Of course Mum doesn't hesitate to give out the gory details.

'. . . car accident ten months ago . . .'

I try to block it out, block her voice out, block the whole world out, focus just on the pedestrian-crossing light. Why the hell hasn't it turned green yet?

'. . . paralysed from the waist down . . .'

11

The dog coughs or sneezes or farts by my feet and I look down at it. He's still sniffing around, nudging my loose shoe-lace with his nose. I tell my feet to give him a little kick, but of course they don't listen. He raises his leg again and starts pissing all over my white Converse.

I shoot forward, away from the pissing dog, away from my mother who can't stop talking about me as if I'm invisible, away from the stranger who thinks she has a right to know everything about me.

I'm on the road now and my heart's hammering, the adrenaline pumping. Cars roar around me and I know one's coming,

closer

closer

closer.

Brakes screech. I wait for Mum to shout, to come running after me, but none of that happens. Am I already gone?

I look to the right and the car is still. The people inside it are still.

It's silent.

And then . . .

BEEPbeepBEEPbeepBEEP.

The pedestrian light has turned green.

When we get home, Mum unloads the shopping while I throw my shoes away. She has to make three trips because she refuses to use the handles on my wheelchair to hang stuff, like I keep suggesting. I told her she could even put stuff on my lap and use me as a trolley, but she just rolled her eyes again. Not one for disability humour, my mother. My therapist, Dr Sterp, says jokes are a coping mechanism a lot of paraplegics adopt. I almost told him that a better coping mechanism would be death.

Almost.

I'm not an idiot; I know he'd tell Mum right away if I said anything suspicious. Lately our sessions have been filled with him talking about all these *inspirational* wheelchair users and me replying with light-bulb jokes.

'What about Jess Stretton?' he'll say. 'Won gold at archery at the Paralympics when she was your age.'

'How many actors does it take to change a light bulb?' I'll ask.

'She even has an MBE,' he'll say, ignoring me.

'One,' I'll say, ignoring him right back. 'They don't like to share the limelight.'

And so on until I run out of jokes or he runs out of examples.

There's no point trying to tell him that maybe I'm not as good a person as these celebrities. Maybe I'm not destined for great things. Maybe that accident should've been the end of me. He wouldn't understand. No one does.

Mum falls asleep on the sofa halfway through *EastEnders*, head flopping to the left, a line of drool down her chin. I listen to her snore for five minutes before deciding it's safe to make my escape. Being with her all day is harder than you'd think; she's like a toddler bursting with energy, trying to get me to play when it's literally the last thing I want to do. I've probably got a half-hour, if I'm lucky, before she wakes up and freaks out that I'm not right by her side.

I go to the bathroom. One of the *many* things people take for granted is just dropping their pants and pissing. I position myself near the toilet and lock my wheels. After moving myself to the edge of my chair, I reach out and place one hand on the toilet seat while keeping the other on my armrest. Then I push myself up and try to pivot my body over onto the toilet seat. My palm slips and I lose my balance, knocking my elbow against the toilet as I tumble down. My cheek slaps against the tiled floor as I land with a thud.

'Shit!' is all I manage to say as the pain shoots through my body. I try to sit up, to roll myself into a more comfortable position, but there's no such thing, just stinging pain all over. All I can do is lie here, waiting for Mum to wake up. For her to pick me up, place me in the tub and clean up the piss that's beginning to pool under my body.

Fucking kill me now.

'Are you sure you don't need anything else?' Mum asks, covering me with the duvet, as if my arms don't work either.

I snatch the material out of her hand. 'I'm *fine*. I just want to sleep.' The soap on my skin reeks of incompetence.

She looks at me for a few seconds before patting my hand and standing up. 'OK, well, shout if you need anything.' She turns the light off and hovers until I settle down under the duvet, wrapping it around myself and closing my eyes.

I force my tears back inside and wait until she goes off towards the living room. As soon as I hear the TV turn on,

I grab my laptop from the bedside table. The sudden brightness of my screen makes my eyes burn and the tears start coming. Pouring, gushing, burning, weak tears. I pull the duvet over myself so Mum doesn't hear me sniffling.

I wipe my nose with the back of my hand and google 'find a suicide partner'. The screen is filled with news articles about dead people and blogs trying to convince me that 'suicide isn't the solution'. The phone number of a charity pops up at the top. As if the Samaritans would understand what I'm going through. I scroll through a few pages of the search results until I find a forum filled with posts from people like me. I read a few of the messages, my tears falling faster and harder when I find one from someone else in a wheelchair.

Amy123: Sun Jan 22 15:53:50
Hi. Looking to die asap. Need someone with a foolproof plan. I can't deal with being in this wheelchair any more. I'm just a burden to everyone and they're better off without me.

I click to reply, but then realise the post is from months ago. Amy123 is probably dead by now. I think about posting my own message, but judging by how few people have replied to previous threads, there's no point. I need a website that's fast and reliable. I go back to the search results and keep scrolling and clicking, to the pages no one ever bothers going down to. I find a website called MementoMori.com. The description reads: *'Fill out a questionnaire to be matched with a suicide partner and have a pact tailored to your needs.'*

A matchmaking service for suicide partners? PERFECT!

This way there's none of that awkward choosing. They'll find someone for me who will *have* to help. That's all I need – just someone to physically help me do it. I feel my heart racing as I click on the link. The website looks like a five-year-old has designed it: pitch-black background, Comic Sans everywhere and a menu bar that's off centre. I can't decide whether it's a joke or whether it's genius – make the website so disgustingly unprofessional that if someone official found it, they'd never think anything of it.

I download the zip file containing an information pack, which I ignore, and a questionnaire, which I begin filling in. I know I should read more about it or whatever, but I'm a real believer in intuition and this website's giving out amazing vibes. Maybe it really is my ticket out of here.

3. OLIVIA

There's a new photo on the mantelpiece.
It sits directly centre;

the smaller frames   pushed to each side so
there's nothing in the vicinity   of this new addition.

In the photo, Mother's hair is down and curled. Her style of
choice for special occasions: dinner parties,

galas,

dates.

Her smile S T R E T C H E S across the picture.
Her head on *his* shoulder.
His arm wrapped around her.
His fingers digging into her arm.
His mouth forming an easy smile.

I pick up the frame. Run my fingers over the sharp corners.

I want to **SLAM** it to the ground. To hear the glass

C   A   K
R   C

against the wooden floor, see the tiny pieces splinter

far   and   wide.

I want to take out the photo and *riiiiiiiiiiiiiiiip* it to shreds.
Set them on fire and **burn** that smile off his face.
  'It's beautiful, isn't it?' Mother asks from the doorway.
  I place the frame back on the mantelpiece, ensuring it's
placed perfectly

>   centre
>   and
>   straight.

  'Just lovely,' I tell her.

We sit down for supper. The smell of lobster permeates the
room as Maria brings the plates in. It's a special occasion,
according to Mother.
He sits at the

H

E

A

D

of the table, <u>*in Daddy's seat.*</u>
I've already had three glasses of champagne. It's a *special
    occasion* after all.
I'm still not drunk enough.

I can still see straight,
            see the way she l
                        e
                            a
                                n
                                    s into him when he
talks, the way she pushes her food around on the plate, no
doubt still stinging from the comment he made about her
weight last week.

He kisses her on the neck.

I pour another glass.

She giggles. Shoots a glance my way. Reminds him that they've
got company.

Company.

I've lived here my whole life and *I'm* the company.

He looks over at me.

I   my head, focusing on the mush on my plate.
  duck

He suggests she tell me the news.

My head **SNAPS** up.

The champagne hits. Makes my head *spin*.

I force myself to look over at her.

                    Fuzzy-faced,
                            oblivious
                                    Mother.

I ask her what news he's talking about.

To her credit, she looks mildly uncomfortable, fiddling with
her pearl necklace.

He reaches over and squeezes her fingers, that **disgusting**
smile

S P R E A D I N G

across his face.

He encourages her to go on.

She straightens her back.

Clears her throat.

She tells me that they've been dating for a while now.

As if I didn't know.

As if I wasn't aware of the

preposterous

amount of time they've been spending together,

the amount of time *he's* spent in my presence.

She says it's time they **took the next step**.

No.   **No.**

No.   **No.**

No.   **No.**

I look up at her.

Pleading.

Begging.

Wishing.

She proudly tells me the lease on his flat is up.

They've rented a van to bring his stuff over.

Next week.

He looks at me.

Smirks.

Winks.

We're going to be roomies, he tells me.

The glass

S H A T T E R S

in my hand.

Champagne goes everywhere.

It's a special occasion after all.

The glass

CUTS

into my fingers.

into my palm.

The sound of cracking glass slices through the silence.
'Oh, Olivia!' Mother chides. 'That's a crystal flute!'
'You really should be more careful, Liv,' he says.

LIV.   **He calls me Liv.**

Maria rushes over dutifully, dustpan and brush in hand.
She tries to smile at me as she clears away the mess, but all
I can focus on is the shard of glass in my hand.

I want to place it against my throat and drag it along

s   l   o   w   l   y

To feel my skin slice open.

                        Y
                      A
                    R
                  P
To watch the blood S   P   R   A   Y
                  P
                    R
                      A
                        Y over everything.

To see it stain the lace tablecloth Mother gets dry-cleaned
every fortnight.

I want to take the glass and **stab** it into my chest
OVER
AND
OVER
'Olivia?' Mother asks, when Maria's out of the room again.

When the mess is gone.

Her brow is creased and I know she's waiting, watching.

But not too closely.

Never   closely   enough.

God forbid she see the truth.

'Congratulations,' I manage to say. 'That's great.'

'Isn't it just?' She puts her hand on his again.

His eyes are on me though.

'You OK, Liv?'

LIV.   **He calls me Liv.**

'Can I be excused, please?'

She doesn't even ask why,

doesn't notice the alteration in my breath,

can't hear the *pounding* in my chest.

She's got what she needed.

We're going to be roomies.

In my bedroom, I unclench my fist, noting the thin, dry trail of red with sadness.

I put the shard of glass to one side

and pull out my laptop.

I open up a Word document.

The list I've been compiling for months.

The list that was supposed to be just a fantasy,
but is now my only option.
~~Line upon line of crossed out websites.~~
Websites where the most hopeless people reside.
People
like
me.
DESPERATE
for a way out.
I click on the first uncrossed website.
MementoMori.com
Please let this be the one.

4. MEHREEN

5th April

'What are you doing here?' Calliope asks as she slides into the chair to my left. 'Aren't Asians supposed to be smart?'

'That's a terrible stereotype,' I reply, shoving the piece of paper I was doodling on underneath my book. 'And you've got the wrong type of Asian.'

I'm hoping this will be the end of it – that she'll go and sit elsewhere, leave me in peace, but instead she takes out her biology textbook and drops it on the table with a thud. She follows this up with an assortment of pens, pencils, rulers and a whole host of other stationery that is utterly superfluous for a single study session.

'Well, at least I have someone to sit with,' she says, placing her phone carefully on the table. 'Can you *believe* they're making us do this in the Easter holidays? That's, like, child abuse.'

'Uh-huh,' I say, reluctantly moving my books and single pen to the side to make space for her stuff.

'Pascha's gone to France and we're stuck at school. *Studying*. This is the worst.' She throws her head back and groans.

'It's only one day.'

'Yeah, but one day of *science*.' She makes a face. 'There's a reason we're failing – because it's the worst, most pointless subject ever.'

'Can't say I disagree.' I slip my phone out from my pocket just enough to see the screen.

No new emails.

It's been twenty-four hours since I signed up to MementoMori. Surely they should have matched me by now?

MAYBE YOUR APPLICATION WAS SO PATHETIC THEY THOUGHT IT WAS A JOKE.
No one even wants to die with you.

I slip my phone back into my pocket and focus on my breathing, like I do every time I feel a panic attack approaching. I read on a therapy website that you're supposed to visualise your lungs expanding and deflating.

'Are you OK?' Calliope asks after a second.

Before I can answer, the door opens and Mr Parker walks in, evidently just as pleased to be here as we are. I shoot Calliope a strained smile before turning to face the front.

CALLIOPE ONLY SAT THERE OUT OF PITY.
You're going to fail all your GCSEs anyway.
MUM WAS RIGHT – YOU'LL NEVER BE AS CLEVER AS AUNT NADIYA'S SON.
SO WHAT'S THE POINT?
WHAT'S THE POINT? WHAT'S THE POINT?

While Mr Parker's back is turned, I slip my headphones under my headscarf and into my ears, pushing the volume as high as it can go without anyone else noticing. Music and prayer are the only two things that help calm me; well, other than cutting. The thrashing of the guitar starts up, vibrating into my eardrums, slowly painting over the Chaos. I slide out my doodling paper to continue sketching. I've drawn Death again, but this time instead of a black-cloaked figure with a scythe, it's my mother. I draw a frame around the sketch, turning it into a panel, and give Mum a speech bubble. Before I can write anything, I feel an elbow in my side. I shove the drawing under my textbook; if Calliope ever saw the dark stuff I draw in my comics, she'd tell everyone I'm crazy. I turn to her when my paper is fully hidden, but she's not even looking at me; her face is still turned towards the front, where Mr Parker stands staring right at me. I quickly straighten my posture, heart now pounding to the beat. I sneak my fingers under my scarf and tug on the cord until the buds pop out of my ears.

'Well, Mehreen?' Mr Parker asks.

'Sorry, sir,' I say immediately.

He tuts, which makes my heart pound harder.

'Surprisingly, "Sorry, sir" is *not* a type of tissue,' he says drily.

Calliope snorts, trying to cover it up by scratching her nose.

I stare at Mr Parker, stuttering for something to say, waiting for him to end this awkwardness. I can feel everyone gawping at me and I want to dissolve. Just completely disappear.

They're all laughing at you. THEY HATE YOU. EVERYONE THINKS YOU'RE AN IDIOT. NO ONE WILL EVEN NOTICE WHEN YOU'RE DEAD.

Mr Parker sighs and says, 'I think it's time we had a break. I need coffee.' He's out of the room before any of us have a chance to move.

I want to shove my headphones back in, to stomp down the Chaos that's pushing its way through again, but Calliope turns to face me and I can tell she wants to talk. I take out my phone and place it on the desk while I untangle myself from the headphones.

'Wanna come over to mine Friday night?' she asks. 'Having some people round, but definitely *not* a party. My parents told me to make sure everyone knows that.' She rolls her eyes.

She's only inviting you out of politeness or pity. YOU LOOK THAT PATHETIC. She doesn't want you at her party. SHE PROBABLY REGRETS SITTING NEXT TO YOU.

'So, you in?' she asks, looking right at me now.

I try to read her face, to gather whether this is a genuine invitation or whether she's just asking for the sake of making conversation. I'd classify Calliope as a friend, but only in the technical definition; we sit together in class, pair up for group work, she passes me the ball in PE sometimes, but there's always been this barrier between us – well, between me and everyone else in school. It's like all of us are pretending. Pretending to be nice, pretending to be normal. It's tough keeping up this facade, but it's the only way to get by.

I suddenly realise I haven't replied to Calliope.

Say something to her!
Why can't you have a normal conversation?
WHY CAN'T YOU BE NORMAL?

Thankfully, before I can answer, my phone vibrates on the table and an email alert pops up.

1 new email from MementoMori.com

28

5. CARA

There's this stupid cliché of waking up in the morning and forgetting, just for a few seconds, about the terrible thing that's happened or is happening to you. It's a standard shot in films; the beautiful, sleepy girl rolls over under her bright white duvet, with a smile, of course. She reaches over to the bedside table for her phone and her fingers clutch at the air. That's when it hits her. The table isn't there because she's not in her bedroom. She's stuck in a hospital with beeping machines and itchy bed-sheets and the pinch of an IV digging into her arm.

I hate that cliché, I really do. But what I hate more is that it's based on truth. I've become that disgusting cliché – a fact that might even be more depressing than the disability itself. Ten months after the accident, I still find myself waking up and trying to kick the covers off, only to find I can't. I still turn to the left, expecting to see the clouds through the skylight in my attic bedroom, but finding the garden instead, from my new bedroom on the ground floor – aka the old dining room. I still sometimes wake up with that same sense of excitement I used to have before everything went to shit.

But today . . . today there actually *is* some excitement in my sad little life.

I reach over to the bedside table, grab my phone and bring it back into bed with me. As I'd hoped, I have an email. From the lovely people at MementoMori.com. There's that weird flutter in my chest – the one I used to get when Sarah McConnell walked past me in school or when Ansel Elgort teased new music on his Instagram. It makes me feel like getting out of bed, and it's been a long time since anything's made me feel like that.

I open up the email, expecting a long detailed message about how this is gonna go down, but instead there's just a few lines.

From: Administrator (admin@mementomori.com)
To: Cara Saunders (SpaghettiCarbonCara@gmail.com)
Subject: RE: Your application to MementoMori

Cara Saunders,

You have been matched with:

- Olivia Castleton
- Mehreen Miah

First meeting: 5th April – 4 p.m. at St Christopher's Church Graveyard, Bridgeport BP8 2HD

Upon arrival, all participants must access the MementoMori website, so ensure there is a device present.

I refresh my inbox over and over, thinking there must be a follow-up email or an attachment or something, but there's nothing else. I open up the confirmation email I got last night after filling in the questionnaire, but that's just another bare-bones message with no details about how or when we're going to do it. I was promised a personalised suicide pact plan, but right now, all I've got are the names of some people who could be made up for all I know. Is there a customer-service helpline for suicide-pact websites? Cos I wanna complain so fucking bad right now.

According to Google, the church is pretty close. It'll take me ten minutes to walk there – ha! See what I mean about those moments of forgetfulness (or should I say delusion)? Let me correct myself, it'll take me ten minutes to *get myself over there*. And that's not even the hardest part . . . How the fuck am I going to get away from Mum?

There's a creak in the hallway outside my room as I'm getting dressed.

'Cara, honey, I thought we agreed no closed doors?' Mum presses down on the handle and pops her head in, eyes already wide and scanning my body. I put on an over-the-top smile as I push my right arm through the T-shirt sleeve.

'Sorry,' I say sweetly. 'Just habit, I guess.'

There's a flicker of surprise in her eyes; she was probably expecting me to bite her head off, like I really want to. But instead I smile so much my cheeks ache.

'Oh,' she stutters, pushing the door fully open. 'Um, well, I made French toast for breakfast.'

'Sounds amazing!' OK, maybe that was too much . . .

There's another pause – Mum must be trying to decide whether I'm having a breakdown or whether she's dreaming this whole thing.

'OK, great!' she chirps. 'Do you need any hel—' She cuts herself off, probably remembering our most recent family-therapy session. Dr Sterp likes to set us tasks and Mum is a proper teacher's pet. Her homework this week is to stop asking that question.

Normally at this point I'd go off on one at her and then we'd eat breakfast with me sitting in silence and her rabbiting on brightly to herself.

'I'm good,' I reply instead. Another big smile, this time with teeth.

Mum actually almost stumbles back at this. I move towards the door, towards her. Would a hug be too obvious?

'This toast is soooooo delicious,' I say with my cheek full of over-eggy mess.

'Oh, thanks. I used brown sugar, just how you like it.' She sips her coffee. 'So what should we do today? Lunch and the cinema? Or how about that new pottery-painting place?'

How's about you let me off the leash for a couple of hours so I can go and plan my suicide with some strangers off the Internet?

It's on the tip of my tongue.

'Um, actually –' I start.

'Ooh, I think there's a fête on in town. Or is that next week? Hmm . . .' She goes over to the fridge, where she keeps tons of leaflets under magnets from all the places she's

32

dragged me to post-accident. She flicks through the adverts, muttering dates to herself.

'Mum,' I say after a deep breath, 'I was actually hoping . . . I could go out today.'

'Yes, sweetheart, I'm sure I remember something about a fête, let me just find –'

'No,' I say, straightening up. 'I meant alone.'

She whips her head round, her hand slipping enough to knock off a dolphin-shaped magnet from the Sea Life Centre. 'Alone?'

'Yeah, I think I'm ready. I mean –' I push my shoulders back so much they hurt, and lock eyes with her (all signs of confidence according to my physical therapist) – 'I *know* I'm ready.'

'Sweetheart, I don't think –'

'Dr Sterp said I should get out more.'

'I don't think he meant . . . alone. Cara, honey, you're not read—'

'I just told you I am!' I push against the table so hard the dishes clink; some juice slops out of the glass.

Mum gasps a little and I snap back into focus. 'Sorry,' I say, forcing the word out of my mouth. I wipe the spilt juice with my sleeve.

'Look, Mum,' I say, 'it's been ten months. I feel like I should be allowed to do some things by myself. I want to get some independence back. You're kinda cramping my style.'

My plan works; she laughs a little.

'I get it,' I continue. 'You're just looking out for me, and um . . . thank you . . . for that. I appreciate it. But you can't keep me wrapped up in cotton wool. I need to . . . I need to find more people like me. I need to be with people who understand what I'm going through, who feel the way I do, who want the same things as I do.'

People like Mehreen Miah and Olivia Castleton.

'I understand that, sweetie. I do.' She plops down in the chair next to me and puts her hand over mine on the table. 'But you're just so . . . fragile right now. I mean, look what happened last night . . .'

Fragile. Fucking fragile. I'm not a fucking snowflake.

'Remember the doctors suggested joining a support group?' I ask, stopping myself from yanking my hand away from hers. 'Well, I found one. That's where I want to go today.'

'A support group?' she asks. I can't figure out whether she's happy or sad or angry.

'There's a meeting today at four, at a church downtown. I just . . . I want to do this alone.'

'Which church?'

'St Christopher's. I can get there myself – you don't need to drive or anything.'

'How long will the meeting last?'

I shrug. 'I dunno. It doesn't matter. Mum. *Please*. I'm ready. I am.'

She doesn't say anything, but she squeezes my hand and rubs my wrist with her thumb. I force myself to look into her eyes, waiting for the moment of judgement. Of course she's going to say no, she's going to tell me to take a long hard look at myself, that I can't even go to the toilet on my own let alone a support group.

'OK,' she eventually says with a nod.

'Really?!'

'Yes, really.' She smiles. 'You're right, Dr Sterp and I have been begging you to go to a support group, so now that you're . . . ready, I'm not going to stop you. Of course I'm not.' She squeezes my hand again and the feeling goes straight to my chest.

'Great. Thanks, Mum . . . I knew . . . you'd und—'

'I'll come with you. They let anyone in to these things, right?'

'Wait – what? No! It's fine. I can –'

'This is a big step you're taking, sweetheart. You need some support.'

'That's why I'm going to a *support group.*'

She laughs. She *actually* laughs.

'I'm serious, Mum.'

'Sweetheart, you can't –'

'Here we go again!' I half shout, finally yanking my hand away from hers. *'No, Cara, you can't do that, you'll hurt yourself. No, Cara, you can't do that, you're not strong enough.'* I mimic her to the point she actually looks away, biting her lip. 'I'm fed up, Mum. *So* fed up of being told that I can't do things any more. I'm fed up of you treating me like I'm about to break.'

'I'm only doing it because –'

'I *know.* I know you're doing what you think is best for me, but, Mum, this is *my* life we're talking about. *I'm* the one who has to live it. Not you, not Dr Sterp or any of the other doctors. You guys . . . none of you has *any* idea what it's like. But the people in this group do.'

She looks down at her fidgeting fingers in her lap and I can tell from her watery eyes that she's on the verge of giving in.

'I can't stay like this forever, Mum,' I say quietly. 'Baby steps, as Dr Sterp would say.'

She smiles. 'No pun intended?' she says in response, like I usually do.

'No pun intended.' I nod.

She leans across and wraps an arm around me, squashing so tight I feel like I might puke up her gross French toast. I let her get on with it, even patting her on the back.

'Baby steps,' she whispers with her snotty nose in my hair. 'I can do that.'

6. OLIVIA

We're meeting at *a cemetery.*
I can't help but laugh at the *irony*.
Me and
      Mehreen Miah
           and
               Cara Saunders.
Mother would say those are ***strong*** names,
lots of vowels.

        We're *meeting* **at a cemetery.**

Cemeteries are strange,
when you really think about it.
Walking over
        the **dead**.
Weeping over
          slabs of stone sticking   out   the
                      of   ground.
Funerals are strange too.
The wailing.
      The black.
         Everyone staring at a body in a box.

The body.

Why anyone would want people to *stare* at their **corpse**
is beyond me.

The body is a husk,
    a vessel to carry consciousness,
        and sometimes not even that.

The body is just **a thing.**
3 layers of skin.
206 bones.
Nerves and cells and tissues and organs.
But all in all
        completely useless.

      It's what's inside that counts, they say.

    No. Not even that.
    NOTHING
     counts

N   O   T   H   I   N   G

The body is a means to an end.
The knee bone's connected to the shin bone.
The shin bone's connected to the ankle bone.
The ankle bone's connected to the foot that lets me move.
  Out of my bedroom,

down the hallway,
ignoring
the giggling coming from the master bedroom.

Down
  down
    down
      down
        down
          the stairs.

Will this be the last time?
What's in store for me at the cemetery?
Will today be the day?

There's a *waft* of cinnamon as I walk into the kitchen.
The *sizzzzzle* of the waffle maker.
A general air of domesticity.

Maria dances from
counter   to   counter
muttering the lyrics to a rap song
        under her breath,
conducting a symphony with her spatula.

There's a **THUD** upstairs.
Maria reaches over to her iPod and,

raises the**volume.**

Maria is the closest thing I have to a
best friend/~~parent~~.
She's the one who makes me soup when I'm ill,
it's *her* room I used to *sneak* in to when I'd had a **bad** dream,
she's the one who taught me how to use tampons.

If I could tell anyone about what's happening to me,
I'd tell her.

But she wouldn't
        /shouldn't
        /doesn't

care.

She's just *the help*.
So instead of confiding in her,
(even though I'm bursting to tell someone
about the two strangers I'm going to die with –
                        about Mehreen Miah
                        and Cara Saunders)
I walk up to the counter
and ask,
    'Can we make croissants?'

7. MEHREEN

The graveyard is empty when I arrive. I was hoping there'd be some fog – that I'd walk into a sea of white mist, with the tops of the headstones just peeking out. It would've made a really apt atmosphere. Instead, it's just an average cloudy day.

Is this a SIGN you're doing the WRONG thing? You should just turn around and go home. THIS IS A SIN - YOU'LL GO TO HELL. NOTHING EVER GOES RIGHT FOR YOU.

I'm early. I check my email for the thousandth time, still expecting to see a message declaring this whole thing a joke, a set-up by some sadist. Or even the two other girls messaging to say they're backing out. I can't stop wondering what these people will be like. What if they're racists? Or just horrible people? I guess that's the point. I don't have a say any more. When I signed up, that's exactly what I was looking for – for someone to take the control out of my hands, to stop me from having to worry about the how/when/what/where.

And look how well that's working out.

*

41

I occupy myself by walking up and down the rows of graves, trying not to visualise the state of the bodies, trying not to think that soon I'll be like them. The headstones vary in size and colour; moss covers the full name on a low rectangular one, so that it just reads 'Rest In Peace'; a tiny white stone depicts the short life of Elizabeth Morgan, and there's even one shaped like a book.

I feel a drop of water on my nose and look up into the grey sky; it's a lot darker now, the clouds looking fit to burst any moment. Still no fog, unfortunately. But the looming rain does have a slightly ominous feel. I look to my left and see a girl in a wheelchair coming up the path towards me. I check the time. 3.58 p.m. Is this one of them? Cara Saunders? Or Olivia Castleton? Or just someone here to grieve for their dead relative?

She looks about my age; her brown hair spills over both shoulders and flicks out a little as she keeps turning her head to look behind her, as if she's being chased. I wait for her by the grave of Timothy Linnighan, who died doing what he loved, apparently. The girl looks up and we lock eyes. I instinctively straighten my posture. This is how I imagine a blind date would be; I feel the need to impress her.

There's no point trying to impress her.
SHE'S GOING TO HATE YOU ANYWAY.

The girl looks back towards the gates one last time and then she's in front of me. My eyes automatically go south, noting the way her thin legs are squeezed together, noting her beaten-up, dirty black Converse shoes and the way her chair looks unscathed in comparison. There's a click as she pulls up to a stop and I force my eyes to focus on her face; her gaze pierces me.

'Are you Mehreen?' she asks tentatively.

'Uh, yeah,' I say. 'Are you . . . Cara? Or . . . Olivia?'

'Cara,' she says with a nod. She holds out her hand and I stand momentarily still. She laughs. 'Don't worry, my hands do work.'

'Oh! No, no,' I say far too quickly. 'I wasn't –'

'I was kidding,' she says. 'Trying to break the ice, I guess.'

'Oh, right,' I reply. 'Sorry, I didn't mean to stare.' I can't even meet her gaze any more.

YOU JUST COMPLETELY INSULTED HER!
She must think you're a *TOTAL IDIOT.*

'It's fine,' she sighs. 'Now, are you seriously gonna leave me hanging?'

I gasp a little.

'Ha! Hanging.' She laughs again and I can't take my eyes off her. 'Didn't even realise.' The way she's talking, joking, seems like . . . like someone who wouldn't sign up to MementoMori. She stretches her hand out further and I finally take it, wrapping my fingers around it and squeezing. There's a faint rustling behind me. Cara and I both turn to find a thin blonde girl in a plaid skirt and white blouse walking

43

towards us. I take another look around the graveyard to make sure we don't have an audience.

'Hello,' the blonde girl says as she reaches Timothy's grave. She has a posh accent – she sounds like the people in the northern part of the town. She's also carrying a large handbag on her shoulder, and for some reason I half expect a Chihuahua to poke its head out.

'I assume you're Mehreen Miah?' the new girl says, looking at me.

I nod, and before I know it, she's got her fingers on my forearm and is leaning in. I tense and suck in a breath as she presses her cheek to mine and makes a kissing sound. She pulls back and repeats the action on my other cheek.

I watch Cara's eyes bulge to impossible levels as Olivia leans down and repeats the motions on her.

'It's lovely to meet you both,' Olivia says when she straightens up again. 'Oh! I brought gifts.'

'Gifts?' Cara and I echo in unison. We share a quick look before returning our open-mouthed stares to Olivia, who's now rummaging through her giant handbag. Before I can even begin to wonder what gift would be appropriate to bring to a suicide-pact meeting, Olivia whips out a clear cellophane-wrapped bundle, with a ribbon wrapped around the neck.

'Freshly baked croissants,' she announces with a huge smile.

'Um . . . thanks?' I say, slowly taking the package from her, the cellophane crinkling under my fingers.

'Mother says to always bring a welcoming gift when you first meet someone,' Olivia explains as she hands Cara her package.

Cara furrows her eyebrows as she accepts the gift, sniffing it before letting it fall onto her lap. Olivia looks from her to me, the smile still plastered to her face. Everything about her is so put together; it's weird seeing this girl with her designer handbag and sparkly clean clothes standing in a graveyard wanting to kill herself. Even weirder that she thinks this is a croissant-worthy moment.

Cara's watch beeps, making me jump. I take another look around the graveyard to ensure it's empty.

'It's four,' Cara says, looking down at her wrist. 'We should probably get started.' She looks over to me, as if I'm the one in charge, but I just nod.

'I've got my iPad,' Olivia says, rummaging once more in her Mary Poppins bag. She pulls the tablet out with a flourish and unlocks it. She types away for a couple of seconds and her eyebrows furrow.

'What's wrong?' I ask, craning my head. 'Are you on MementoMori?' It's weird saying the name out loud. To real people.

Olivia turns the device around; the screen is black with three equidistant white circles running horizontally. 'We have to put our fingers on at the same time,' she explains, looking at each of us in turn before placing her index finger on the left circle.

I take a step forward and press my finger in the middle.

'Sure they don't want us to cut our fingers first? Like a blood pact or some shit?' Cara asks, inching herself forward.

I might be imagining it, but when all our fingers are on the circles it feels like there's a jolt of electricity. There's a

45

flash of white on the screen, and the suddenness of it makes me pull away. A message appears, bright white words appearing on the black background like letters from a typewriter. Slowly the letters spell out our names. Goosebumps erupt all over my skin, and I get the weird feeling that we're being watched, but I don't want to look away from the screen. In fact, I don't think I can.

Olivia Castleton
Mehreen Miah
Cara Saunders

Date of Termination: 18th April
Location: Bossfort Beach, Bridgeport BP8 4TG
Method: Respiratory impairment from submersion in and inhalation of water

You will meet regularly at predetermined times and locations. MementoMori will provide you with a task at each meeting, to help you prepare for the Termination. You must submit photographic evidence of having completed these tasks **together** before the next meeting.

Task 1: Suicide notes are a way to ensure your last words are meaningful. Write individual suicide notes to leave behind when the time comes.

Next meeting: 8th April, 10 a.m.

Location: Westgate Shopping Centre, Bridgeport BP5
1UH

**Reminder: MementoMori requires all users to
complete tasks <u>together</u>; otherwise no further
assistance will be provided. Failure to adhere to
our rules and regulations will result in further
action, as stated in our terms and conditions.**

8. CARA

Writing suicide notes. Seriously? I signed up for a suicide pact, not a bloody creative-writing class. I can't help but feel pissed off at all this faff – the meetings, the tasks. Why is this website forcing us to do all this stuff? Why can't it just let us get on with it?

Mehreen and Olivia's eyes are still glued to the iPad. I can't tell whether they're really slow readers or they weren't expecting this either.

'What do they mean?' Mehreen asks quietly. '*Respiratory impairment from submersion in and inhalation of water?*' She looks up at Olivia and I swear she's on the verge of tears. Great, I *would* get stuck with a cry-baby.

'Drowning,' Olivia replies matter-of-factly. 'They want us to drown ourselves.' All said with no emotion whatsoever.

'How original.' I roll my eyes. 'I was hoping for something cooler.'

'Cooler?' Mehreen asks.

'Yeah,' I reply, fiddling with the hem of my T-shirt so I won't have to look at her cry-baby eyes. 'I mean, wouldn't it be awesome to be . . . attacked by a shark? Or eat Krispy Kremes until we burst? Or y'know, something different. Drowning is so *lame.*'

Olivia laughs. 'I don't think there are sharks at any English coasts. And is it even possible to eat yourself to death? I assume you'd just vomit, maybe then choke . . .' She trails off, as if she's actually considering the technicalities of it, and this makes me laugh out loud.

'Is that really how you'd do it?' Mehreen asks me. 'I mean, if you had the choice . . .' She doesn't finish, as if scared to say the rest.

I shrug. 'I can't decide on a favourite method. I just want something so bizarre that everyone talks about it for years. Like that guy who took out his own intestines and hung himself with them. That'd be awesome, right?'

As I expected, Mehreen's eyes pop. It makes me want to keep pushing her buttons to see how far I can go.

'What about you?' I ask her. 'How did you wanna do it? Have you tried before?'

'Um, no, I haven't tried yet,' she says, tugging at her sleeves. 'I mean, I've been thinking about it for ages,' she adds quickly. 'Like, just constantly really. As for how . . .' She pauses for a second, looks up at the sky, closes her eyes, then continues quietly, but confidently. 'I wanted to fly.' There's a small smile on her face as she opens her eyes and looks back down at me. 'There's this building in town, seventy floors, tallest in Bridgeport. I wanted to jump.'

'Sounds painful,' Olivia says.

'Not to burst your bubble,' I say, 'but I don't think any method of dying is pain-free.'

Mehreen's head snaps up, and the discomfort on her face gives me a teeny, tiny thrill.

'So how are we going to complete the task?' she says quickly, not looking at me.

'Well, we've got three days,' Olivia says. 'Maybe we could go home, each draft our note and then meet to workshop tomorrow or the day after?'

'Can't we just do it now?' Mehreen asks. 'I'll overthink it otherwise. Obsess over it.'

'Can't we just skip to the drowning part?' I groan. 'This whole task thing is ridiculous.'

'We can't go against the rules,' Mehreen says, like a four-year-old.

'She's right,' Olivia says. 'Their rules state they won't help us any further if we don't follow their precise instructions.'

'It's not like they're gonna know!' I say.

'You agreed to follow all instructions when you signed up,' Olivia says.

'Plus, the lack of control is rather freeing, don't you think?' Mehreen asks.

They're both staring at me now, like Mum and Dr Sterp do during therapy sessions when I refuse to talk. Like the nurses used to in the hospital when I refused to let them treat me like a kid. Everyone's always fucking staring.

'God, fine, whatever,' I say.

'Great,' Olivia says, her face transforming instantly to a smile again. She digs through her bag. 'We'll do it now then. I think I've got some paper and pens in here.'

It's like we're being mothered, or teachered. People sometimes call me immature for my age, but Olivia is like some stuck-up middle-aged housewife; it's really creepy. And annoying.

We set up camp at a grave with a headstone almost taller than me. I force myself not to read the name. I don't wanna know whose carcass I'm on top of. Olivia has a notepad in her bag (of course she does), but lets us down by only having two pens. I just about stop myself from telling her she's a disappointment. Thankfully Mehreen manages to save the day with a key-ring pen. They sit on the grass, and I take another look around to see whether Mum's followed me. I wouldn't put it past her.

'So we just write?' Mehreen asks.

'Sure,' I say. 'What d'you want? Tips?'

'Actually, yeah,' she replies. 'I don't really know what to say.'

'Just talk about how you can't cope, that you're sorry, blah blah blah. Have you told anyone else about wanting to do this?'

She shakes her head. 'My family don't . . . they don't *get* . . . depression. It's not really a thing in our culture. They'd probably blame it on black magic or tell me to pray it away, as if I haven't already tried.'

Olivia reaches over, puts a hand on Mehreen's thigh and squeezes. 'That sounds rough.'

Whoa, over-friendly much? I make a note to stay away from Olivia's wandering hands; she's totally not my type anyway, even if she was gay (which she's obviously not, cos look at that hair). It's weird, actually, how chilled she is, how normal she seems. Mehreen's practically in tears, I'm desperate

51

to get it over with, but Olivia . . . she seems like she's chatting with her mates. There's something not right with her.

Mehreen chews her lip for a second before beginning to scribble away. Olivia and I do the same. We sit in silence for a few minutes, writing, crossing out, writing some more. Mehreen starts sniffling after a while and I try to ignore it. I decide to play along and pour out my anger, imagining Mum's face when she reads my note, when she realises that my bad mood isn't something that I'll get used to, like I have the chair. I don't know whether it's because I can still hear Mehreen's crying or because I've just noticed that the grave in my eyeline is a really fucking tiny one, but I start to feel my chest ache. I scrunch up the angry note I've written and start a new one. If I'm going to do this, I should do it properly. It's better to leave Mum with something nice, right?

'Is everyone done?' Olivia asks, like the teacher she is.

I roll my eyes and nod. Mehreen says, 'Yes.'

'The instructions say we need to upload a photograph.' Olivia gets out her phone. 'Do you think just the notes will be enough or do we need to be in it?'

'I assume they want to see our faces,' Mehreen replies.

'Hmm.' Olivia looks around, then jumps up and walks across to the tiny headstone. She places her phone on top of it and angles it so the camera is pointed right at my face. 'Five seconds!' she says, jogging back. 'Hold up your notes.' She gets on her knees.

'Everybody say "suicide",' I singsong, just before the click sounds.

Olivia rushes over to check the photo. 'Looks good,' she says, typing away on her phone as she walks back. 'I've sent it. We should probably upload our individual notes to the system too, just in case.'

I pull my phone out of my pocket and take a snap of my paper; I'll post it on the website later.

'OK, so shall we read them out?' Mehreen asks as she puts her phone away.

'Wait – what?' I ask. 'This shit is personal.'

'We're supposed to do this together, Cara,' Olivia says in her mother voice as she sits on the ground again.

'I think it'll help.' Mehreen perks up. 'Like a team-building thing.'

'Aren't you supposed to ask what someone's favourite colour is? Not "Why do you want to kill yourself?"'

'I just meant,' Mehreen says quietly, as if I've just told her off, 'I think it'd help me to know why you guys are doing it, if that makes sense.'

'You can read yours out if you want,' I tell her. 'There's no way I am.'

She looks sad and I know I should feel bad, but I don't. We're not here to become bezzie mates.

'Go on,' Olivia says. 'Read yours out, if you think it will help.'

Mehreen nods and fiddles with her paper for a second before unfolding it.

Mum, Dad, Imran,
   I guess if you're reading this then I'm gone. You probably

haven't noticed, but I'm miserable. I have been for a long time. I know you'll think I'm taking the easy way out, but you aren't inside my head. You don't know how hard it is to pretend to be OK for your sakes, for everyone else's sakes.

I've tried so hard to stop the thoughts hammering around in my head, to stop feeling like this, to just be normal, but I can't do it. I can't fix myself and I don't think I can be fixed. I know you won't respect my decision, that what I'm doing goes against everything we believe in, but I honestly don't see any other option.

I wish things could have been different, that I could have been different. I just . . . can't bear it any more.

Sorry,

Mehreen

'Um, OK,' I say slowly. I try not to focus on the tears now streaming down her cheeks, although Olivia takes care of patting her on the back. I always feel awkward around crying people. It's like they *want* everyone to look at them. I can't stand that much attention.

'Sorry.' Mehreen sniffs, wiping her eyes. 'I didn't mean to get so emotional.'

'Olivia, you wanna take the spotlight?' I ask quickly.

Olivia looks up. 'Oh, I could never top that.'

'Top?' I ask. 'It's not a competition.'

Olivia yanks out a blade of grass and runs it through her fingers.

'Please?' Mehreen says. 'It'll make me feel better.'

'It's nothing grand, just a quote from *Hamlet* – Mother loves that play,' Olivia explains.

'I'd still like to hear it,' Mehreen says. 'If that's OK.'

Olivia sighs, but picks up her piece of paper.

Mother,
To die, to sleep – perchance to dream.
I'm sorry.
Yours,
Olivia.

'You ended a suicide note with *yours*?' I say.

Olivia shrugs. 'That's how you're supposed to end a letter.'

Mehreen and I look at each other; I bite my lip to stop from laughing.

'It's a bit short,' I say. 'Doesn't really explain why you're doing it.'

'You shouldn't really criticise,' Mehreen says. 'Especially since you're refusing to read yours at all.'

'Whatever.'

'It's rather obvious what Cara's reason for doing this is,' Olivia pipes up. 'The wheelchair, no?'

I whip my head towards her, ready to punch her in the gob.

'It must be tough,' she continues, giving me her pity eyes, 'being limited like that.' She stares at me as I try to come up with the right words to cuss her out.

I can feel the anger bubbling in my stomach and I glare

at her, trying to make her burst into flames. She just stares right back, judging me like the cow she is.

'You don't know a fucking thing about what it's like,' I finally say. My fists are clenched in my lap.

'So tell us,' Olivia says. She turns and sits cross-legged (fucking rub it in much?), facing me, still staring. 'Honestly, I'd like to know how it feels.'

'Y'know what? Fuck this. Fuck you both.' I throw the pen and paper at her stupid perfect face and turn to leave. I can't even have a bloody tantrum with this chair, so I settle for huffing lots as I head off towards the gate.

'*Dear Mum,*' I hear Olivia say behind me, '*You and I both knew this was gonna happen sooner or later.*'

Wait . . . those are *my* words.

My note.

That bitch. That fucking bitch.

'*You know I've never really got over what happened. And as much as you keep saying you understand, you don't.*'

How fucking dare she?! I turn around and try to speed back. If my legs worked, she'd be eating grass right now.

'*You don't know what it's like to have killed someone –*'

I bash into her side and yank my letter out of her hand as she screams.

'Just stop! You fucking –'

'You're hurting me!' Olivia shrieks, and I realise my chair is still pushing against her. Part of me wants to keep pushing, to hurt her as much as I can, but the look on her face – like a little kid about to be slapped by a parent – causes me to pull back.

'Stop it!' Mehreen shouts.

'You had no right – *no right* to do that,' I tell Olivia as I roll back slightly.

'So you thought you'd stop me by attacking me?' She rubs a spot on her thigh.

'You deserved it,' I say, though I do start to feel a bit bad, seeing how red her skin is.

'You need to stop being so defensive,' Olivia says, her voice sharper than usual. 'These pacts are designed so people can *help* each other. We're on the same side, Cara.'

'I agreed to kill myself with you,' I say, 'not sit around telling stories about how shit our lives are. And not to have you pity me. I get enough of that already, thank you very much.'

She finally starts to look guilty, but I can tell there's still pity beneath it all.

'Fuck this,' I mutter, before turning to leave.

'Hey, wait!' Mehreen calls after me. 'You can't just leave.'

'We'll see you at the Westgate in three days,' Olivia says calmly, confidently, as if she's certain I'm coming back.

I can't wait to prove her wrong.

9. CARA

Mum's waiting outside the gates. Of course she is. I should have known when she asked what church the meeting was at that she'd come to spy. It doesn't look like she got out of the car though; her head's down and she's flicking through some papers.

I make sure the others haven't followed me out, begging me to come back, saying they can't do this without me, before finding a dropped kerb and crossing the road. Mum doesn't even pretend to look guilty when our eyes meet through the windscreen. She just smiles and gets out of the car.

'You said I could come alone,' I say.

'And you did!' she says happily. She opens the passenger door and waits for me to get into position. 'How was it? You're done earlier than –'

'How long have you been sitting out here?' I ask, super-pissed now. 'Don't you have anything better to do than spy on your own daughter?'

'It's not like that,' she says. 'I was worried, Cara. I have a right to be worried. This is the first time you've been out alone. I just . . . I wanted to be on stand-by. I didn't come in, did I? I let you do it on your own.'

'Whatever,' I say, manoeuvring myself into the car and

waiting for her to put my chair in the back. I know I should bite her head off, tell her to stop babying me, but I guess it worked out well that she was here; at least I can get a lift home.

Mum chatters away the entire drive, trying to get me to tell her what happened, if I made any friends, if I 'feel better'. I ignore her and go to the MementoMori website on my phone. I can see the photo Olivia uploaded – the three of us posing in the middle of the graveyard, looking like actual friends. Olivia has a huge smile on her face, and seeing it makes me want to smack her.

God, what a let-down this whole thing was. When I found MementoMori, I honestly thought it was the answer to everything, that they'd find me people who weren't dicks, and let us get on with it right away. But they're bloody useless, making us wait thirteen days to do it. And all these weird tasks. I mean, honestly, what is the point?

I scroll through the entire website looking for a button to cancel the pact or even delete my account, but there's nothing. I try to sign up again to see if I can get paired with someone less annoying, but an alert pops up:

A pact is already underway for you. You must stick with your original partners.

I try signing up with my old email address, but the same message pops up. God damn this shit. Before I can return to Google to look for another suicide-partner website, a Facebook notification pops up on my screen.

Mehreen Miah sent you a friend request.

I stare at it for a minute, squinting to make sure the photo is really her, wondering why she'd even bother with this. I know I should ignore it, delete the request, but I'm curious. I must get my nosiness from Mum (who's still rabbiting on to herself). I spend the rest of the drive home snooping on Mehreen's profile. She has over two hundred friends, which I'm surprised by. People with that many friends don't generally go looking on the Internet for strangers to kill themselves with. She doesn't seem to post much and there are barely any photos of her. I notice that she's friended Olivia too, but before I can snoop on her profile, another notification appears on my screen. A DM from Mehreen.

Cara,
  I didn't like how we left things, so I just wanted to message and say it was nice meeting you today. I'm sorry if Olivia and I came on too strong, but I guess it was a weird situation for all of us. Please forgive us for being so rude. I'm looking forward to seeing you again on the 8th.
  Mehreen

How weird. Like . . . literally what the hell? *It was nice meeting you*?! She's acting like we went on a first date or something. But other than that . . . it's quite sweet of her to have reached out. I feel slightly bad about being mean to her (but not about being mean to Olivia, the bitch). I should probably reply, but what would I even say?

'Cara?' Mum asks suddenly.

I look up to see we've stopped at a Burger King drive-through.

'Did you decide what you want?' Mum asks.

10. MEHREEN

I replay the meeting over and over in my head as I walk home. I'm the type of person who imagines every outcome to a situation in order to be prepared, but even in my wildest dreams I didn't expect anything like *that*. I assumed it would be a somewhat formal meeting, for the website to just give us the necessary information and set us on our way, not that someone would admit to murder. I can't help but wonder what the rest of Cara's note said. There must be more to the story – Cara didn't seem dangerous to me. I feel so bad about what happened; I think Olivia eventually realised she had been rude. She didn't want to go after Cara and apologise, like I suggested, though. I check my phone to see if Cara has responded to my message, but there's nothing there, even though I can see she's read it.

As I walk through the front door, I'm hit by the smell of frying onions. There's a pile of shoes by the stairs and Aunt Nadiya's shrill laugh emanates from the kitchen. Oh, great. She's probably here to gloat about the extravagance of her daughter's wedding. I realise it's one of the many things I won't get to see. Not that I'm sad about that in any way. I also realise that one of the pre-wedding ceremonies is on the eighteenth. So I'll be upstaging the bride, which does make me feel a bit bad.

I close the front door as quietly as possible and creep up to my bedroom. I've started trying to minimise my impact in the house, leaving no trace. Preparing my family, I guess. Though it's not really any different than normal. I've become so accustomed to being ignored that I pretend it's my own doing, rather than acknowledge the fact that I've left no imprint, even on my own family. I often wonder how long I could go, hiding away in my room, not making a sound, before someone would realise. Sometimes I wonder what would happen if I were to kill myself in my room. How long it'd take them to find my body. I imagine that someone would only come in when my blood started seeping into the carpet, down through the floorboards and dripping from the living-room ceiling. Or maybe it'd be the smell that would finally get their attention. Once my body has disintegrated so much that the acrid stench would infect their lives.

Even then, they wouldn't care.
THEY'D PROBABLY BE GRATEFUL FOR THE SPARE BEDROOM.

I know there'll be hell to pay if I don't go downstairs; Aunt Nadiya would tell the whole world how rude I was, hiding upstairs while Mum slaved in the kitchen. I hide Olivia's croissants in my cupboard to eat later, change into a shalwar kameez, fix my headscarf again and take a deep breath before leaving my room.

'Only thirteen more days,' I tell myself. 'Just push through this and it'll all be over.'

Imran's bedroom door is wide open and as I walk past I can hear him in there laughing with our cousin Wasim as they play on the Xbox. My chest constricts at seeing how easy it is for Imran to get on with anyone and everyone, how he seems to breeze through life. It's not fair that I'm lumbered with a messed-up brain and he turned out so normal.

'Oi, loser!' he calls out as I pass his doorway.

I turn my head and just look at him, not even having the energy to bite back.

'Bring us up some samosas, will ya?' he says, without even taking his eyes off the screen.

Wasim catches my eye and offers an apologetic smile, but it only lasts a split second before he's back to the game. I turn around without a word and go downstairs.

'*As-salaam-alaikum*,' I say to Aunt Nadiya as I walk into the kitchen.

'*Wa-alaikum-salaam*,' she replies, her eyes already flicking up and down my body.

She's going to tell you how fat you're getting, how her son is doing better in school than you. SHE'S GOING TO TELL YOU THAT OUTFIT DOESN'T SUIT YOU.

'Where were you?' she asks, digging for dirt, for flaws, already.

'Oh, just out,' I reply. I've never been a good liar. It goes against my moral beliefs for starters, so I've had to learn how to bend the truth; vagueness usually works. Before she can say anything else, I walk over to the stove where Mum is frying samosas. She wordlessly passes over the plate and spoon, leaving me in charge as she goes to sit at the table with her sister.

'Kids these days,' Aunt Nadiya says. 'Always out with their friends, no time for family, never helping their mothers.'

SHE'S RIGHT - YOU'RE A TERRIBLE DAUGHTER.

'Mehreen's been attending study sessions at school, haven't you?' Mum asks.

I nod. Still not a lie. I *did* go to a study session today.

'You know how it is,' Mum continues. 'She's so far ahead with her schoolwork that they gave her these special sessions in the holidays. She's on track to get great grades.'

Mum obviously has no moral hesitation about lying.

'Hmm, well *my* Wasim doesn't need anything like that; he's just naturally smart. Did I tell you the school is letting him take *extra* GCSEs? He's the only one in his year taking thirteen.'

Mum shoots me an accusatory look before distracting Aunt Nadiya with a plate of food. I look down at the boiling oil, half wanting the pan to tip over onto me. I pick up a cooked samosa and take a bite. I can't help but wonder if this is the last time I'll eat Mum's fish samosas. Whether this is the last time I'll see Aunt Nadiya and be subjected to her scorn. The next thirteen days are going to be filled with lasts, and I feel like I need to notice all of them.

11. CARA

8th April
(10 days until Date of Termination)

I always used to have tons of notifications on my phone when I woke up. People tagging me in memes, Hana and Cerys sending me links to songs they wanted us to lip-sync to on our YouTube channel, people just messaging for the hell of it. But that was before I became someone no one knew what to say to. Before all they could see was the chair.

Nowadays I'm lucky if I get even a couple of notifications. But today one stands out. An email from MementoMori.

From: Administrator (admin@mementomori.com)
To: Cara Saunders (SpaghettiCarbonCara@gmail.com)
Subject: Reminder

Meeting today at 10 a.m.
Location: Westgate Shopping Centre, Bridgeport BP5 1UH

Reminder: MementoMori requires all users to complete tasks **together**; otherwise no further

assistance will be provided. Failure to adhere to our rules and regulations will result in further action, as stated in our terms and conditions.

I wonder whether Mehreen and Olivia will have to cancel their pact if I don't show up. It doesn't look like this bloody website lets you have a second chance either. I feel a bit bad if I'm ruining their chances. Well, mainly I just feel bad for Mehreen. She was decent. Awkward, but decent.

I load up her message and read it over and over at the table while Mum does something at the stove. She's chatting away, as usual. I'm not listening to a word, as usual.

It was nice meeting you.

I can't remember the last time anyone used the word 'nice' for anything to do with me. Mehreen wouldn't be the worst person to help me die, I guess. And Olivia . . . well, she probably hates me enough that she'd make the perfect partner.

I'm looking forward to seeing you again.

Mum slides a full English breakfast under my nose and sits next to me with her coffee.

'I already had breakfast.' I push the plate away.

She laughs. 'Pop-Tarts *don't* count as breakfast.' She doesn't move the plate back though. 'Plus, these are organic. Good for you.' She picks up a knife and fork and starts cutting up a sausage.

I look back at my phone, but before I can switch to another app, Mum raises the fork and hovers it in front of my mouth. I look at her and she smiles, pushing the chunk of sausage towards me.

'Are you literally trying to feed me right now?'

She laughs. 'You're busy with your phone, it's fine, I don't mind.' She pushes the fork further until it touches my lips.

I'm tempted to eat it, because damn that sausage does smell good, but I'm honestly a bit freaked out by how casually this is happening. What next – she follows me into the bathroom to wipe my arse? I wouldn't put it past her after the other day, to be fair.

I push myself away from the table quickly. 'Um, I've just remembered . . .' I say, looking up at the clock on the wall; there's still time. 'I made plans with some people from support group today. I need to be at Westgate in twenty minutes.'

Mum frowns, dropping her fork. Finally. 'What people? Why didn't you tell me this before?'

'I forgot about it till now. It's just some girls I met at the group the other day. Mehreen and Olivia. We were going to . . . go shopping for a bit.'

She just stares at nothing, pushing the food around the plate without looking at it. 'I don't think so,' she says eventually. 'I've got a deadline today and I'm *so* behind. I need to work.'

She's behind because of me. I'm the reason she can't work like normal people any more. The reason she had to give up her dream of writing and get this crappy job instead. That's what she wants to say, what she's thinking.

69

'Exactly!' I say, forcing the cheer into my voice. 'You can just get on with that without me distracting you for a couple of hours. All I'm asking for is a lift; you don't have to wait at the shopping centre or anything. Just drop off and pick up.'

'I'm not comfortable leaving you with people you've just met. They could be serial killers for all you know.'

Ha! How ironic. I bite my lip to stop the laughter. 'That's exactly it. I'm hoping they'll teach me their tricks. This shopping trip is really just an initiation, Mum. You guessed it.'

'I'm being serious, Cara,' Mum huffs, crossing her arms into her signature angry-mother pose. 'What do you even know about these girls? You've only met them once.'

I take a deep breath through my nose and put on the sad pout she can't resist. 'I know that they're the only ones who really understand what I'm going through. That they feel the same things as I do. I know that I need their help.'

Mum's eyes get less angry and she lifts her thumbnail into her mouth, which means my strategy's working.

'And I'm like ninety-five per cent sure they're not serial killers. Their fingernails were too clean.'

She laughs. 'Well, you certainly seem happier than you've been in a long time.'

'I am,' I confirm. Ten days left, if this goes to plan. Very happy indeed.

'So what condition do these girls have then? Are they in wheelchairs too?'

'Um, no . . .'

'I thought you said they were just like you?' She narrows her eyes, stuffing some toast in her mouth.

'I meant they understand what it's like for me,' I say through gritted teeth.

Must resist urge to be a snarky bitch. Snarky bitches don't get permission to go out and plan their deaths.

'Well, how can they? If they're not –'

'They have invisible disabilities!' I blurt.

I watched a YouTube video about invisible disabilities a few weeks ago, and it's been stuck in my mind ever since; they were talking about how having an invisible disability is just as bad. Total bullshit of course.

'Invisible disabilities?' Mum asks. The sarcasm in her voice is the first thing I've been able to relate to her about in ages.

'It's like disabilities that aren't . . . visible.'

'Yeah, I got that, thanks, Sherlock,' Mum says, nudging the plate towards me again.

'We were talking about it at group,' I say, pushing the plate back, hard. 'It's things like epilepsy and chronic fatigue syndrome. And invisible conditions can be just as disabling. Just because you can't see a person's pain, doesn't they're not suffering.'

Mum tilts her head to the side and looks at me. I'm worried she's gonna call me out on my bullshit, say she can tell when I'm lying, but instead she smiles. This isn't her fake smile either, when her eyes stay fixed and the corners of her mouth just twitch. This is her real smile, the one she gets when she goes for a shower and there's actually some hot water left,

71

or when she treats herself to fancy chocolates after getting paid for one of her writing gigs.

'What?' I say after she doesn't say anything for a few seconds.

She shakes her head, looking down at the plate instead of at me. 'No, nothing. You just . . . You sound so much like . . .'

So much like your father.

'You sound really grown-up, that's all. I can't believe that group has had such an impact on you from just one meeting.'

'Oh yeah – I told you it was great.' I nod, pushing out my own smile as far as it'll go, forcing back the thoughts of Dad that have started to creep into my mind. I take a dramatic breath, look down into my lap, fiddle with a hole at the bottom of my T-shirt. 'These two girls are the only ones who've shown an interest in me since the accident, Mum. Cerys and Hana stopped visiting after, like, a month. They've even unfollowed me on Twitter and Instagram. It would be nice to have friends again, to feel normal again. And I want to start doing more normal things. Shopping, lunch, cinema – you know, that teenager shit you keep telling me to do.'

'Oh God,' Mum groans. 'How can I say no to that?'

'You can't,' I say with a grin.

12. MEHREEN

9.55 a.m.

Cara and Olivia seem to be making a name for themselves as people who don't know the importance of being prompt. The baristas at Costa keep looking at me as I wait; at first it was those sly looks people give when they're pretending to do something else, but now they're just outright staring and whispering to each other. I tug on the edges of my headscarf, making sure no stray strands of hair have come loose. I can see the server with the lip ring edging closer towards the phone, as if to call security and alert them to the shifty-looking Muslim girl with a backpack standing next to the cash machine. I feel the eyes of the customers beginning to turn on me too.

THEY'RE NOT GOING TO SHOW UP.
Olivia and Cara don't like you anyway.
THEY'VE PURPOSELY DITCHED YOU.
The Costa girl is going to call the police on you.
What if there actually is something in your bag that could be used to make a bomb?

'Mez? Is that you?' a voice squeaks behind me.

73

I turn to find Calliope and Pascha standing there with their hands full of shopping bags. I instinctively plaster on the smile I always adopt when I'm around them, transforming into the Mehreen they expect me to be. The Mehreen who just about passes off as normal.

'Oh, hey, guys.' I make sure to keep my voice steady. 'I thought you were in France, Pascha?' Normal Mehreen remembers such details about her friends.

'Got back yesterday night. I texted you?' She cocks an eyebrow, like she does at school when I don't focus on anything she says because the Chaos is so bad.

'Oh, right, yeah, sorry,' I gabble. 'I forgot.' The mask slips slightly and I inwardly curse myself.

It's a shame really. Calliope and Pascha are nice. They deserve a proper friend. God knows why they put up with me. Though I'm grateful they do. I can't imagine how unbearable school would be without their coat-tails to ride on.

'What're you doing here anyway?' Calliope says. 'And how come you didn't come to mine last night? I was looking for you.'

NO, SHE WASN'T.
She's lying to be polite.

'Are you on your own?' Pascha asks, thankfully taking away the spotlight. 'We're going to the cinema. Wanna come?'

'Uh, I'm just . . . waiting for someone.' My voice wobbles slightly.

'Is it a *boy*?' Calliope gasps. 'Is he from school? Do we know him? Is that where you were last night? On a *date*?'

It's at times like this where I wish I could lie without feeling guilty. How easy it would be to concoct a fake boyfriend that would get me out of any and all social situations, one who'd impress Pascha and Calliope and make everyone think I was a semi-normal teenager.

YOU COULDN'T EVEN GET A FAKE BOYFRIEND.

'No, idiot!' Pascha whacks Calliope on the arm. 'She's not *allowed* to date, remember?'

'I thought they weren't allowed to drink?' Calliope muses. *They*.

Pascha and Calliope get into a mini-whisper-fight, discussing who's right and wrong about my religion. I want to back away quietly, just fade into the walls.

I check my watch again.

9.57 a.m.

Crap. They're going to be here any second. If Pascha and Calliope see Cara's black clothes or Olivia's shiny perfection, they definitely won't stay quiet about it.

'You guys have bought loads!' I say, flicking my eyes to their bags.

'I know!' Pascha squeals. 'I don't know how I'm going to fit everything into my wardrobe.'

I force a laugh, looking over their shoulders. There's a girl who looks like Olivia a few shops down. 'Have you guys been to River Island yet?' I ask quickly. 'They have a *huge* sale on. It was pretty empty in there too.'

It works; their eyes light up.

'Really?' Calliope asks.

'Yeah, I think they had that jacket you've been after, Callie.' I know I'm being so completely obvious, but I also know that once you mention River Island to Calliope, that's all she'll be able to think about.

She squeaks. Actually squeaks.

'Ohmygod, Pascha, let's go!' Calliope tugs on her arm and begins skipping away.

'Bye, Mez!' Pascha calls as she's dragged away. 'Have fun on your date!'

I roll my eyes, clenching my fists at being called 'Mez', then turn around, only to come face to face with Cara. Well, chest to face.

'Jesus, I didn't see you there!' I half scream.

'Did you just say *Jesus*?' Cara laughs. She's wearing another baggy black top. This one's got a print of skeletons posing in the letters of the alphabet.

'Um, maybe? Why? I mean, we do believe in Jesus.'

'Well, sure,' Cara says. 'But you don't call him Jesus.'

'Since when are you an expert in Islam?' I ask, clenching my fists again. Why does everybody think they know more about my religion than I do?

Cara shrugs a little and looks away. 'I read up on it last night.'

'You read up on my religion?'

SHE THINKS YOU'RE A TERRORIST.
You have that look about you.

She shrugs. 'Didn't wanna offend you or anything.'

'Oh,' is all I can say, touched that she'd go to that much trouble.

There's a bit of silence between us and, as usual, I feel the need to immediately fill it.

'I'm sorry for what happened the other day,' I say. There's a tiny voice in my head repeating the line 'you don't know what it's like to have killed someone' over and over.

'Don't worry about it,' Cara says flatly. She raises her hand to Olivia, who's now walking towards us. If she's waving at her, that's a good sign, right? That she's not mad any more?

'Morning!' Olivia chirps as she reaches us. She does her half-hug, double-kiss thing on me, then pauses for a few seconds before repeating it on Cara. To my surprise, Cara accepts the gesture.

The awkward silence resurfaces, bringing the tension from the last meeting back with it.

'I was just saying to Cara how bad we feel about the last meeting,' I tell Olivia, hoping she'll jump in to apologise and make everything OK again.

She doesn't. 'Right,' she says instead. 'Yes, that was very rude of me to read your letter without your permission, Cara.'

That's almost an apology, right?

'Can we just forget that day even happened and get on with it?' Cara asks, determinedly not making eye contact with anyone.

77

'Sounds perfect!' Olivia says, with far too much glee in her voice.

Ever since the day at the graveyard, I've been trying to figure out her life, figure out *why* she'd want to do something like this. On the surface she seems so happy . . . I don't get it.

WHAT DOES IT MATTER?
Why are you trying to befriend these girls?
YOU JUST WANTED TO USE THEM TO FEEL LESS GUILTY ABOUT YOUR DECISION.

'We're not doing it here, are we?' I ask, looking around. There are far too many people nearby. Too many people with ears pricked up for any mention of anything out of the norm, especially when it comes out of the mouth of a brown girl in a headscarf. I can just imagine the lip-ring girl from Costa overhearing me say the word *suicide* and immediately calling 999 and MI5 and the Prime Minister and God knows who else.

'I know where we can go,' Cara says.

I trail behind Olivia as she follows Cara into a long corridor that's off to the side, hidden behind the lifts. My imagination's going into overdrive, imagining a secret clubhouse or an apocalypse bunker. But then I see a sign leading us to the toilets.

Cara laughs when she sees the look on my face. 'You wanted privacy, right?' she asks, pushing open the door to the disabled toilet. 'Well, ta-da!' She seems a lot more relaxed today, which is good.

Olivia helps her with the door and I traipse in behind

them. The room is a lot more spacious than I'd expected. I've always been one to abide by the rule of not using disabled toilets, even as a last resort. Cara wheels herself into one corner and Olivia glances at the toilet seat. She rummages through her handbag – another designer one, of course – and pulls out a packet of wet wipes. Cara and I share a look as Olivia lowers the lid of the toilet and wipes it thoroughly before sitting down. She pulls her iPad out of her bag and begins tapping away.

'We need fingerprints again,' she says after a few seconds.

I look down at the screen and the three circles are waiting. Cara rolls forward and places her index finger on the left circle, Olivia occupies the middle. I step up and take the last spot. There's a nervous buzz in my stomach, the anticipation somehow less nauseating than the first time we did this. The screen flashes white, and I force my hand to stay. Goosebumps erupt over my skin and I swear I feel someone breathing on my neck. The others seem unconcerned and just keep their fingers on the screen until the black screen returns. A message begins to appear, typed out a letter at a time.

Task 2: Funerals are important for those left behind. To ease the burden, you should plan your funeral as fully as possible. Leave these plans in an easily accessible place before your Date of Termination.

MementoMori requires you submit photographic evidence of having completed this task **together**, to

be submitted to the website before the next meeting.
Failure to do so will delay the next step, and the
process as a whole.

Next meeting: 11th April, 10 a.m.
Location: The Sundowner Cafe, Bossfort Beach,
Bridgeport BP8 4TG

**Reminder: MementoMori requires all users to
complete tasks <u>together</u>; otherwise no further
assistance will be provided. Failure to adhere to
our rules and regulations will result in further
action, as stated in our terms and conditions.**

13. CARA

OK, I gotta admit, this task business sort of makes sense now. I mean, I still wish we could just skip ahead to the end, but if we've got to do *something*, it's good to ensure Mum doesn't try and bury me in a dress. To tell her not to bother with a church, but to use the cash to fix the leak in the garage instead. The whole 'collaboration' thing is still weird though; they've used the word 'together' like a million times. Why are they so obsessed with teamwork? What do they get out of it? And what's up with wanting photos as proof of everything?

'So, how are we gonna do this?' I ask, nodding towards the iPad. 'I mean, we don't exactly have the money to be able to, like, *book* anything. Well, *I* don't anyway.' I look at Olivia's handbag. 'Think it's enough to just leave a plan of what we want, rather than spending money?'

'I guess so.' Mehreen shrugs. 'Although our funerals are really different to Christian ones. I don't need to find a church, or choose flowers. We have really simple ceremonies. Barely a ceremony, actually. So, um, I don't really know what to do.'

Olivia pipes up. 'You still need an outfit, right? Or . . . do they bury you naked?'

'Um, wrapped in a cloth, but, yeah, naked under that.'

'Oh no, what a shame!' I say. 'Guess we can't go shopping after all.' I start moving towards the door, hoping we can just go home, but Olivia holds out her hand to stop me. Like she's a traffic controller and I'm a car.

'Wait, we can work around this. How about an outfit for your last day? That should be special too.'

'I guess?' Mehreen shrugs again.

'Excellent!' Olivia chirps. 'Looks like we're going shopping then!' She seems legit over the moon, as if shopping isn't literally hell on earth.

'Can't we just buy everything online?' I ask.

'Oh, don't worry about it,' Olivia says. 'We can totally find something that works for you.'

'That *works* for me?'

'I just mean,' she continues with a small laugh, 'have you ever thought about . . . wearing something less . . . *angsty*?'

I look down at the skeleton print T-shirt I changed into especially for this meeting. It's one of my favourites – doesn't even have any holes in it yet.

'Not to brag,' Olivia continues, crossing her legs, 'but choosing clothes is my superpower.'

'What happened to plain old saving the world?' I mumble.

'Oh, fashion can totally save the world,' Olivia insists. 'I actually think a dress would look lovely on you.'

'Is there anything else on the website?' Mehreen asks, thankfully stopping the conversation, and stopping me from punching Olivia in the gob. I've been forcing myself to be nice today, to not be a snarky bitch, because I now know I can't do this without them, but there's a limit to how far I can be pushed and she's getting really fucking close.

Olivia taps the screen back to life, scrolls up and down. 'No, just those instructions.' She stashes the iPad back in her gigantic handbag. 'So, where shall we start?'

'So that was a firm no on doing this online?' I ask, looking at Mehreen, hoping she'll back me up.

'We're supposed to do this together. I guess we could make a day of it. Lunch afterwards?'

They're acting like we've been put together for a fucking play date. To brush each other's hair, give each other make-overs and talk about boys. Not to help each other drown.

'Sounds like a plan,' Olivia says, jumping off the seat. 'Let's go!' She pulls open the door and basically skips out.

'Seriously,' I say to Mehreen as she holds the door open, 'just fucking kill me now.'

14. OLIVIA

Mother always used to tell me
that the way you *dress*
says *more* about you
than the words you **say**.

Presentation
is key.
People know within *seconds*
           of first **SEEING** you
whether they
       like
       trust
       respect
         you.

I ***desperately*** want
Mehreen Miah
and
Cara Saunders
to like me.

I also want to
        help

them.
And if there's **one thing** Mother has taught me,
it's how to look

        Dignified
        Elegant
        Respectable.

                'No way.'
            That's Cara.
       'I'm not fucking wearing a dress.'
'But you have such beautiful long legs,'
I tell her.

           'Even if they don't work?'

I look away.
Mehreen looks away.

           'No fucking dresses.'

    'Funerals aren't for your comfort.'
      That's Mehreen.
    *'They're for **other** people.*
    *It's their way of **coping**,*
      *of getting **closure.***
    *If it'll make your family **happy**,*
    then why not?"

       'I'm not fucking going against myself.'
         Cara again.
       'I'm not having some
        strangers

make up their minds about what kind of person
I am **I was**
based on a stupid piece of fabric.
*That's not **me.***
*I'm not going to let **them***
bury
*or **burn***
me
*as someone I'm **not**.*
I've got principles.'

What do principles matter when you're dead?

'So no dresses,'
I confirm.
'What's your stance on skirts?'
Her glare
shoots
through me.
'Top and leggings it is.'

She rolls her eyes
again,
but this time
she **smiles** too.
A **smile** from Cara is so **rare**
that it **infects** me too.

Mehreen is easier to shop for.

She *trusts* my judgement,
is open to anything.
I get the feeling
she likes being told what works for her,
what looks **good**.
As if no one's given her a compliment before.
As if she doesn't realise how **extraordinarily**
beautiful she is
inside
and
out.

Things are more **difficult**
when it comes to me.
The Westgate Shopping Centre
brags
Primark
and
New Look
and
River Island.

Not the
Vivienne Westwood
and
Armani
and
Michael Kors
I'm accustomed to.

The material of the clothes feels
coarse
and
cheap
in my hands.

The styles look either
garish
or
bland.

The others play stylist now.
Cara tries to sell me a *minidress.*
Black, of course,
but surprisingly
<u>**no skeletons.**</u>
I tell her it's too *short,*
that it'll draw too much **attention.**

'Show off those legs,'
she tells me.

'I want something more *refined,*
more **elegant**,'
I tell them.
I don't want to look like an attractive **corpse**.

Mehreen pulls out a dress.
The dress.
Navy blue.

Down to the knees.
No frills. No beads. No gaudy sequins.
Understated.
Subdued.
Perfect.

After an hour or two
of browsing through
rack
    after
        rack,
Mehreen buys a
        simple
           black, long-sleeved dress.

Cara buys skinny   jeans and a loose   blouse.
        black   black
No skeletons!
And I pair my dress with a grey blazer.

The woman at the counter **looks** at us,
smiles the perfunctory smile,
asks the **customary**
    'Did you find everything you were looking for?'
When we all *smile* back at her,
she asks,
    'Are you three shopping for prom?'
I'm the first to laugh.

15. MEHREEN

The food court is pretty busy, even though it's barely lunchtime. The number of people and the closeness of the tables makes me slightly anxious. Crowds are one of my big stressors; I feel like I'm constantly in the way or inconveniencing others. Someone pushes past me and I apologise immediately; they don't even look at me.

'Where should we eat?' Olivia asks.

'Is anywhere here halal?' Cara asks me.

I'm taken aback by the thoughtfulness of this question. I've been out for lunch countless times with Calliope and Pascha and not *once* have they suggested we go somewhere that serves halal food.

'Oh, it's no trouble, honest,' I say. 'I don't mind where we go. I can just eat veggie.'

'Don't be silly,' Olivia says, at the same time Cara says, 'Fuck veggie.' They look at each other and smile, which makes me smile too.

We end up choosing a restaurant that sells a variety of cuisines. I order a burger and chips, literally *thrilled* at the fact I can eat meat. Olivia fiddles with her food when it arrives, poking and prodding her burrito with her cutlery, turning it over, unwrapping it and trying to identify all the ingredients inside.

'Today was fun,' I say, squeezing a sachet of ketchup onto my plate.

'That sounds weird.' Cara smirks, opening her can of Coke. 'You had *fun* picking out the last set of clothes you're ever going to wear?'

'I don't think I *picked* anything,' I say with a laugh. 'Project Runway over here didn't give me much choice.'

'Superpower, I told you,' Olivia says, wiping her cutlery on a napkin.

'If you could have any superpower, what would you choose?' I ask Cara.

'Super-strength, obviously,' she says without hesitation. 'What about you?'

'Telepathy probably,' I say.

'You really want to hear what's going on in people's minds?' Cara asks. 'I can tell you, it's not a great place to be . . . up here.' She taps on the side of her head.

'OK, maybe selective telepathy,' I amend. 'A lot of what . . . *gets* to me is imagining what people are thinking. The Chaos in my head tells me they're thinking the worst, that I'm inconveniencing them, that they'd rather I wasn't around. If I knew what people were thinking, I wouldn't have to worry about that.'

'The Chaos in your head?' Olivia asks, brows furrowed. 'What do you mean?'

I wipe my fingers over and over on a napkin, trying to come up with the right words. I've never even *tried* to tell someone about my Chaos before, but if anyone would understand, it's these two. I hope, anyway.

'It's just what I call what happens in my head, my anxiety. It's like . . . like all my thoughts are a bunch of voices in my head. A cacophony of voices screaming, yelling horrible things, telling me I'm useless, that everyone hates me, that they're laughing at me. And then that triggers my depression, leading me to actually *believe* I'm useless and that everyone would be better off without me, and basically just makes me want to not exist. And, like, when it's *really* bad, I can't . . . I genuinely can't function. It feels like I'm physically being weighed down and I just want to shove my hand into my brain and pull the plug. Like I'd do anything to just make the Chaos stop. Does . . . ? Does *any* of that make sense?'

They're staring at me intently and I can't read their faces at all. Are they laughing at me? Or does someone finally get it?

They have no idea what you're on about.
THEY THINK YOU'RE AN IDIOT.

Before the Chaos can rise in volume, Olivia speaks up. 'I understand,' she says quietly. 'I don't have precisely *that*, but I know what you mean.'

I sag with relief, almost wanting to cry. *She gets it. She actually gets it.*

'What about you, Olivia?' Cara asks. 'Your superpower?'

'Invisibility,' Olivia replies without missing a beat, as she cuts into her food. (Seriously, who eats a burrito with a knife and fork?!)

'How come?' Cara says, taking a bite of her pasta.

'It's just common sense,' Olivia says. 'Being able to disappear on a whim, not having to be subjected to other people's company, not having to deal with their wants and demands.'

'Is that why you're doing this?' Cara prods. 'Because people *want* too much from you?'

Olivia looks up from stabbing her burrito. Her face is slack and shows no emotion. 'Sure.' She shrugs.

'I don't get why you're being so secretive about it,' Cara says. 'It's no big deal.'

'Is that why you made such a fuss about your letter the other day?' Olivia retorts, cocking an eyebrow.

Cara immediately drops her head down to look at her food.

I know I should let it pass, since she looks so uncomfortable, but I can't stop myself from asking, 'Did you really kill someone?'

She looks up quickly, and I'm worried she's going to be mad at me, but instead she looks on the verge of giving in.

'It's OK, you can tell us,' I say to her.

'Collaboration, remember?' Olivia prompts. 'Also, I think there's an implied confidentiality clause in this whole situation.'

Cara sighs. 'It was my dad. He died in a car crash about ten months ago. A car crash I caused. It's also how I got into the chair.' She gestures to her legs. 'I keep thinking about how the anniversary is coming up and I couldn't . . . I can't . . . it's why I joined the website.'

I'm speechless. It's not only the shock revelation that's getting to me, but the rawness in Cara, the vulnerability I'm seeing in her for the first time.

'What happened?' Olivia asks.

'He was driving,' Cara says after a second. 'I was in the front seat. We were coming back from the cinema. It was dark and pissing down with rain. We'd just watched some soppy film he thought I'd like.' She pauses for a second and I'm worried she's about to start crying, but then she shakes herself back to life. 'We were having an argument about it, but, like, a joke one, y'know? Dad was all about the cute animals, but I thought the film was offensive to women. He made some comment about me only saying that because I'm gay, and I shoved him on the shoulder. The car swerved and . . . uh, yeah.'

'Oh,' is all I can say.

I see Olivia start to put a hand on Cara's shoulder, but she thinks better of it.

'What great last words, eh?' Cara says. '"*You're only saying that because you're gay.*" He meant it as a joke, obviously, but I read this book once where a person's last words meant a lot in the afterlife.' She ducks her head again and sniffs ever so quietly. I can tell she's on the verge of tears.

'Do you believe in it?' I ask to distract her. 'An afterlife?'

Cara shakes her head after a second, raising her gaze to me; her eyes are red, but no tears fall. 'Nah, seems too easy, doesn't it? You leave this crappy world and go off into a land of sunshine and rainbows?'

'I actually find it reassuring,' I say. 'We believe that all of our time on Earth is a test. That what we should be looking forward to is the afterlife.'

'How can you be sure that whatever comes afterwards is any better than this piece-of-shit life?' Cara asks.

'That's what faith is.' I shrug. I've never been comfortable explaining my beliefs to others; it's as if I have to justify things way more than people of other, or no, religions.

'I guess I don't really *get* religion,' Cara says. 'I told you I googled around, right?' She pauses for a second, as if scared to continue. 'I was reading some list on Wikipedia about things Muslims believe in . . .'

'And . . . ?'

'I just mean . . . you're *so* religious, and yet you're here . . . with us . . . doing this.'

'Ah,' I say, thrown by the direction. 'You mean about suicide being a sin? I'm totally aware of that; I had so much trouble coming to terms with my decision, you have no idea.'

'So what made you change your view?' Olivia asks. 'You're going against your religion.'

'I reasoned that doing it with someone else makes it . . . less problematic, I guess? Like, I wouldn't be taking *my own* life.' I try and gather my thoughts, but fail, as I do every time I try to rationalise this. 'I don't know – trying to explain it makes me see the flaws in my plan.'

'You want me to shove your head under the water first?' Cara smirks.

There's a sharp stab in my chest, a reminder of what we're really gathered here for, what we're striving towards. Sometimes the reality of it punches me in the gut, causing me to freak out a little. An image of Cara and me in the water infiltrates my mind and I can practically feel the lack of oxygen in my body.

I force myself to smile in response.

'I think I've got something,' Olivia starts, thankfully distracting me from my thoughts. 'Anxiety and depression are illnesses, right? Not everyone accepts that, but it's scientifically correct. So *anxiety* is making you feel like this and *depression* is making you want to do this. The thing with mental illness is that it dominates your mind, pushes out everything that was originally there. So you could argue that it's not *you* making this decision, it's the anxiety and depression. Or your "Chaos".'

'Hmm,' I say, considering it. 'I guess that makes sense. I do genuinely feel like I'm not *me* any more.'

'See, this is why I don't believe in stuff. Too much thinking about things,' Cara says.

'And that's a *bad* thing?' Olivia laughs.

'Sure. I mean, how much easier would this have all been for you, Mehreen, if you could've just offed yourself alone and not felt guilty about it?'

'Easier, sure, but by no means *better*,' I say. 'And in all honesty, I don't think I would've been able to do it by myself.'

'How about you, Olivia?' Cara asks. 'You believe in God or any of that shit?'

Olivia shrugs. 'We go to church every week, but I haven't decided on my level of faith. I believe in a higher power, that we have souls, but heaven? I'm not sure. Although, as you say, Cara, anything's better than this shithole.'

I choke on my drink, the Coke shooting up my nose and burning a trail out. 'Oh my God,' I splutter, picking up a handful of napkins and shoving them up against my watering nose.

Cara cackles and I can hear Olivia begin to laugh too.

96

'Cara's having a bad influence on you,' I say when I've recovered.

'I wouldn't necessarily say *bad*,' Olivia says. 'Mother doesn't allow crude language at home. She says it's unladylike. It's rather freeing to be able to curse now.'

'Curse away, my friend,' Cara says, raising her drink for a toast.

We all clink cans.

'So what's our next step?' I ask, placing a napkin over my plate. 'What else can we plan for this task?'

'I'd like to try to book my church,' Olivia says. 'I could use Mother's credit card.'

She starts describing the intricacies of her church, the stained-glass windows, the lavender plants by the door, just as a woman begins walking towards our table. She's not wearing a uniform, so I assume she doesn't work here. I nudge Olivia to get her to stop talking, just in case something incriminating slips out, but the woman soon reaches our table.

'Hello there, girls,' she says, placing a hand on Cara's shoulder.

16. CARA

A hand lands on my shoulder and I can smell Mum's perfume.

Oh shit.

Shit. Shit. Shit.

Mehreen and Olivia look up and smile, probably thinking it's just some waitress coming to clear our dishes.

'You OK, Cara?' Mum asks with a shoulder squeeze.

I watch as Mehreen stops smiling and stares right at me. My stomach twists, knowing that they're about to see an episode of the Cara Pity Party, courtesy of my biggest fan. I should've known she'd come along to spy.

'I'm fine,' I say quietly.

Mum removes her hand, and I'm hoping this means she's going to get lost, that seeing me alive and breathing is enough for her. But of course, she pulls out the spare chair and plonks her butt down at the table with us.

'Seems like you girls have been busy,' she says, looking at the bags under the table.

Mehreen laughs a little. 'Yeah, we might have got a bit carried away.' She smiles at me and I can't help but smile back.

Mum notices and stares from Mehreen to me and back.

'You must be Mehreen,' she says, stretching her hand out.

Mehreen takes it slowly. 'Um, yeah. Hi.'

'Cara's told me all about you.'

Mehreen's eyes pop and I try to shake my head without Mum noticing.

'Hello, Mrs Saunders,' Olivia says, reaching out her hand. 'I'm Olivia Castleton – pleasure to meet you.'

'Lovely to meet you too,' Mum says, shaking Olivia's hand. 'So how *are* you girls?' she asks in that same pathetic voice she uses on me after every minor slip I have. The same voice the nurses used on me the whole time I was in hospital.

And that's when I remember what I told her this morning. About Mehreen and Olivia having invisible disabilities.

'I thought you had lots of work to do at home?' I ask before the others have a chance to respond to her question.

'Cara, sweetheart, don't interrupt. I'm trying to get to know your new friends.' She doesn't even look at me.

'So is the support group helping you two? Cara seems to really love it, and that's after just one session.' She's gone back to pretending I'm not there.

Mehreen looks confused and opens her mouth to say something. I wish I could give her a kick under the table, but thankfully Olivia notices my expression and cuts in.

'It's really wonderful,' Olivia says. 'Being around others with the same problems.' She side-eyes me and I relax. She's unpredictable, this girl. She looks like a perfect goody-two-shoes, but here she is, bullshitting to a woman she's just met. Unpredictable and interesting.

'Are there many people like you?' Mum asks.

I cringe at her wording, wanting to melt into the floor.

God, I hope Mehreen and Olivia don't think I'm anything like her.

'I mean,' Mum says quickly, leaning in a bit, 'I'd never even heard of *invisible disabilities* until Cara mentioned it to me earlier.'

'Invisible disabilities?' Olivia says.

Shit. This is where it all falls apart. I start to try and distract Mum again, but Olivia beats me to it.

'It's actually a really misunderstood category of disabilities,' Olivia says, making her face look like those people on the adverts with the starving children. 'It's far more common than you would assume. One in ten people suffers with an invisible disability of some kind.'

'Really?' Mum asks, totally into the conversation. 'Wow.'

I can't help but stare at Olivia. She doesn't even have a tell. When I bullshit, I can't keep my hands still, but Olivia is a freaking pro, keeping up the sad face while looking Mum straight in the eye. I look over to Mehreen and she's as stunned as I am.

'What the hell?' she mouths at me.

I have to bite my lip to stop my laugh. I shrug and tune back in to Olivia and Mum's conversation just as Olivia starts going on about how people sometimes think people like her are making their illnesses up, because there aren't any visible symptoms. Mum's leaning so far into the table it looks like she's going to fall off her chair.

'That's *so* interesting,' she says, as if she's just heard the latest gossip about one of her favourite reality-TV shows. She leans back and turns her attention to Mehreen.

'And what about you? What's your official diagnosis?'

Mehreen's eyes go wide again and she fumbles for something to say. I can tell she's about to blow this whole thing apart.

'Mum, can we go?' I say quickly.

'In a minute, sweetheart, I'm just –'

'No, Mum, I need to go *now*.'

That does it. She finally turns to look at me, her eyes going from my head to my legs, as if they might have somehow got *more* paralysed.

'What's wrong?' she asks, concerned mother/nurse voice returning.

'Oh, um, I just . . . feel weird.'

'Weird?'

'I'm just really tired. Can we go?'

'Oh, are you sure you're ready to leave? You were having so much fun. I don't want to spoil that.'

I can't stop myself from rolling my eyes. As if she didn't ruin it by coming over.

'It's fine, Mrs Saunders, we were done anyway,' Olivia says. 'Are you still coming round to mine tomorrow?' She looks at me with an innocent smile on her face.

'Tomorrow?' I ask, looking over to Mum, trying to flutter my eyelashes a bit.

'I don't know,' Mum replies. 'Your schedule's been all over the place lately. I think we need to get you back into a routine.'

Get me back under your thumb, you mean.

'Oh, it won't be for long, I promise,' Olivia says. 'We've just got a project for support group we need to finish together.'

101

'A project?' Mum asks. 'They make you do *work*?'

'It's for us to get to know each other better,' Olivia says, not missing a beat.

God, I need to learn how to bullshit like this girl.

'Don't worry, my house is totally accessible.'

My mouth drops a little at that. She sure knows how to play parents. It makes me wonder once again why the hell she wants to kill herself. If she can manipulate people this well, she'd get far in life if she tried. I kinda want to ask her for some tips. I think we could've been good friends actually. Pre-accident, I mean. Mehreen too. They're good people, easy to get on with. The first ones I've met who haven't been weird around me, where I haven't felt like they're thinking about my disability all the time. It's like they see me first, and then the chair. They didn't even mention the whole 'killing someone' business until it came up in conversation. Maybe they're not so bad after all.

Mum looks at me and I put on a pout, sad eyes and all.

'Oh, go on then,' she says.

17. OLIVIA

9th April
(9 days until Date of Termination)

There are days
where everything seems *fine*.
                    Better than fine.
Where I wake up
and it's almost like time has
                    turned

BACK
to
- before Daddy left us for the woman he'd been having
  an affair with for months
- before Mother buried herself in work, designing other
  people's perfect homes instead of fixing ours
- before the students of Blithe Academy started shunning
  the girl with the treacherous father
- before the monster took residence
                    in my brain.

<u>**Today is one of those days.**</u>

Today the *'family'* calendar has both green
and red pen,
which means they're **both** busy.

There's a pile of boxes in the hallway.
c r e e p i n g their way into the living room
the bedroom.
Creeping his way
F U R T H E R
into
our   lives.
I **PUSH** past them on the way to the kitchen.
The silence in the house is
the BEST sound
I've heard in months.

I put on Maria's apron,
place my iPod on the docking station,
and bake to my heart's content.

Raspberry macarons.
Lemon-zest shortbread.
Chocolate cheesecake.
Custard slices.
Chocolate-chip cookies.
Fairy cakes with sprinkles.

The doorbell chimes at 12.55.
Mehreen Miah is *always* prompt.

She looks taken **aback**
when she sees my
flour-dusted hair
and tatty gingham apron.
I kiss her hello,
laugh
when some flour *smudges* onto her black scarf.
Mehreen looks around
> at the gold-flecked wallpaper
> at the chandelier
> at the vintage rug Mother imported
> from Turkey

and I start to feel
embarrassed
at the life
my abode says I have.

Cara has the same reaction,
but I distract her with the *delicious* scent from the kitchen.

We take the food and *settle down* in the living room.
We start looking for churches
> and burial plots.

Cara selects songs she thinks **represent** *me*,
and I'm honestly **so** touched,
even though the first song is
> 'Rich Girl' by Gwen Stefani.

But soon . . .
soon we switch over

to watching YouTube videos
        of cats being scared by cucumbers,
        of Cara
                lip-syncing to songs
                with a group of girls
                who don't look anything like
                        people who Cara would be friends with.
Crumbs fall *down* the sofa cracks
and I know Maria will be **mad**
when she comes back from leave.
But for now
NOTHING
        matters
except the **laughter**.

But the laughter
is not **LOUD** enough
to cover the sound
                of the front door
                                opening.
Of *him*
        hollering,
                'Anyone home?'

                No.

NO   *NO*   *NO*

He's going to **ruin** it all.

They're going to *see* him.

They're going to KNOW.

He looks *confused* for a second . . .
(I've never brought **friends** to the house,
not since he and Mother got together.)
But his face soon
C   O   N   T   O   R   T   S
into that *grin*
that makes my **stomach turn**
and my heart **POUND.**

'Well, hello there, girls.'
NO NO NO NO NO NO NO NO NO NO NO NO NO

'Oh, um, hey.'

That's Cara.

'I didn't know you were planning to have company, Liv.'
LIV.   **He calls me Liv.**
I can't speak.
Can't even take my eyes away from him.
He's still grinning.
His eyes f l o a t
to Cara
then **LOCK**
onto Mehreen.

His eyes travel

up

     and

          down.

He steps *forward*,

arm **out.**

'Hello, I'm Dominic.'

Mehreen reaches out too.

They touch . . .

his hand

in her hand

        'NO!' I shout.

Everyone's heads

    TURN

        towards me.

Heart

pounding

pounding

pounding

'Let's go to the guest room,'
I say.
~~Too eager.~~
I stand up.
The laptop H
         U
         R
         T
         L
         E
         S to the ground

~~Too quick.~~

'You're being very rude to your guests.'

I need it to be **over.**
For him to **LEAVE.**
For it to just be **US** again.
For me to pretend.
For me to forget.

I know I should apologise to him.
Let it happen.

                    ~~Relax and it'll be OK.~~

But then I remember
              his hand
          in **Mehreen's** hand
       on its path **UP** her arm

into her **hair**
or onto her **breasts** . . .

'Come on, let's go.'
I look at the girls
through my thin *shield* of tears,
mouth the word

please

(Please. Please. Please. Please.)

Cara's eyes are fixed on mine,
her eyebrows furrowed,
her mouth **tight** in a scowl.

Please.

She moves forward,
almost **knocks** him over
on her way to the door.
Mehreen picks up the laptop off the floor,
says,
'It was nice to meet you,'
before leaving too.
I follow quickly.
Don't look at him.
Don't look at him.
Don't look at him.

Don't look at him.

'You know your mother and I can't abide rudeness,'
he whispers as I pass.

'We'll discuss this later.'

Later

Later

Later

Before Mother comes home.

Later

I shut the door behind me,
step into the hallway,
d   r   a   g   the girls into the guest room
and lock that door.
They're both staring,
and my first **sob** comes out
like a *whimper.*

A cry
for help.

18. MEHREEN

Olivia ushers us into a room just as opulent as the last, but apparently not enough to be the main living room. She's bawling, almost hyperventilating. I wrap my arm around her shoulder and lead her to the soft grey sofa. Her body is shaking, shivering, shuddering underneath my touch. I'm so confused as to what's triggered her; I've never seen her lose her composure.

'Shh, it's OK,' I tell her, rubbing her shoulder as she sits down.

She covers her face with both hands, her sobs wracking her entire body.

'Olivia, it's OK,' I say again. Although I have no idea if that's the right thing to say. Is it OK? Or is she having a panic attack? I've never been on this side of a panic attack. I don't know how to help.

'Do you want to lie down?' I ask.

Her sobs are quietening now and she manages to shake her head. Her body turns from shuddering to just quivering as she sniffs over and over. Cara grabs an ornate box of tissues and holds it out to Olivia.

'Thank you,' she says as she grabs one tissue after another after another.

A minute passes with her just wiping her nose, me rubbing her back and shoulders, sometimes stroking her hair, and Cara opposite us, almost glaring at Olivia.

'It's him, isn't it?' Cara asks quietly. 'He's the reason you're doing this.'

There's a brief pause. I turn to Cara to find a thunderous look on her face. Olivia's hands are still over her face, her body bent at the waist so her long hair curtains down around her head.

She nods slowly, before breaking out into a new wave of tears.

'That fuck,' Cara spits. 'That motherfucking fuck.' Her voice gets louder with every syllable until it's loud enough for Olivia to raise her head.

'Please,' she begs, looking at the door. 'He'll hear.'

'Let him!' Cara shouts. 'That motherfucking prick. I'm gonna kill him.'

'Cara, please!' Olivia reaches out to grab her wrist. 'Please . . . don't.'

They have a silent stare-off and I flick my head between them, trying to figure out what they're talking about.

'What does she mean?' I ask Olivia. 'That your dad's the reason?'

She burns me with her stare, her eyes wide and watery and red. 'He's *not* my father!' she yells.

I'm so shocked by this outburst that I take my hands off her.

Olivia's posture softens. 'Oh, Mehreen,' she says quietly. 'I'm sorry, I didn't mean to shout.' She reaches out for my

113

hand and I let her pull me close again. 'I just . . . he's Mother's boyfriend. *Not* my father. Daddy left a few years ago. He's . . . just her boyfriend.'

'Sorry,' I say.

I wait for her to go on, to tell me what they both seem to know, but she just lowers her head, takes her hand out of mine and begins ripping her tissue into shreds in her lap.

'So what has he done?' I ask again. I look at Cara this time.

'He's been abusing her!' Cara almost spits.

This brings on a new wave of tears from Olivia. I feel her body shaking against me.

Abuse? That's the type of thing you read about in books, see in films. Not something that happens in real life. Not something that happens to people you know. I can't believe she's been hiding something this big. Olivia always appears so composed, so . . . *normal* . . . I just . . . I can't get my head around it. So instead I wrap my arms around her fully, feeling her collapse into me, disintegrating completely. It's like the life has completely been drained out of her. I feel tears slip from my own eyes and run down into her soft hair.

The front door slams. Olivia's mother's boyfriend didn't say anything before leaving, which I think is for the best. If he'd come into this room, I honestly think Cara would have attacked him. She sits, still seething, in front of Olivia, whose eyes are now glazed over and staring at the bare white wall. We've all been silent for God knows how long, but as soon as we hear the door, it's like the room fills with air again.

Olivia's phone chimes, making all of us jump. She blinks a few times before reaching into her pocket to pull it out. She lets out a little gasp as she reads.

'What? What's wrong?' I ask.

'It's Mother,' she croaks. Her voice is raw. 'Her conference ran late so she's . . . she's going to stay the night there.'

'She's leaving you alone with that prick?' Cara asks, her fingers tightening on her armrests.

Olivia shrugs. 'It's not the first time,' she says quietly. 'It's OK, I'll just . . .' She trails off.

'Just what?' Cara asks. 'Lock your door and hope he doesn't come in and try to rape you again?'

The word ricochets around the room, bouncing off the walls and striking us all in the chests. I can feel Olivia start to crumble again, a teardrop falling onto her lap.

'No,' I say, sitting up straight. 'There's no way you're staying here with him tonight.'

'Mehreen . . .' Olivia starts, looking up at me with her glassy red eyes.

'No,' I say more forcefully. 'You can stay at mine. I can sneak you in – my parents won't even notice.'

'Mehreen, honestly, it's fine,' Olivia says.

'This is the complete *opposite* of fine,' Cara says. 'There's no way we're letting you near that monster again, right, Mehreen?' She looks over to me and I nod. 'You can both just come to mine,' she adds. 'Mum will be *thrilled* to see me doing something as normal and *girly* as a sleepover.'

Olivia begins crying again, but this time I swear I see a faint smile beneath it.

19. OLIVIA

Believe it or not, we actually got **on** *at first*.
I *trusted* him.
We **laughed**,
      went out as a FAMILY.
After years <u>without</u> a **father figure** in my life,
I *relished* his presence.

He bought me a dress for my fifteenth birthday.
White. Down past my knees. Elbow-length lacy sleeves.
Beautiful.
I *loved* it.
Wore it to my party.
I was wearing it the first time he came into my room.
The first time we were *alone* in my room.
The first time I started to feel scared.

<u>First times</u> are funny, aren't they?

The <u>first time</u> he *touched* me:
- in the kitchen
- his fingers trailing across my backside as he passed behind me.

o · He smiled as he reached up for a plate, pressing himself against me.

The <u>first time</u> he **kissed** me:
- He was **drunk**.
- I was tipsy.
  - It was another *special occasion*.
- He said he thought I was Mother
  - because I'm just *that* pretty.
- He made me promise not to tell her.
  - *'It'll be our little secret.'*

The <u>first time</u> *it happened:*
- I was fifteen
- in *my* bedroom
- I couldn't breathe, let alone scream.
- Mother had rushed out for a work emergency.
- I was just fifteen.

He told me it was *my* fault,
that I'd led him on,
thrown myself at him.
He said Mother would **disown** me,
        that I'd be a disgrace,
if I told anyone.
As if I would.
As if I ***could***.
*As if anyone would **believe** me.*

Respected lawyer vs delusional young girl

Mother never noticed
                    or perhaps just ignored
the way I retreated into myself,
how I didn't speak for days on end
                              after each time.
How I'd scrub myself *raw*,
trying to get the traces of **him** off **me**.
How I'd *flinch*
    any time he was near me.

The <u>first time</u> I tried to kill myself:
  • Mother found me in the front seat of her Audi.
      o Ignition on.
      o Windows open.
      o Garage door closed.
  • Found me far too early
      o Unharmed
      o Barely conscious, and **unfortunately** still very
        much alive
I couldn't speak.
Couldn't tell her
              WHY
                  I had done it.
Couldn't tell her
              WHAT
                  was going through my head.
I knew it would change everything.

That it would *ruin* everything.

But none of that even mattered.

Because Mother loves to jump to conclusions.

And she was

ADAMANT

that it was just an innocent mistake,

that I had just fallen asleep,

while listening to the radio.

The next attempts were foiled before Mother even realised:
- Scarves that were tied incorrectly
- Slit wrists where the blood clotted
- Vomiting up half-digested pills

And always

always

always

waking up

getting through it

surviving

but never truly

healing.

No matter what I *did*,

what I **tried,**

he kept coming

into my room

and each time
my soul   **br**   **oke**   a little more.

That's why I **need** this pact,
              need Mehreen and Cara.

I need **someone**
              to make sure the next attempt is the **last.**

                         'What about the police?'
                              That's Mehreen.
                    'Or a counsellor, or **someone***?'*

It's sweet
how naive she is.
So
DESPERATE
to find a solution.

She's like me,
like I *was*
before he *sucked* the **life** out.

                         'They wouldn't believe me.'
                              'We can back you up.'
                    'It's my word against his. He's a lawyer.'
                    'There's got to be *something* we can do.'
              'It's futile. Trust me, I've considered everything.'
       'OK, but now you're not alone. Now you've got *us*. We

must be able to help in some way.'

Us.
Two letters.
Such a *simple* word,
but such a
foreign
concept.
I've never been an **us** before
Never been a **we.**
Never had someone want to *help*
as much as Mehreen does.

She reaches out,
holds my hand.

'It's going to be OK.'

I **wish**
I could believe her.

'Right, that's sorted.'
Cara comes back into the room.
Her *scowl* has softened.
'You're both staying at mine tonight.
Mum's so happy she's out buying snacks, so you can't even
back out.'

The way she's **looking** at me,
the way they're **both** looking at me . . .
it isn't *pity*
or *disgust*.

It's love.
And the idea that these two girls
love me,
care for me
enough
to do this
warms my heart so **much**
I can't help but cry.

20. CARA

'Oh my God, she's so bloody embarrassing!' I shove my face into a cushion and scream. I can still hear the others laughing though.

'Your mother is *adorable*,' Olivia says, popping another Haribo into her mouth.

I forgive her for liking Mum, since it seems to have put a smile on her face. She and Mehreen are wearing my pyjamas; the trousers end halfway up Mehreen's legs and I can't help but laugh every time she tries to pull them down. I was expecting Olivia to complain that I didn't have silk PJs on hand for her, but it's like she's a different person now, as if us finding out about that fucking pervert made her feel OK enough to show us the real her. She wiped her make-up off as soon as we got here, and I swear I didn't even recognise her when she walked out of the bathroom. Without her make-up, it's easier to see how sad she really is.

The door opens and Mum walks in with another bowl of food.

'Jesus, Mum, remember what *knocking* is? That thing that gives other people *privacy*? Do you even know what *privacy* is?' I say.

Mum huffs. 'I just thought you might like some crisps to

'go with the sweets,' she says, pushing aside my open laptop to make space on the table.

'There's enough food here to feed Somalia,' I groan.

Mum frowns, leans in and whispers, 'I thought her name was Mehreen?'

Olivia chokes on her sweet. Mehreen bites her lip to hide her smile. Weirdly, just seeing their amusement makes me hate Mum a little bit less. I don't even say anything, just roll my eyes and move closer to the table covered in snacks.

'Are you done force-feeding us junk food?' I ask. 'What about all your lectures about healthy eating and taking vitamins?'

'It's only one night,' she says. 'Plus, it's not a proper sleepover without junk food.'

'This isn't a sleepover! We're not seven.'

'Your friends are *over* and you're going to *sleep*, so it *is* a *sleepover*,' Mum says, laughing and practically nudging Olivia with her elbow. If there was a prize for most embarrassing mother, she would win it, hands bloody down.

'OK, bye, Mum, see you later, Mum, get the hell out, Mum,' I say, fake happy, herding her towards the door.

'I'll check up on you in a bit,' she says as she walks out of the room, leaving the door half open, of course.

'How will we ever cope without you?' I ask loudly, closing the door behind her.

Olivia bursts into giggles as soon as we're alone again, and just hearing that sound makes me both want to laugh and cry.

'You're kind of mean to your mum,' Mehreen says, folding up her crisp packet into a little triangle.

'I'm not *mean* to her,' I say. 'It's just banter.'

'Mother would never stand for such backchat,' Olivia says, carefully unwrapping a Snickers bar.

But she'll stand for her daughter getting raped under her nose.

'Mine neither,' Mehreen agrees. 'Although I don't think I'd ever have the confidence to speak to her like that.'

'I'm not *that* bad,' I say. 'It's not like I'm calling her a whore or hitting her or anything.'

They both stare at me, wide-eyed. 'What?'

The laughter starts up again. It's weird how comfortable we feel around each other, considering we only met four days ago. I like them better than I've liked any of my 'real' friends, and when I'm with them I don't feel like 'the girl in the chair with the dead dad'; I'm just Cara.

I manoeuvre myself onto the sofa and then realise that's probably the first time I've ever transferred out of my chair in front of people other than Mum or the doctors. I look at them both, expecting them to be staring or shocked or *something*, but they're flicking through Netflix on my laptop.

There's a loud chime and Olivia picks her phone off the table. I hear her suck in a breath.

'What is it?' I ask.

'It's *him*,' she says, looking up at us. 'Telling me to come home right away.'

'Don't reply,' I tell her. 'You can pretend you didn't hear your phone or something.'

She nods slightly, still clutching the phone in her hand.

'What are you going to do?' Mehreen asks after a few

seconds. 'I know you said you don't want to tell anyone, but . . . what else is there to do?'

Olivia ducks her head and it seems like she's not going to say anything. I want to push her a bit, get her to face up to it, to make a decision, but that seems kinda mean, considering.

'Nothing,' Olivia replies quietly. 'That's what I'm going to do. Nothing.'

'What?' I ask. 'You can't just do *nothing*. You can't let him get away with –'

'What good is telling anyone going to do?' Olivia glares at me. 'They'll just blame me. *Why didn't you scream? Why didn't you push him off? Why didn't you tell him to stop?* As if I could have. As if *anyone* could understand . . .'

I'm really not a touchy-feely person, but I have such an urge to reach out and touch her, to hold her hand or something. She always does that with me and Mehreen when we're talking about the hard stuff, so I assume she'd like it back.

'It's not going to get rid of what's up here,' she says, pressing a finger to her head. 'It's not going to make me . . . forget, get closure or anything. I have to live with this . . . seeing it all playing out in my head . . . for the rest of my life . . . there's no . . . nothing's going to change that.'

I put my hand on her knee and squeeze. She puts her hand over mine and lets out a sad laugh that's almost like crying. 'It's funny – sometimes I feel as if the way he's affected my head is worse than . . . than actually . . . what he does. Do you understand what I mean?' She looks at Mehreen and she nods right away.

'He's your Chaos,' she says softly.

Olivia smiles a bit. 'I told you I understood.'

Mehreen basically launches herself onto Olivia, wrapping her arms around her neck.

'I'm so sorry, Olivia,' Mehreen says. 'I know it's a stupid thing to say, but I'm *so* sorry this is happening to you.'

'It's OK,' Olivia sniffs. 'It doesn't matter anyway. I guess I don't have to endure it for much longer. Although, I have to say . . . it helps, knowing you two believe me, and that you would listen if I ever . . . wanted to talk.'

'Of course. Collaboration and all that shit, yeah?' I say.

She begins to laugh, but stops when her phone pings again. Before she can even check it, I snatch it out of her hand and launch it across the room, into the laundry basket in the corner.

'What was that for?' Olivia shrieks.

'We're forgetting about that crap and just having fun tonight. You need a distraction.'

'So does that mean *no one*'s allowed a phone? Are you going to throw yours into the dirty washing too?' She raises her eyebrow at me – a challenge.

I shrug. 'Sure.' I slip my phone out of my pocket and chuck it into the basket. Mehreen stares open mouthed, as if I've thrown it on the ground and run over it. 'C'mon, Mehreen, you too. We're cutting ourselves off.'

'From what? The hordes of friends we have begging to socialise with us?' Olivia laughs.

'Exactly,' I reply. 'Shouldn't be hard then, should it? C'mon, Mehreen.'

She holds her phone to her chest. 'But . . . I mean, I'll just keep it here but won't use it.'

127

'Why? What's so special on there?' Olivia asks, leaning over to look.

Mehreen pulls it closer. 'No, nothing bad. I just . . . I'm playing a game I need to keep on top of.'

Olivia and I burst into laughter.

'What's that saying?' I ask Mehreen. 'One for all and all together?'

She laughs. 'All for one and *one for all*.'

'There you go, you just agreed to it,' I say. 'Phone, basket, now.'

She groans, but eventually tosses her phone onto the pile too. 'Not fair, I've been putting time into that game for *months*. You've just ruined my streak.'

'Your priorities are whack,' I tell her. 'Anyway, enough of this crap – can we get a film on already?' I snatch the laptop off the table and scroll through the menu.

'Ooh, my fave, let's stick this on.' I hand Olivia the laptop and shove some popcorn into my mouth.

They both start giggling. I look over and they're staring at me.

'What?'

'*You* like *Titanic*?!'

Oh shit.

'Um, crap, I think I clicked the wrong film.'

They fall back laughing and I can't help but join in.

21. MEHREEN

10th April
(8 days until Date of Termination)

The first thing I notice when I wake up is how stiff my neck is. Then I realise how much my back hurts. And my arms. And literally my whole body. I roll over and realise I'm not even in bed, just lying on top of a duvet on a wooden floor, with a thin blanket covering me. I automatically feel around for my phone to check the time, but it's nowhere near me. I can see the daylight pouring through the windows and realise I missed dawn prayers without my phone as an alarm. Crap.

I push myself up to a sitting position and see Cara is spread out on her bed, lying on her back, her face turned sideways into the pillow. Olivia is fast asleep too, curled up on the sofa. My heart sinks at the peaceful expression on her face. I can't even begin to imagine what she's been through, what must be going through her head. I can't believe she's been keeping such a terrible secret. I remember how rattled she was at her house yesterday, and the possibilities of what could have happened if Cara and I hadn't been there. But, of course, we can't always be there with her. This thought makes my heart hurt too much so I slowly stand up, stifling the urge to cry out in pain from the soreness of my aching body. I walk over to Cara's en suite, trying to pull down her ridiculously short pyjama bottoms on the way.

The bathroom has a handrail on the wall and a chair in the shower. I feel uneasy, just in case Cara wakes up and needs to use it, but my bladder's about to burst and there's no way I'm going to go walking around her house – imagine if I walked into her mother's bedroom unannounced! As I wash my hands I find myself thinking back to last night. A smile springs to my face at the memories of Cara screaming, 'There's enough room on that door for both of them!' at the TV, of Olivia seeing how many gummy sweets she could fit in her mouth at once. It was probably the best night I've had in years. It's like something's shifted – as if we've gone from people forced to be in each other's presence, to *wanting* to be.

I expect the others to have been woken by the sound of the toilet flushing, but when I get back to the room they're both still fast asleep. I could quickly do my prayers in the corner, but what if they wake up and think it's weird? It's probably better to just save them for when I get home.

Cara lets out a little snort and turns her head so she's facing the ceiling. Her breath evens out again. She reminds me a bit of my brother, as weird as that sounds. Imran and I used to be super-close, since he's only a couple of years older. We shared a room when we were kids, and I'd always try and wake him up accidentally on purpose: dropping things, coughing fits, loud alarm music. But he always slept like a log. Spread out right across the bed like Cara. I notice a pack of felt-tips on the floor (we were using them to play *Who Am I?* last night) and without even thinking about it, I grab a black pen and creep over to the bed. I nudge Cara lightly on the arm, then a bit harder, then harder still. Just like Imran, she doesn't move an inch. I uncap the pen and press the inky tip to Cara's upper lip, then stroke it from side to side. I pull away after the first line, but she's still motionless. I smirk and continue my masterpiece. By the time I'm done, Cara has a handlebar moustache, a small goatee and a unibrow. I place the cap back on and hide the pens with the empty chocolate wrappers and crisp packets. Before I can get back under my blanket, Olivia starts rustling.

'Morning,' I say, adding a fake yawn to make it look like I just got up too.

Olivia blinks herself awake and stretches out. 'Morning,' she mumbles.

Cara's still snoring away when Olivia and I finish getting dressed.

'We should wake her up,' Olivia says.

'You think?'

'I'm starving, and we can't really go looking for breakfast without her.'

'I guess.'

Olivia steps over to the bed, ready to shake Cara awake, but I stop her with my arm.

'I've got an idea.' I grin, thinking of another prank I used to play on Imran. I gesture for Olivia to go to the opposite side of the bed. As I sneak up to Cara's pillow and lean my

131

face in, Olivia catches on to my plan. She grins and does the same on the opposite side, so we're both a couple of inches from Cara's face.

'Caaaa-raaaa,' I call softly. 'Wake up.'

Cara's head shifts slightly, so that we can see her newly decorated face. Olivia's eyes dart to mine and I purse my lips to stifle the laughter. She does the same. When we've composed ourselves, we take turns trying to wake Cara. Our slowly rising voices do the trick; Cara's eyes flutter slightly, and then snap open. She lets out a scream as she sees our faces so close and tries to scoot back in the bed, hitting her head against the headboard instead.

Olivia and I fall on top of each other laughing.

'What the fuck?!' Cara screams.

We just continue rolling around laughing as Cara whacks us with her hands and eventually some pillows too, all the while showering us with insults.

'What's that on your face?' Cara's mum asks when we all go into the kitchen.

Cara's spent the last fifteen minutes scrubbing her face, but hasn't managed to get all the pen off. (How was I supposed to know it was permanent?!) My stomach drops when I notice how hard her mum is staring. It was meant in fun, but what if she thinks I'm a bad influence? I expect the Chaos to reappear and convince me that I've ruined everything, but it doesn't make a peep. I actually can't even remember the last time my Chaos was present, the last time it overpowered me. Noticing this is like lifting my head above water for the first time.

'Slept funny,' Cara replies, side-eyeing me. I'm sure she's mad at me, but then she smirks and I relax.

'C'mere, I'll get it off,' her mother says, grabbing a tissue and wetting it at the sink.

'No, Mum, it's *fine*,' Cara says, annoyance already in her voice.

I frown. Her mum's just being attentive; I don't understand the aggression.

Mrs Saunders walks over with her tissue and begins dabbing Cara's brow.

Cara swats her away. 'Oh my God, Mum, *stop*.'

They struggle for a few seconds, each pleading with the other. I can't help but smile at the interaction, but I feel an undertone of irritation towards Cara. She complains so much about her overbearing mother, but I would give *anything* to have either of my parents pay this much attention to me. My own mother saw the marks of my self-harm and yet the enormity of it didn't even register. I can't remember the last time she showed anything near the amount of affection as Cara's mum's simple 'I'll get it off'.

We're served freshly made American pancakes for breakfast. Mine and Olivia's are drenched in syrup and cream whereas Cara's just has berries. It looks like something you'd see in a recipe book. Even Olivia tucks right in without the usual inspection I've noticed every time we've eaten together – even last night she broke apart the chocolate bars to see the inside before committing to anything. Breakfast itself is the epitome of an idyllic family meal. It's like Cara, Olivia and I are actually sisters, with Cara's mum asking us all questions about our likes, dislikes, our lives in general.

'So how come you haven't got your scarf on?' Mrs Saunders asks. 'Do you not wear it while you're eating, in case something drops?'

'Oh my God, Mum, *stop*,' Cara says.

'I'm just asking!' she says defensively.

'Oh no, it's fine, honestly,' I say. 'I don't have to wear it all the time, just around men I'm not related to.'

'It's so you don't attract their attention, right? But what about if you're gay?'

Olivia chokes on her juice. Cara slides a hand down her face.

'It's more the idea of modesty,' I say, hiding my smile. 'It's a lot to do with how we conduct ourselves around everyone, women too.'

Mrs Saunders opens her mouth to reply but her phone rings and she excuses herself to another room.

'Sorry about that,' Cara says. 'She could work for the police with her bloody nosiness.'

'Don't worry,' I say. 'I'd prefer her to ask than make assumptions. I really like her.'

'Yeah, she's hilarious,' Olivia says.

'Hilariously embarrassing,' Cara replies, sneakily squirting some syrup onto her plate while her mum's back is turned. 'But she does make good pancakes.'

'She *is* just looking out for you though – give her some credit,' I say.

'She *smothers* me. You have no idea. Have I told you about the time she literally tried to spoon-feed me?'

Her mum rushes back into the room, as if on cue. She looks over at Cara with an almost pained expression on her face. I expect her to say something, but she just watches, not noticing me noticing her. She's clutching her phone to her chest as if trying to crush it into pieces.

'Is everything OK, Mrs Saunders?' I ask.

The others turn to look at her now and she shakes herself out of her trance, bringing the phone down and sliding it into her pocket. She plasters on a smile and walks back into the kitchen.

'It was a work call,' she explains to Cara. 'I'm going to have to pop out for a bit.'

Cara stiffens and stares at her mum.

'I'm sorry, sweetheart. It's an emergency.'

'An emergency you can go to *alone*,' Cara says slowly. 'Right?'

'Sweetheart –'

'Oh, c'mon, Mehreen and Olivia are here. They know how to call an ambulance if I randomly catch on fire. We won't answer the door to strangers. We're not kids, Mum. We *can* be alone for a few hours. Unless you're planning on leaving the country or something?'

'No,' she replies slowly. 'It's just . . . something I have to deal with.'

'And you don't want *me* getting in the way. Just *go*, we'll be fine. Right?' Cara looks over to us and widens her eyes.

Olivia and I pipe up on cue.

'Oh, yeah totally,' I say.

'Of course,' Olivia says. 'I used to be in the Girl Guides; I have great leadership skills.'

I can tell Mrs Saunders is having a hard time trying to make up her mind and I realise that she probably hasn't left Cara home alone since the accident. It breaks my heart a little, seeing Cara so desperate for her mother to say yes.

The phone starts ringing again and Cara's mum flicks her eyes between her pocket and her daughter.

'Remember what we talked about the other day?' Cara asks softly. 'Baby steps?'

Her mother smiles softly. 'No pun intended?'

'Exactly.'

It takes a second, but eventually she pulls the phone back out of her pocket, looks at it, frowns and cuts the call. Then she jumps into action.

'I'll only be an hour. Less than, probably,' she says, rushing into the living room and snatching her coat off the hook. She's putting her arms through the sleeves as she comes back over to us, chattering on like her life depends on it. 'I'll keep my phone in my hand *the whole time*, OK? Call me if anything goes wrong, and I mean, *anything*, yeah? And don't forget to take your vitamins.' She pauses in the kitchen, staring at Cara.

'Yes, Mum,' Cara says, more placatory than I've ever seen her. I can tell she wants to say something sarcastic but is forcing herself not to.

Mrs Saunders grabs her keys and pauses in front of us. 'Maybe I could –' she starts.

Her phone rings again and she gives Cara a huge hug, clutching her way too tight. Surprisingly, Cara doesn't complain. Or even roll her eyes. Her mum pulls back and looks at her again, just holding her by the arms. Her eyes are watery.

'*Go,*' Cara says. 'You're gonna be late.'

She picks up her handbag and rushes out of the door.

There's silence for a moment before Cara whispers, 'She *actually* left.'

'You OK?' I ask.

She begins to laugh, starting from quiet chuckling to full on maniacal laughter, head thrown back and everything. I turn to look at Olivia, wondering if we should stop this, whether Cara has actually blown a fuse or something, but she's just smiling at her.

'She *left,*' Cara repeats, turning around to face us. 'This is . . . This is the first time she's left here without me since the accident. I can't . . . I can't freaking believe it . . .' She goes quiet again, but there's a humongous smile on her face.

'So what do you wish to do with your newfound freedom?' Olivia asks.

'God, I don't even know,' Cara laughs. 'Let's get some drugs or crack open the wine! Let's smash shit up!'

'Whoa there.' I laugh. 'I assume you want this to become a regular thing? Not going to happen if she comes back to find the entire house demolished.'

'Hmm, good point,' Cara says, deflated.

'You can still have fun without going to extremes,' Olivia says.

'Maybe we could watch *Titanic* again,' I tease.

There's a familiar chirp from Cara's bedroom. An email alert on my phone.

'Whose is that?' Cara asks, twisting her head.

Another chime comes from the same direction. And then

another. We all look at each other before moving into the next room, towards the laundry basket; I'm a step ahead of the others.

'Itching to get back to your farming game?' Cara laughs as I begin rifling through.

'Ha ha,' I say, handing the others their phones before looking at mine.

1 new email from MementoMori

I look up just in time to see Cara's expression fall. Olivia seems unaffected as she scans her screen. No one says anything, so I swipe to open the message.

From: Administrator (admin@mementomori.com)
To: Mehreen Miah (mehreenmiah@hotmail.co.uk)
Subject: Reminder

Reminder:

We notice you are still to upload photographic evidence of having completed Task 2 as detailed below. Failure to adhere to MementoMori's policy of evidence provision contravenes our terms and conditions.

Task 2: Funerals are important for those left behind. To ease the burden, you should plan your funeral as fully as possible. Leave these plans in

an easily accessible place before your Date of Termination.

MementoMori recognises that you three, as teenagers, do not have the means to plan as thoroughly as someone of more advanced age and wealth could do. However, find below a list of suggestions tailored for you:

- Choose location - request price list and ask about services included
- Choose any service specifics - e.g. music playlist, hymns, readings
- Purchase funeral outfit

Reminder: MementoMori requires all users to complete tasks <u>together</u>; otherwise no further assistance will be provided. Failure to adhere to our rules and regulations will result in further action, as stated in our terms and conditions.

I look up at the others as soon as I finish reading; their faces are still aimed at their phone screens and I can't decipher their emotions. I can't decipher my own emotions.

I agreed to this.

I wanted this.

I *want* this.

And yet . . . reading this email, being reminded of what I've committed myself to . . . it's causing a . . . *weird* feeling in my stomach. A sinking, swimming, butterfly-like feeling.

'Oh, we forgot the photo,' Cara says. I can't tell whether I'm imagining the tinge of hesitation.

'I've got a photo of us from yesterday,' Olivia interjects. Her voice sounds normal. 'From the dressing rooms.' She starts tapping away.

All I can do is stare, flicking my gaze between the two of them to watch for any changes in their demeanour. Surely I can't be the only one feeling suddenly uneasy?

'We can get together again this evening to plan everything else?' Olivia suggests.

'Why tonight?' Cara asks. 'Why not now? Mum's not here; it's the perfect time.'

Olivia smiles a little, but it seems like her fake one again. 'Your mother has left you alone, just like you've been wanting for months, and your choice is to spend that time researching churches and hymns? What happened to *smashing shit up*?' She makes air quotes with her fingers.

This time when Olivia swears, none of us laughs.

I can barely even smile.

22. OLIVIA

The television is on
when I walk through the front door
at lunchtime.
But no one is watching it.
The Castletons would *never* be so **idle**.

I can hear Mother **bustling** around in the kitchen,
but other than that
it's quiet in the house.
His shoes aren't by the door.
His car isn't in the driveway.
His coat isn't on the rack.

I could have stayed at Cara's house.
Maybe I **should** have . . .
I could be picking out wreaths now,
writing a note to request a closed casket.
But even though Cara's mother *smiled*
and said it was **fine** to stay another night,
I know **deep down**
she didn't *mean* it.
Deep down

she wanted to know **WHY.**
Deep down
she was trying to figure out
what's **wrong** with me
and
deep down
I'm scared that she would have
prodded until
she found out.

> '. . . *A group of teenagers*
> ***died***
> *after being hit by a train . . .*'

I turn my head to the screen
where a woman in a **bright** red blouse and **bright** red lipstick
reads with no expression

> '. . . *We go over now to Andy Perkins who*
> *has the full story . . .*'

The reporter appears outside a train station.
Next to him stands a woman
who speaks of watching the teenagers [jump],
holding hands,
just as a train sped by.

'It was on purpose, totally on purpose.'

Next to her is
a girl.
A tiny
beautiful
innocent
little girl.
She **grasps** the belt hook of her mother's jeans
and leans in *so close*
that she's almost consumed by the

SHADOWS.
I can tell by her face,
pale
and **blank**
and **wide eyed,**
that she saw them *jump* too.

Mother calls from the kitchen,
'Is that you, sweetie?'
I don't know whether she means me
                                        any more.

I can't help but **wonder**
whether **he's** already told her
about how *rude* I was to him yesterday.

I take one last look at the TV,
at the girl

who's now chewing on her pink beaded necklace
as her mother *flails* her arms
and describes
the **THUD** of the bodies
against metal,
and I think
about the fact that
every time this girl **closes her eyes,**
all she will see
is the image
of those people
jump^{ing}
The train
H U R T L I N G.

The bodies.

The **thoughts**
and *images*
and ***memories***
will CONSUME her,
DEVOUR her.
It'll turn out to be
the **strongest** memory
she'll have of her *child*^{hood}.
Maybe of her whole life.

'It *is* you,' Mother says when I walk into the kitchen.
Maria is still on leave,

off *back home* as she calls it.
Because this is *definitely* not a **home.**
But the air smells of smoke
and burnt sugar
and mother is in

         . . . an apron.

An apron?

'What are you trying to cook?'
I say this
because mother *can't* cook.
It's a **known fact.**
It's why she hired Maria.
I'm also hoping I can distract her
enough
to **avoid**
bringing up *yesterday*.

Just thinking about
the fact that
he's going to be **back,**
that he's
ACTUALLY
moving in next week
makes me want to
vomit.

'I'm trying to bake some chocolate fondants.'
I look around the kitchen

and it's like a bag of flour has
E X P L O D E D.
Mother also has flour in her hair,
        on her cheek,
        on her clothes.

        We're **alike,**
        Mother and I.
        Baking is our release;
        I bake when I'm **HAPPY,**
        she bakes when she's sad.
        The only *difference* is that
        the treats I make actually taste **good.**

I look up at her,
at the red eyes
that she's tried to **cover up**
        with a full face of make-up,

at the hair that's been tied back in a rush
but still has loose tendrils
   c

       a

          s

            cading down
'Is anyone else home?' I ask.
Because I **don't** want to
       can't

won't

say **his** name out loud.

'Just us.'

She seems sad about this.

Doesn't see

that it fills me with **JOY**.

'Dominic had to go on a business trip,'

she says with a hint of annoyance

that makes my glee ^{SURGE}.

I can tell by her *tone*

that she's not *happy* about his trip.

Then I remember it ***clashes***

with the weekend away they had planned.

The weekend away I was *SO* looking **forward** to.

But this is better.

Much

much

better.

'When is he back?' I ask,

hoping

praying

wishing.

It's not within

eight days.

'Not for a fortnight,' she says.

I almost **Colla**pse

with **joy,**

almost
squeal
with *relief*.

But **instead,**
I pick up a few eggs
and teach Mother how to make fondants.

23. CARA

Mum was in a ratty mood when she came back from her work thing; she went straight upstairs to have a bubble bath. I decided not to rock the boat and ask to go out to meet the others again. If I want her to keep up this whole trusting-me-enough-to-be-a-normal-human-being thing, I need to take it slowly. Baby steps and whatever.

Cara: Soz, can't come round. Mum's being weird.
Cara: We can just plan online tho rite?
Olivia: *though *right
Olivia: Well, we've already sent the photo, so technically we've completed the task.
Cara: Yeh thats true
Olivia: *yeah *that's
Cara: *eyeroll*
Olivia: Mehreen? Are you OK with that?

Mehreen's been really quiet all day, and it's starting to worry me. She's normally yapping away in our group chat, telling us about the comic she's making about us. She showed me a sketch she did of my character and I was honestly speechless. She's so fucking good. Not that I know

149

what comics are supposed to look like, but I'd definitely pay for one drawn by her (especially if I'm in it). I can't figure out why she's gone mute all of a sudden. She looked a bit sad when she left this morning, but I thought that was because she was going home after a great night. Maybe she's got something going on with her too, something as big as Olivia . . .

Shit.

Cara: Mehreen! Where are you?
Cara: ?
Cara: ????

I spend the night in front of the telly with Mum, with my phone in my hand, waiting for Mehreen to reply. There's something up with Mum too; she's not making her usual comments about how disgusting the food on *Come Dine with Me* looks or how badly decorated people's houses are (as if ours is any better). I try to cheer her up by adding in the commentary instead.

'Nothing says "sophisticated dinner party" like a dress code of "prostitute", amirite?'

Nothing.

Mum keeps checking her phone and texting. It's weird. She has no friends, so her work must be picking up or something. I guess that's good, right? It'll keep her occupied when I'm gone.

It's weird thinking that.

In just eight days, she'll be sitting here alone.

I push that thought away and just focus on the TV, where a man is telling the woman who won to get out of his house. It's the most dramatic *Come Dine with Me* moment I've ever seen, but it feels weird to laugh.

24. MEHREEN

My phone keeps buzzing on the table. I know Olivia and Cara are waiting for me so we can sort the rest of our plans out, but every time I let thoughts of the pact enter my head unease starts bubbling around until my mind is clouded. But not with Chaos. Surprisingly, my Chaos has yet to resurface.

I distract myself from the buzzing phone with my laptop. I listen to the latest episode of my favourite podcast, *Dear Hank and John*, as I catch up on social media. There are tons of photos from my classmates on their holidays. Group shots from the bowling alley/cinema/dessert bar. I'm not the kind of person who gets jealous about this sort of thing, or the kind of person who *wants* a large group of friends – I've made do with the couple of close friends (if you can even call them that) I've had since the start of school – but I've never really had a *best* friend, someone I could tell anything and everything to. I don't think I've ever been as close to anyone as I am to Cara and Olivia. It's made me realise how much I was missing out on. More than that, I feel *different* around them; I don't feel the need to put the best version of me on show. I like that I can talk to them about anything, without them thinking I belong in a psych ward. I've always hated the cliché that 'talking about problems helps', but apparently it's true. My

Chaos seems to have disappeared ever since I started recognising it, rather than just putting up with it.

My phone lights up with more messages.

Cara: Mehreen! Where are you?
Cara: ?
Cara: ????

I feel bad for not replying, but what can I even say? They're booking churches, organising playlists, and me? I can't even think about the pact without feeling sick. How can I tell them I'm having doubts?

'Imran!' Mum shouts from the loft. 'Can you come here? I need some help!'

'Ask Mehreen. I'm busy!' he yells back. I can hear the click of his gaming controller across the hall.

'Mehreen!' Mum shouts again. 'Come here!'

I close all the windows on my laptop, clearing my browser history out of habit and shutting the lid before walking over to the stairs leading up to the loft.

'What do you need?' I ask from the foot of the pull-down ladder.

'Come up here – I need to move these boxes.'

The air is filled with dust particles, and I can't help but scrunch my nose as I climb up through the small hatch. I've always been scared to come up here; it feels like the floor is going to collapse any second. Mum's in the nearest corner, rummaging through one of the boxes that have been a permanent fixture in our loft for as long as I can remember.

'Your father is such a hoarder,' she moans, pulling out a backpack. 'God only knows why he wants to keep all this tat.'

'What's in it?' I ask, tiptoeing across the fragile floorboards.

Mum kneels on the ground, pats off the dust from the green and black backpack and unzips it. She begins to laugh as she pulls out pieces of creased paper. 'It's from when Imran was in nursery. Oh, look at this family picture he drew!' She thrusts a stick-figure drawing at me: Mum, Dad, and little Imran in the middle. Bright colours and the sun shining down on them.

'Oh, and this is the Mother's Day card he made me when he was five.' She stares at a yellowing piece of paper that reads 'Happee Motha's day'.

I don't even bother asking if there's anything of mine in there. When you've already got cards and drawings from the perfect son, why would you keep anything from the defect child? As she continues reminiscing, I kneel down next to her and begin rummaging through the rest of the boxes.

'What's this?' I ask, pulling out an A3 sketchpad similar to the ones I use.

'Oh my God, he kept my sketches?!' Mum exclaims. She snatches the book out of my hand.

'Your *sketches*?' I ask, craning to see as she opens it up on her lap.

'Drawings, doodles, whatever you kids call it. I don't even remember packing them when we moved from Bangladesh.'

I suck in a breath when I see the first page. I almost don't recognise Mum as the subject of the charcoal drawing, but it's her unmistakable eyes that pop out from her youthful face. She turns the page and there's a sprawling landscape watercolour of a paddy field.

'Wow!' I breathe. 'Mum, these are incredible.'

She continues turning the pages and I'm blown away by how talented she was. While I stick to one style in my drawings, Mum's experimented with so many different techniques and media. I want to snatch the book out of her hand and absorb the details of each individual piece, but she's flipping the pages so fast it's like she can't bear to focus on anything for more than a few seconds.

'Whoa, Mum, slow down.'

'Should've thrown this junk out years ago,' she mutters to herself. 'Look how much space it's taking up.' She throws the book back into the box and moves over to start unpacking another one.

I take the book back out while Mum's distracted, and open it towards the middle. Another watercolour painting, this one of a mosque in Bangladesh. The sharpness of the lines and softness of her shading has stood the test of time, even in this dusty loft. I flip to the next page and there's a pencil portrait of another face, someone I don't recognise.

'Who is this?' I ask.

Mum twists around and I half expect her to chide me for still looking at the book when she's dismissed it, but instead she just stares at the woman on the page.

'It's your grandmother,' she says softly, taking the book back and running a thumb over the lines of her cheek. 'I don't even remember drawing this.'

Grandma passed away before I was born; Mum barely talks about her and I realise that I've actually never seen a photo of her. I feel like I should make some remark, ask about her, but I also feel like Mum wouldn't notice if I did; she's utterly transfixed by the drawing. I take out another sketchpad from the box and leaf through the pages, forcing myself not to stop and stare at any one for long because otherwise I'll never get to see them all. There are a few more of Grandma and I feel bad for not lingering on them like Mum is, but I'm filled by an insatiable desire to see more and more.

'These are all amazing,' I tell Mum. 'I didn't know you were into art.'

'Where else did you think you got it from?' she replies, her voice returning to normal.

'What?' I ask, surprised. I've never shown anyone at home my comics or drawings. I wouldn't have thought Mum even knows I'm taking art GCSE.

'You think I don't notice you drawing away all the time?' she says with a smile. 'Some papers slipped off your desk when I was cleaning the other day. Your cartoons?'

'Uh, yeah,' I stutter. 'Comics. I like . . . drawing comics . . . and stuff.'

'They're good,' she says. 'I liked the one about the cat in the park.'

I smile automatically, inwardly grateful she didn't find any of the darker ones I've started hiding in my school bag.

'Thanks,' I say, feeling super-awkward. Mum and I rarely talk about anything real; it's always just practical things – shopping for school, when the holidays are, that sort of thing.

156

I'm shocked she's even noticed my passion, enough to acknowledge it out loud anyway.

'Is that what you want to do as a career?' she asks. She's turned around so she's facing me again; the first sketchpad is still in her lap, open to the portrait of Grandma, who stares out at us.

'I'm not sure,' I reply. 'It's a really hard field to get into. I'd have to take specialist classes and stuff.'

'So what?' she asks. 'Every job requires a specific set of skills. That's not a valid excuse not to do something.'

'I just mean –'

'Mehreen, I've seen how talented you are. You can't let that go to waste.'

'You mean like you did?' I cringe immediately after saying it. I'm not the kind of person who talks back, let alone to my parents. Cara must be rubbing off on me.

Mum drops her gaze back to her pad.

'Sorry,' I say quickly. 'I didn't mean . . .'

She shakes her head, caressing the portrait again. 'I wanted to take classes too. I spent all my spare time drawing, painting, making things, but then when it came to qualifications . . .' She looks up at me with the softest eyes I've ever seen, then reaches out and takes my hand. 'In my day, back home, girls weren't exactly . . . encouraged to study. My parents took me out of school after I'd done the required years. I wanted to go to college, university. I wanted to study too . . .'

'But they said no?'

She nods. 'Girls were supposed to stay at home, look after the house. They thought I wouldn't find a husband if I was

157

"too educated". And on top of all that, I wanted to study *art*! In their eyes, that was just a frivolous hobby, no money to be made, that sort of thing.'

'Wow,' is all I can say. My grandparents sound just like my Chaos.

Mum squeezes my hand. 'But it's different for you,' she says almost desperately. 'We're not in Bangladesh any more; you have *so* many options. I know your aunts and uncles and even me and your dad can be a bit old-fashioned, but I'm telling you now, Mehreen, don't let anyone push this down, push *you* down. You're talented, I've seen it, and you're also lucky enough to live in a time and place where you can nurture that talent. What I wouldn't give to have had that.'

I'm speechless, literally speechless. It's so weird having such a deep conversation with my mother, one where she's encouraging me to do something I'd convinced myself she would hate.

'Promise me you won't let it go to waste like I did,' she says, almost desperately. 'You know your dad and I will support you with whatever you want to do.'

'Really?'

She gives me a sad smile. 'I just don't want this to be you in thirty years, looking through old sketchbooks and thinking about what *could* have been. I want so much for you, Mehreen. You've got everything laid out in front of you – don't take it for granted. Don't make the same mistakes I did.'

She reaches up and cups my cheek, using her thumb to caress it. There's so much written on her face – pain, regret, sorrow, but most of all, hope. She has hopes for me. This

158

realisation makes my eyes immediately well up, and a smile appears on my face.

'I won't, I promise,' I say, taking her hand off my cheek and kissing it.

25. MEHREEN

11th April
(7 days until Date of Termination)

Bismillah hir-Rahman nir-Rahim . . .
In the name of Allah, the most gracious, the most merciful . . .

I take a deep breath and step onto the prayer mat. Mum follows my lead. She's got a slight smile on her face, a visual representation of the serenity that she embodies every time she prays. I smile too, starting to feel the same. We stand side by side and begin the dawn prayer together. I take my time, breathing deep, elongating the words, losing myself in the rhythm.

Mum finishes her prayers before me as usual, but today before leaving she kisses me on the head while I'm still knelt on the mat. This gesture makes me almost burst into tears. I start my personal prayer.

Allah . . . Alhamdulillah, thank you. For everything. Thank you
for bringing Cara and Olivia into my life. Please keep them safe
and ease their suffering. Please keep my mother safe and happy.
Somehow, please let her reignite that passion she had for art.

Please remind me not to be so hostile towards her in the future. Remind me to be more grateful because I know I have so much to be thankful for. Please help me find a way through this.

I get changed and go downstairs to help Mum cook breakfast. At first we stick to our own sides of the kitchen; she beats eggs at one counter, I grate cheese at another. But eventually we come together to make the omelettes and by the time Dad and Imran come down to eat, we're moving in sync, deep in a conversation about our favourite artists.

'Since when do *you* know how to cook?' Imran asks as he slides into a seat.

'It's not exactly rocket science,' I reply, sliding the last omelette onto a plate. 'You should try it sometime. Even *you* should be able to make breakfast.'

He looks up from his phone to glare at me.

'There's an idea,' Mum says, sitting down at the table. 'Imran, you can make breakfast for everyone on Saturday.'

'What? No way. That's unfair. I don't –'

'Know how to use the stove?' I suggest.

'Shut it.'

I take a bite of my omelette to hide my smile.

'I think it's a great idea,' Dad chips in. 'Imran, you take breakfast. I'll do dinner. We'll have a whole day of food cooked by men.'

'So we're having cereal and Pot Noodles?' I say.

Mum and Dad turn to me. At first I assume it's because they're shocked I'm so talkative, but then I realise they're just laughing at my joke.

Dad nods. 'It could become a nice tradition.'

'I'll stock the freezer with ready meals, just in case,' Mum says, glancing at me with a smile.

I smile back.

On my way out of the kitchen, I notice something new on the whiteboard we keep on the wall; the reminder about my dentist appointment has been erased and replaced with four faces: a family portrait. Mum and Dad beam from the middle, with Imran and me on either side. The detail in everyone's features is astounding, topped off by the fact she's drawn this with only a rubbish marker. Just looking at it makes me smile.

I take the pen and draw a few love hearts in the blank spaces before walking out of the front door, on my way to meet Cara and Olivia for our next MementoMori meeting.

26. MEHREEN

The sun's out in full force at the beach today, as are the families. There are sandcastles every few metres, and discarded plastic buckets and spades. Mothers fuss to apply sunscreen to children who just want to run into the sea. It's ironic that what these children do for fun is going to be the end of me.

Was going to be the end of me.

I have to keep repeating it in my head to make sure I don't lose my resolve.

I'm not doing this.
I'm not doing this.
I'm not going to kill myself.

I repeat the mantra in my head as I make my way over to the cafe we've been told to meet at. I'm not the first one here today; Cara and Olivia are already settled in at a table that looks out onto the beach. They notice me approaching and wave. They seem enthusiastic enough, waving with such vigour that anyone would think it's been months since we've seen each other, not just hours. That we've been friends for years, not mere days. I practise the words over and over as my flip-flops slap against the pavement.

'Listen, guys, I've been thinking . . .'
'I'm not the same person I was when I joined the website . . .'
'It's down to you two, really . . .'

'Unlike you to be the last one,' Olivia says as I sit down.

'Sorry,' I say automatically.

'Don't be, it's nice to change things up,' Cara says, pushing her sunglasses onto her head.

'So you'll be early from now on?' I try.

'Whoa, don't get too crazy,' Cara says, raising her palms.

'How're things at home?' I ask them both.

Olivia sits up straight. 'He's *gone*,' she says, with as much glee in her voice as a child being given ice cream for breakfast.

'What?' I ask, a shiver running down my body. 'Really?'

'Only for a couple of weeks for work,' Cara butts in. 'Don't get too excited.'

'No, *do* get excited,' Olivia says. 'A whole *fourteen days*. That's the longest he's been away since they got together.'

'That's amazing,' I say with a grin.

'I think they had a fight,' Olivia says quickly. 'I heard them on the phone last night. Raised voices throughout.'

'So what do you intend to do with this newfound freedom?' I laugh.

'Well, I only plan to be around for seven of those days,' she says. She sounds so blasé, it makes my heart skip. 'Speaking of freedom,' she continues, turning to Cara, 'how did you manage to escape Diane?'

'You're calling her *Diane* now?!' Cara shrieks.

'She said I could!'

'Well, *Diane* was too busy on the phone to really give a crap about where I was going. There's something going on with her; I woke up this morning and she was gone. Ten months she keeps me locked up, then all of a sudden she's leaving me alone without even mentioning it?'

'Isn't this what you wanted?' I ask.

'Well, yeah, sure, I guess. But I mean, it's weird, dontcha think?'

'Maybe she's seeing someone,' Olivia says. 'Mother was like that at the beginning – the secret phone calls, the random errands that took her hours.'

'What? No way. She wouldn't,' Cara says. 'It's hasn't even been a year since Dad –' She's cut off by a shriek loud enough to reach across the entire beach.

All three of us turn towards the sea, where a little girl about five or six years old in a *Shimmer and Shine* swimming costume is screaming her head off, pointing at something by her feet. I crane my head to investigate, but the girl is dancing around on the spot, obscuring my vision.

'Children are the worst,' Cara says, covering her ears. 'They should have muzzles.'

A crowd forms around the girl and I watch as more people start pointing at the ground.

'Something's washed up,' I say urgently. I stand up, the chair scraping hard behind me, but the little girl is still blocking my view of whatever's on the ground.

Cara and Olivia try to see.

'What is it?' Olivia asks quietly.

The mother of the little girl leans down to pick her up, stroking her hair and hugging her tight. The small crowd begins to disperse, leaving behind just a small boy. He pokes the thing on the ground with his spade.

'It's just a jellyfish,' Cara says, turning back and picking up her drink.

Olivia and I continue staring. We watch as another mother comes along to drag this boy away, leaving the carcass to be swallowed by the water.

After a moment Cara's watch beeps. Olivia catches my eye and I can see fear in hers. I wonder if we're having the same thought: that it could've been something much worse than a jellyfish.

I sit back down and Olivia looks away quickly as she takes her iPad out from her handbag. This is it. The perfect moment to tell them. But . . . how?

Before I know it, Olivia has the MementoMori website loaded up, her finger already resting on the screen. She gestures it towards me, but I hesitate.

'Guys, I . . .' I start. 'I don't . . .'

They're both staring, but my mouth has gone dry.

Just say it, Mehreen.

Say the words.

I don't want to do this any more.

They're looking at me, waiting. Wondering what the heck has happened to me.

'C'mon, Mehreen,' Cara says. 'Finger on. Let's get on with it.'

'I don't . . .' I sputter.

Words, Mehreen. Simple words. One sentence and it's over.

'I think something happens if we're not on time,' Olivia warns.

And so of course I reach over and place my finger on the screen, because that's the kind of pushover I am. The type of person that can't stand up for themselves enough to say, *Actually, I don't want to kill myself any more*.

The screen flashes white, as usual, and a jolt of energy runs through me, accompanied by a shiver of fear. I instinctively look around us, but this time sort of *wanting* someone to be watching us. If someone caught onto this, they could stop it.

A woman with a huge baby bag jostles past. Her bag hits Olivia on the shoulder and then knocks into the back of my head. The woman apologises profusely but it's as if she knocked some sense into me.

'I don't want to do this any more,' I blurt.

There.

It's done.

'It's fine, you can take your finger off now,' Olivia says.

'No,' I say. 'I mean *this* . . . everything. I want out of the pact.'

27. MEHREEN

'What?' Cara asks.

They're both staring at me now and I swear I can see a trace of contempt in Cara's eyes.

'What do you mean, Mehreen?' Olivia says.

I fiddle with my hijab pins and try and form the right words. 'I just . . . I'm not in that place any more. I feel like . . . maybe we're making the wrong choice?' I catch a glimpse of the *Shimmer and Shine* girl running up and down the beach and sit up in my chair. 'No, I *know* we're making the wrong choice.'

'What do you mean? What's changed?' Olivia asks.

A small laugh manages to pass my lips. '*I've* changed,' I say. 'You two . . . our friendship . . . it's changed me.'

'The fuck you on about?' Cara asks, brow furrowed.

'When we first met, I was at rock bottom. I guess we all were. And joining MementoMori seemed like the only way out. But after getting to know you guys, hanging out, talking everything through . . . I honestly feel like it was fate, meeting you at the lowest point in my life. As if God pushed us together to stop us making the biggest mistake of our lives.'

'You've been reading the Quran again, haven't you?' Cara asks flippantly.

'I never stopped. What's that got to do with anything?'

'It's brainwashing you – can't you see that? You were fine a few days ago, then you go read some passage about –'

'No, stop,' I say forcefully. 'You don't get to hate on my faith, right? This has got *nothing* to do with religion.'

'You're talking about fate and God's plans and whatever – of course it's to do with fucking religion.'

Olivia puts a hand on Cara's arm. 'Let her speak,' she says softly but authoritatively.

Cara rolls her eyes and crosses her arms. Olivia smiles at me and my heart leaps at the possibility that she might be understanding me.

'OK, so –' I take a deep breath – 'I told you guys about my Chaos, right? How my brain is basically my worst enemy? Well, ever since I met you two, it's not as bad. My brain is quiet. It's not telling me I'm useless, that everyone hates me, that I'd be better off dead. With you guys . . . I feel like you understand. And I can't tell you how much that helps. I feel like I can . . . *breathe* now.'

They're both still just staring at me. I know I'm rambling, but I need them to see, need their eyes to light up with realisation, with understanding.

'Can you both honestly say you feel the same as you did when we first met? That you still feel as bad? That you still want to . . . kill yourselves?'

Cara's still scowling; Olivia's biting her lip. I feel like she's on the verge of giving in, so I focus my attention on her; if she caves, we can make Cara see sense together.

'Remember when we first met? We talked about *why* we

were doing this, right? Olivia, what happened to you . . . what's *happening* to you . . . I can't even . . .' I shake my head and reach over to squeeze her hand. She doesn't resist. 'But it doesn't have to break you. You're *so* strong, Olivia. Stronger than the rest of us – no offence, Cara.' I look over and Cara cracks a tiny smile.

'I just mean . . . don't let him beat you, Olivia. You . . . you *can* get through this. We'll help you. We can come with you to talk to the police, your mother, a counsellor, *someone*. Just because this has happened to you . . . it doesn't mean you have to end everything. You can't let him win. If you die without reporting it . . . what's to stop him forcing himself on someone else?'

28. OLIVIA

NO.

Such a *simple* word,

yet so

HARD

to say.

'I don't want to do this any more.'

The words R

   O

    L

     L off her tongue

with such *ease*,

that I'm

S T U N N E D.

How is it so *easy* for this girl

to speak out
without **fear**

       of repercussions,
       of being shunned,
       of being cast out?

'Can you both honestly say you feel the same as you did when we first met?'

I can't.

'You're so strong, Olivia. Stronger than the rest of us.'

I'm not.
I'm weak.
I can't do this.
I can't do ***anything***

without them.

'We'll help you.'

Mehreen Miah
and
Cara Saunders
will **help** me.
They're on *my* side.
They *believe* me.
They believe **IN** me.

'If you die without reporting it, what's to stop him forcing himself on someone else?'

The twelve-year-old girl next door,
his young, blonde assistant,
my own mother.

NO.

29. CARA

She's gone crazy. Total flip-shit crazy. I know people always call anyone with a mental illness crazy anyway, but Mehreen has gone *literally* crazy.

'You're crazy,' I tell her. 'We can't . . . we can't just *stop* this.'

'Why not?' Olivia asks.

'Oh great – you too?'

It feels like being in the hospital again, being outnumbered by people telling me what I should be doing, what's *best for me*.

'Have you really thought about what comes after?' Olivia asks, like one of those hippie meditation people Mum dragged me to a few months back.

'It doesn't matter what comes after. We'll be gone,' I say, avoiding eye contact.

'You've seen what grief does to a person, Cara,' Mehreen pipes up. 'Do you really want to put your mother through all that again? Do you think she'd cope with losing your dad and then you too in just one year?'

I clench my fingers into a fist, thinking about Mum sitting on the sofa watching *Come Dine with Me* on her own, wanting to comment on how crap someone's food is, but having no one to say it to.

'Think about how much has changed,' Mehreen urges. 'I know no one can push the guilt about the accident out of your mind. But your mum – you almost fell down laughing with relief the other day when she went out without you. Does that not make you see that things can get better? You're starting to get what you wanted.'

I feel like storming off. Throwing my glass against a wall and stomping my feet so hard into the boardwalk that it splinters. But of course I can't. Mainly because Olivia and Mehreen have me trapped into a corner. But also . . . there's a part of me that knows she's making sense.

'There was something on the news yesterday,' Olivia says quickly. 'About a group of teenagers jumping in front of a train – did anyone else see it?'

I squint at her, trying to figure out what the hell she's on about. Mehreen shakes her head.

'A woman, a bystander, was giving an account of what happened. And there was this . . . little girl standing next to her. And you could just tell . . . that she saw them jump. That she saw their bodies collide with the train. Can you imagine how that's going to affect her?' Olivia's voice starts to go quiet and she looks over my shoulder at the beach. She nods her head in the direction of the brat who was screaming earlier. 'What if that had been our bodies instead of a jellyfish? I know you say you hate children, Cara, but you of all people know how much trauma affects the mind. You wouldn't be here if you didn't.'

I look over my shoulder towards the kid too. She's digging a hole with her hands, throwing the sand every which way

176

like a dog trying to find a buried bone. From the way she screamed earlier, you would've thought she was literally about to die, and now it's like it never happened.

'So you agree?' Mehreen asks Olivia. 'I mean, you think we should stop too?'

I turn back round and can't decide what I want her answer to be. What do I want *my* answer to be?

'I agree that circumstances have changed.' Olivia nods. 'And that we should reconsider the pact.'

Mehreen basically launches herself onto Olivia. 'Oh thank God! I thought I was the only one feeling like this. I was so scared you'd both still want to go through with it.'

Olivia laughs as Mehreen pulls away. 'We haven't convinced Cara yet.'

They both turn to look at me. 'What if I say no?'

'No what?' Mehreen asks.

'No to your no. What if I still want to go through with it?' I pick up Olivia's iPad from the table. 'Do you think MementoMori will find me new partners?' I tap the iPad and the screen comes to life. I'd forgotten we even logged in. I begin to read the message.

Task 3: When planning to die, most forget to consider the physicality of it. To prepare yourself for the pain of your final moments, try inflicting pain on each other. Learning to cope with pain will help you push through in your last moments.

MementoMori requires you submit photographic
evidence of having completed this task **together**, to
be submitted to the site administrators for checking
at the next meeting. Failure to do so will delay the
next step, and the process as a whole.

Next meeting: 15th April, 8 p.m.
Location: Hillingdon Park, Bridgeport BP7 8RT

Reminder: MementoMori requires all users to
complete tasks <u>together</u>; otherwise no further
assistance will be provided. Failure to adhere to
our rules and regulations will result in further
action, as stated in our terms and conditions.

'What the fuck?' I say, cutting off something Mehreen was
saying. I turn the iPad around and push it towards them.
'Look at our next task.'

Mehreen looks like she's gonna say something, but eventually she looks down and starts reading with Olivia. They
both gasp.

'No way,' Mehreen says quietly. 'They can't be serious,
right?'

'Surely that's not legal,' Olivia says. 'Inciting people to
physically harm each other?'

'You realise this is from a *suicide pact* website?' I say. 'People
that like telling others how and when to *kill* themselves?'

'Who do you think runs the site?' Mehreen asks, now
swiping across the iPad and tapping away. 'It seems weird,

178

doesn't it? To have a job that's literally just helping people commit suicide.'

'Why anyone would *want* to set up a website like this is beyond me,' Olivia says.

It's weird – I never thought about there being a person behind this. I just assumed everything was done by computers, but I guess it makes sense that there must be someone controlling it, especially since they marketed it as 'personalised'. It's scary as fuck to think that someone could be enjoying all this.

'Nope, nothing on there about the creator,' Mehreen says, letting the iPad drop back down to the table.

'This whole thing's getting pretty freaky,' I say. 'The first tasks were logical enough, right? But this? What's next? Asking us to practise waterboarding each other? It's fucked up.'

'Another reason to walk away,' Olivia says in her teacher/ mother voice, raising an eyebrow at me.

Walking away means having to live with Mum and her smothering. Having to keep remembering how Dad's dead because of me. But Mehreen's right, things *are* getting better. I'm here, without Mum hovering, for starters.

I roll my eyes. 'Fine, fine, I give in.'

'Really?' they both ask together, sitting up in their seats like kids being told they don't have to do their homework.

I shrug, trying not to show how relieved I am. 'I just don't want to follow some faceless website that thinks telling people to hurt each other is a good idea. One that wants photos of it too.'

They're both still watching me.

'We can still hang out though, right?' I ask quickly, then hate myself for sounding so desperate. 'I mean, I can't go back to being stuck at home with *Diane* all day long.'

'Totally,' Mehreen says. 'I was thinking we could try to help each other out? Our lives were miserable before, and I've sort of come to rely on you guys as an escape. It's been great to just get away from everything. Can we try and keep that up?'

'You mean we cured your depression?' I ask, raising my eyebrow.

'No, no, of course not. I just think it's really helped, having people who feel the same, who understand. I can talk to you two about things I wouldn't mention to anyone else, and you don't make fun of me, for *that* anyway.' She laughs and nudges me.

'So what are you suggesting?' Olivia asks. 'We form a real support group?'

'Yes! I guess so?' Mehreen says. 'I mean, like I said before, we can come with you to . . . tell your mother. And Cara and I mainly just need to get out of the house and talk about things.'

Olivia reaches over and puts her hand on Mehreen's. 'That sounds doable,' she says softly.

They both turn to look at me, so I put my hand on top too. 'Well, now that I'm not killing myself any time soon, I suppose I've got nothing better to do.'

They both laugh and they try to do a group hug over the table, but I'm having none of it.

'Can we get something to eat then?' I ask, rolling my chair back a bit. 'I'd kill for a fried-egg sandwich.'

'Oh!' Olivia almost jumps out of her seat. 'I've just had the *best* idea.'

'Full breakfast instead of just a sandwich?' I ask, looking to see if the breakfast menu is still out.

'This decision is huge,' she says, ignoring me. 'We need to mark the occasion.'

'I swear to God, if you suggest a picnic or some shit –'

'You don't believe in God,' Mehreen says, 'so that makes no sense.'

'Neither does your face,' I say, sticking my tongue out at her. She sticks her tongue out at me too, making me laugh.

'No, no,' Olivia says. 'I mean something *significant*, not just sandwiches on a blanket.'

'What did you have in mind?' Mehreen asks.

'I know *just* the thing,' Olivia replies with a huge grin.

30. OLIVIA

When Mother and Daddy ~~separated~~

> divorced,

Mother didn't cry,
> didn't **SCREAM,**
> didn't **break** things.

> Well, not right away, anyway.

Instead she took Daddy's clothes,
> his golf clubs,
> the bottle of thirty-five-year-old Scotch he was saving
and threw all of it into
the firepit in the back garden.
She said it was *symbolic*
since he'd left her for a <u>Fire Risk Assessor</u>.

We roasted marshmallows over his burning possessions,
she *slurr*

> *r*

> *rr*
> *rred*

> that men weren't *worth it*,
> that I was better off

ALONE.

She told me never to get married.

> I was ten . . .
>
> Hadn't even had a crush.

His clothes began to *shrivel* immediately,
spurred on by the alcohol.
But the clubs were resilient,
Unwavering.
Like Daddy's love for the woman he called his soulmate.
> the woman he'd been cheating on Mother with.
> the woman who said she was 'too young' to take on a
> stepchild.

The next day,
Mother woke up
bright and *sparkling*
(with perhaps a well-disguised hangover).
She told me the *ritual* from last night
had left her *cleansed*.
That she felt she could now
~~draw a line~~
under all things
Daddy.

I didn't want her to ~~draw a line~~.

I wanted him to move back **home**,
for our family to be *whole* again –
even if the love wasn't there.

                    (Had it **ever** been there?)

But she just said,
'Now I really feel like I can move on.'
(Although she didn't. She cried and drank and begged him to come
back for weeks afterwards.)

But the *poetry* of the fire
STUCK with me.
And so I tell
Mehreen and Cara
to meet me at the beach
tomorrow morning
for a *ritual* of our own.
So that we can finally
~~draw our own line~~
under all this unpleasantness.

31. MEHREEN

12th April
(6 days until Date of Termination)

I've never been on the beach at dawn before. It's completely deserted. There aren't even any seagulls, although maybe that's because I don't have any food. I really thought more people would be here – maybe not for the same reason as me, but . . . aren't sunrises on the beach supposed to be a thing?

I pull up the backpack strap that's slipped off my shoulder and continue walking towards the slipway that runs from the pavement down to the sea, where I can already see Cara waiting. I check my watch, worried I might be late, but somehow she's the one who's early today. I duck my head, hiding my smile, and continue walking up to her. It doesn't look like Olivia's arrived yet, which is weird considering she lives only a few minutes away.

'Geez, about time!' Cara moans, rolling her eyes as always.

I stop short when I get close to her. 'Are you wearing a dress?!' I practically squeal. I eye her bare calves and the grey material that stops at her knees.

Cara surveys her body casually, then looks back up at me with a smirk. 'D'you like it?'

'Olivia will be *thrilled*,' I laugh.

She laughs too. 'I know, right?'

I thought Olivia told us to come in our funeral outfits. 'What happened to the clothes you bought the other day?'

Cara shrugs, fiddling with her armrests. 'She keeps going on about how *special* today is meant to be, so I thought I'd make it *really* special.' She nods towards my backpack. 'You got everything she asked for?'

'Yeah. Any ideas what she's got planned?'

'I guess we're about to find out.' Cara waves to Olivia, who's now at the top of the slipway.

'Morning!' she chirps when she reaches us.

'The sun's barely up. Don't think you can call it morning yet,' Cara mutters.

Olivia starts to respond, but stops almost immediately when she registers Cara's outfit. Her eyes go so wide I'm sure it must be painful. 'Is that . . . a *dress?*'

Cara and I laugh.

'Well, you wanted symbolism . . .' Cara says. She looks to Olivia, who's now frowning. 'I always said I wouldn't be *seen dead* in a dress . . . Get it?' she expands.

Olivia bursts out laughing – so loudly I wouldn't think it possible from someone so petite. I feel my heart constrict slightly, and a smile spreads across my face from seeing her so happy.

'That's *perfect*,' she splutters. 'I love it.'

Cara does a mock bow.

'So are you going to tell us exactly what this *anti-suicide ritual* entails?' I ask.

'You mean you've never done one before?' Cara jokes.

'Did you bring our notes and funeral plans?' Olivia asks, ignoring her.

'Yeah,' I reply, shrugging my backpack off one shoulder and swinging it round to my front. 'All in here.'

'And you have no sentimental attachment to that bag?'

I cock an eyebrow at her. 'I have no sentimental attachment to *any* bag.'

'Excellent!' She grins. 'Now we just need to get some stones.'

'Stones? What for?' I ask.

'Are you gonna tell us what we're doing or what?' Cara asks. 'I'm freezing my balls off here.'

'OK, so,' Olivia says, tucking a strand of hair behind her ear. I swear her eyes light up. 'I was thinking that to draw a line under everything, we need to erase the evidence. A purge, if you will. I was thinking it would be rather poetic to let the sea wash this experience away. Both physically and emotionally.' She turns to look at Cara and me in turn; we must both be looking really confused because she sighs dramatically.

'I wanted us to put everything in that bag with some stones and drop it into the sea,' Olivia says in a flat tone.

'That's *it*?' Cara exclaims. 'You got us up at the butt crack of dawn, made us get all dressed up, to come and toss a backpack into the sea?'

'C'mon, go easy on her.' I nudge Cara. 'I think it's a great idea, Olivia. I'm all for symbolism.'

'It's fine, we don't have to,' Olivia mumbles, looking down to the ground. 'I should have discussed it with you first.'

I glare at Cara, nodding my head towards Olivia.

Cara rolls her eyes. 'No, it's fine. I guess it sounds cool. Kinda like a "fuck you" to the idiots who run the website?'

'Yes! Exactly,' Olivia squeals, back to her chirpy self.

'OK, I'm in,' Cara says.

'Ditto,' I say with a smile. 'So, stones?'

We stand in a line at the edge of the concrete slipway, watching the waves rushing towards us, pausing, then retreating. Teasing. Inviting. Begging. I've always been enchanted by the sea, the soft call, the refreshing spray, the slight salty tang that lingers for days. When the website deemed this the place of our death, I took it as a sign that I was doing the right thing. But now . . . now it seems like fate chose this place to show me the way out. The *real* way out. A sharp gust of wind makes my headscarf flap in the air like a white flag. I try to fix it back in place but the force is relentless, pushing and pulling it in every direction. After a while I give up trying and just enjoy the feeling of the breeze and seeing everything tinted in white.

'Are we ready?' Olivia asks.

'I feel like we should say something soppy,' I say, fixing my scarf. 'Seems appropriate, don't you think?'

'People are gonna start showing up soon,' Cara says. 'If they catch us, they'll call the police right away.'

'She's right,' Olivia says. 'It would be nice to do speeches, but we're cutting it fine.'

The sea gurgles a soft call, an invitation. I look out to the endless stretch of water and feel a sense of wonder filling me. I match my breaths to the ebb and flow of the waves and begin to see myself as an extension of it. The kaleidoscopic sunrise today really is breathtaking; the pinks, purples, oranges and blue all shimmer on the mirrored surface, the sea looking like the gateway to Paradise.

'Right, step one,' Olivia says. She picks a stone out of the backpack and pulls a Sharpie out of her pocket, then passes both items down the line to Cara. She gives me a pair too, and keeps a set for herself.

'What's this for?' I ask.

'I read about it online,' she explains. 'You're supposed to write the thing you want gone from your life. Whatever's causing you the most distress. When the sea engulfs it, it takes the problem with it too.' She uncaps her pen and starts scribbling on her rock.

'So we're all writing Justin Bieber, right?' Cara asks.

I giggle, but Olivia tuts. 'You've got to take this seriously, Cara,' she admonishes. 'Otherwise it won't work.'

'Just humour her,' I whisper.

Cara rolls her eyes, as expected, but begins to write.

I uncap the pen with my teeth and place the tip on the smooth surface.

Write the thing you want gone from your life. Whatever's causing you the most distress.

I don't even need to think about it. I scribble 'The Chaos' and trace the letters over and over so that the words are as angry as the voice in my head. The others look up a few

seconds later and we all nod at each other before taking turns
to throw the stones into the sea. A flock of seagulls squawks.
The stones are easily swallowed and we all watch as the
ripples fade to nothing.

'Nice,' Cara appraises.

'Right. Next,' Olivia says. She picks up the backpack filled
with stones, our suicide notes and our funeral plans and holds
it to her chest. She begins wading into the sea, letting out a
loud gasp as the water hits her.

'Are you OK?' I ask. 'Want me to do it?'

'Y-you s-said you're a t-terrible swimmer,' Olivia chatters.
She's waist deep in the sea now. 'Not r-risking it.'

I feel bad just standing here, watching her in pain. But
then I hear a giggle escape from her mouth. She's up to her
neck now, and turns to face us, the biggest grin on her face.
It's infectious.

'You doing all right in there, Little Mermaid?' Cara asks.
There's a hint of bitterness in her voice.

Olivia nods before taking a deep breath and sinking under
the water. I try and peer in to watch her drop the bag, but
she's too far out and the water is too murky. There's a tense
few seconds of silence, and I expect Cara to say something,
but she doesn't. Then Olivia's head emerges and she's moving
her arms to stay afloat.

'Do you feel all *cleansed* now?' Cara teases. The bitterness
has gone up a notch.

'No, but I will in a few seconds,' she says, before swooping
her arm to splash Cara and me with a wave of ice-cold water.

'Oh my GOD, that's freezing!' I say, shrinking away.

Olivia's laughing again, and that spurs me to run into the water to join her. I scream from the blast of cold invading my body, but it's mixed with a squeal of laughter. I feel myself being pulled in by the waves and look back to see Cara sitting in the same place, looking all glum. I turn and wade towards her.

'Cara, what's w-wrong?' I ask, shivering all over as I emerge from the water.

She sighs, looking out at the sea instead of at me. 'I just . . . I miss it. I miss being able to splash around like that. Not that I was a good swimmer or anything, but it just hits me sometimes, that I'll never be able to feel that again.'

'Oh, Cara, I'm so sorry,' Olivia calls out. 'I didn't think.' She swims back to the shore and comes out to stand with us.

'No, shit, *I'm* sorry.' Cara shakes her head. 'I didn't mean to bring the mood down.'

'Don't be silly,' I say, placing a wet hand on her shoulder and squeezing. I look around the beach, trying to think of a way to cheer her up. A thought pops into my head when I spot a discarded toy bucket. I rush over, pick it up and fill it with water, before returning to Cara.

'I know it's not the same . . .' I say.

Cara turns to look at me but before she fully realises my intention, I throw the water over her in one swift movement.

She screams instantly, but I can hear the laughter start to come through soon enough, peppered with a few choice swear words of course.

'F-fucking hell,' she says, wiping the water out of her eyes. 'Yep, j-just as cold as I r-remember it.' She laughs.

I fill up the bucket again, and this time hand it to Cara. 'Here,' I say. 'You can get me back.'

Cara takes the bucket and looks at me mischievously.

I wait for the splash attack, but it doesn't come. Instead, Cara throws the pail of water right at Olivia's face. I hear her cackling as Olivia squeals.

Cara's returned enthusiasm makes me smile. I take the bucket and fill it up again before wading into the sea and trying to splash her from there. A water fight ensues and by the time people start coming onto the beach for their morning run, we're all drenched and laughing so hard that any little thing sets us off again.

It's honestly a wonderful way to start the day.

32. CARA

When I get home, nothing has changed. The whole place still looks as if an eighty-year-old decorated it, and downstairs stinks of last night's curry. I mean, I wasn't expecting a sneaky sixty-minute makeover, like on those awful daytime TV shows, but coming back here reminds me that really nothing has changed. And yet *everything* has.

Mum's still asleep, which is understandable since it's crazy o'clock in the morning. It feels weird, sneaking into my own house. I close the door quietly and go straight to my room. It's like the sound of my chair on the wooden floor is a million times louder today, and I keep expecting Mum to come running down. I think up an excuse, just in case.

'Just getting a drink, Mum.'

'Why are you fully dressed?'

'Um . . . I fell asleep like this. The make-up too.'

God, Mehreen's over-preparedness/paranoia is starting to rub off on me.

I change my clothes in the bathroom, getting annoyed when a strap of the dress gets stuck on my chair. It takes me forever to get changed and I feel completely exhausted after. I wrap the dress in another top and shove it down to the bottom of my hamper. I know I'll never get back to sleep, but it makes sense to get back in bed, just to keep up the sneak factor. You'd think I'd gone out to snort coke or go to a rave, not for some poncey anti-suicide ritual at the beach. Thinking about this makes me laugh. My phone vibrates with a text from Mehreen filled with just a string of hearts. I reply with a line of aubergine emojis.

I can hear creaking from upstairs, so I quickly stash the phone and pull my duvet over myself. The creaking eventually turns into footsteps on the stairs. I can hear Mum whispering as she moves into the living room, on the phone to someone, I'd say, guessing by the pauses between her talking. Judging from the way she's tiptoeing, she's up to something shifty. I try hard to catch what she's saying, while being ready to pretend to be asleep. Who the hell would she be on the phone to at this time?

'. . . But it said on the form . . .' I hear her say as she rifles through the drawers of the cabinet near the TV. She sounds on the verge of tears. Probably a missed deadline or something.

'*No*,' she says forcefully. 'There's no way I'm telling Cara.'

Wait – what?

I push myself up in the bed, hoping she doesn't hear the bedsprings.

'It hasn't even been *a year*,' she hisses. 'She's just getting used to things, why would –'

She moves further away and I can't hear her any more. What is she talking about? The accident? If it's the doctors she's speaking to, she'd be sucking up to them, not fighting them off. Or is she talking about Dad? I think about getting

194

back in my chair so I can go closer to the door, but her steps are closer now; she could walk in any second.

'OK, OK,' she says. '*Fine*, yes. Can you just take care of it, please? I've kept the letters here somewhere.'

She pauses outside my door. I can feel her about to come in, so I get under the covers again, but not before I hear her end the conversation.

'Thanks, love, I don't know what I'd do without you.'

33. OLIVIA

They've **definitely** had a fight.
Mother no longer **mentions** him at
every opportunity,
no longer calls him
every night.
Not even to *argue*.

The photo
on the mantelpiece
has also **disappeared**.
The boxes of his possessions have been
relegated to the **spare** bedroom.

Could it be?
*Is he finally being **pushed** out of our lives?*

At **breakfast**
I *try* to tell Mother my secret . . .
But
she's baking **again**.
She *meticulously* measures out

- sugar
- flour
- butter

All the while
humming.

I can't very well tell her *that* when she's humming.

At **lunchtime**,
I try to pluck up the **courage**,
but Mother suggests
we go out to eat:

just her and me –
something we haven't done
in a
L O N G
                             L O N G
                                               time.

And then by **supper**
I've decided
I'm not going to **ruin** this
amazing
beautiful
BOND
we now have
by telling her the *truth*.

34. MEHREEN

I dip my brush into the cup of water and swish it about until it's clean. Then I flick the tip up and down on the blue block in my palette of watercolours before spreading it across my page. I repeat this action, mixing pinks and oranges into the blue, trying to recreate the sky from this morning, but failing. I'm not used to watercolours; they're not traditionally associated with comic books, but there was no way I was going to be able to capture that sky with anything else.

I leave the top half to dry and focus on the bottom, using a Sharpie to draw over the pencil sketches of Olivia, Cara and me hand in hand at the edge of the sea. When I'm done, I stretch back in my seat and admire the completed picture. It's the most fitting end to my comic. I pull across the rest of the pages I've been working on since the pact started and flick through them, noting how they show my journey, not only through the narrative, but through my style; scratchy and heavy at the beginning, ending with the fusing of what looks like every colour on the planet. I can't wait to get a copy over to Cara and Olivia. I just hope no one else finds it and questions us about it. Or at least that they believe it's all fiction.

I can't stop looking at the watercolour picture. Just thinking about this morning makes me break out into a smile. How weird to think an 'anti-suicide' ritual could turn out to be such fun. Mum even picked up on my changed mood; at dinner she asked me why I was so smiley. I just had to pretend the food was extra delicious. Even Imran's comments about my weight didn't spoil my mood, which is a first. Maybe I really can draw a line under all the bad stuff.

I take a photo of the painting and text it to the girls with the caption 'Just the front cover to go!' They both message back almost instantly, gushing over my picture.

Mehreen: I miss you guys.
Cara: You saw us literally twelve hours ago.
Olivia: Were you serious about the support group idea?
Mehreen: Totally!
Mehreen: First meeting tomorrow?

We make plans to meet at the graveyard again. Olivia and her symbolism. I put my phone down but it buzzes straight away. I assume it's Cara or Olivia, but it's not.

1 new email from MementoMori.

My stomach sinks. The sense of dread I feel on a Monday morning with PE first period invades me. With everything that's been happening today, spending time with the girls, putting everything behind us, I never even stopped to wonder what would happen with the website. I hesitate for a second before deciding to open the email, my curiosity getting the better of me.

From: Administrator (admin@mementomori.com)
To: Mehreen Miah (mehreenmiah@hotmail.co.uk)
Subject: Reminder

We notice you are still to upload photographic evidence of having completed Task 3 as detailed below. Failure to adhere to MementoMori's policy of evidence provision contravenes our terms and conditions.

Task 3: When planning to die, most forget to consider the physicality of it. To prepare yourself for the pain of your final moments, try inflicting pain on each other. Learning to cope with pain will help you push through in your last moments.

MementoMori recommends starting small and increasing your pain levels as you progress.

Reminder: MementoMori requires all users to complete tasks together; otherwise no further assistance will be provided. **Failure to adhere to our rules and regulations will result in further action, as stated in our terms and conditions.**

I can't help but wonder how many people signed up to

MementoMori before we did, how many people actually went through with it, and who's behind the website. Who sits on the other end and sends out these emails inciting people to kill themselves. It's not as if they get paid, so why do they care? What do they get out of it? Just sick pleasure from seeing photos of people doing these tasks?

Mehreen: Did you just get another email?
Cara: Yep. Just stocking up on plasters before I start harming myself.
Mehreen: They can't actually do anything about us stopping, right? Legally?
Cara: As if they'd have a leg to stand on. 'Your honour, I'm suing these underage teenagers because they didn't kill themselves in the way I told them to.' Sounds legit.
Olivia: Cara's right – this wouldn't stand up in court without them looking like the villains.
Mehreen: So there's nothing to worry about?
Cara: Nah, just ignore their emails. They'll stop when the deadline passes.
Olivia: By the way, did either of you look up what Memento Mori means?
Cara: Um, no. We're normal.
Mehreen: It means something? I thought it was just a made-up name.
Olivia: It's Latin for 'remember that you will die'.
Cara: Cheerful.

I stare at the email for a few seconds before deleting it. I make sure to remove it from my trash folder too before returning to chat to the girls about our meeting tomorrow.

Mehreen: Olivia, any chance of you bringing some more of those macarons?
Cara: Cupcakes too!

35. CARA

13th April
(5 days until Date of Termination)

I miss cereal. I used to love Shreddies with hot milk and like three spoons of sugar, or Coco Pops that had been soaking for so long the milk was dark brown. But the doctors forced Mum to put me on a health kick, so now she's all about porridge and avocado toast and bloody quinoa for breakfast. Quinoa isn't even a food. I've noticed recently, though, that she's not been so bad. Pancakes the other day with the girls, French toast, a full English. She's slipping, and I've figured out why. She's been trying to butter me up so I wouldn't be pissed she's basically cheating on Dad. I know it's not *technically* cheating, but c'mon, the guy's been dead five minutes and she's already calling someone else 'love'? I bet he's a dick. And hairy. I bet he has a scraggly beard he can't keep crumbs out of. And fat fingers. Oh God, what if she's a cougar? What if this is her midlife crisis and she's dating some twenty-year-old just because that one time some guy said she looked like my sister. God, I can't even.

'More eggs, sweetheart?' Mum asks from over at the stove. Her back is turned to me so I can't tell whether she's smiling or wearing make-up, can't figure out whether she looks different in some way.

'No,' I reply, dragging a string of scrambled eggs through the ketchup on my plate.

'You sure?' she asks, cracking another egg anyway. 'I made them just how you like them.'

I wonder how *he* likes his eggs in the morning. Does she know? Has she spent the night with him? Has she been fucking him this whole time? Wait – what if it started before Dad even died? No, she wouldn't . . . would she?

She's standing in front of me now, frying pan in her hand. I stare at her face. She's not wearing any more make-up than normal. I can't smell any new perfume, her hair's still a fucking state. Which is good. Or is it bad? Does it mean that she's comfortable enough with him to meet him looking like crap?

'I said, "Is that OK?"' Mum asks a bit louder, as she scrapes more eggs onto my plate.

'I said I didn't want any more!' I shout, shoving my plate towards her. It knocks into my glass of juice and sends a loud TING bouncing around the room.

'Honey, what's wrong?' she asks. 'Did something happen between you and your new friends?'

'What? No, *God*, you're so . . .' I stop myself from going off on one, from telling her what I'm really thinking. I need to keep her on my side, keep up this *best friends forever* crap if I want her to keep letting me out of the house alone.

'Sorry,' I force myself to say. 'I . . . didn't sleep well, I guess.'

'Should I call the doctor? Are you getting the flu or something?' She tries to put her hand on my forehead but I wriggle away.

'*No*. Jesus, Mum, give it a rest.'

'I'm only looking out for you. Your habits and schedule have changed so much recently, it wouldn't be a surprise if it made you sick.'

'You're acting like I'm one of those bubble kids leaving the house for the first time. I'm just trying to get my life back to normal. What's wrong with that?'

She sighs, putting down the pan and sitting across from me. 'Nothing. Of course there's nothing wrong with that. It's just . . . this has been our norm for so long it's . . . it's tough for me.'

'For you?' I scoff. She frowns and I remember the deal about being a good little girl. 'I mean . . . yeah, of course. It must be . . . hard . . . for you.' I sit up straight. 'But I mean, this is good, right? If I can start getting back to normal, then so can you. You can get *your* life back too. Start, y'know . . . going out, joining clubs, meeting people . . . maybe even get a . . . boyfriend?'

She whips her head up, her eyes wide open. 'What?'

'I'm just saying, most people in your position would be out there, dating or whatever. Tinder's pretty big now, even for oldies like you.'

She stares at me for a few seconds and I'm *sure* she's going to crack.

'I . . . I . . . don't . . .' she stutters. I can see her eyes getting watery, probably because she's realised what a cheating bitch she's been. I lean forward, waiting for her to admit it, to break down and cry about what a terrible human being she is, but she just shoots up from her chair, frying pan still in her hand. 'More eggs?' she asks again. She shoves the pan in the sink though and starts scrubbing away. I half want to say yes to more eggs and see how she freaks out, but by the look of things, she might have a legit breakdown if I push her any more.

'What are your plans for today?' she asks in a high-pitched voice.

I'm about to ask her permission, no *tell* her that I'm going out with Mehreen and Olivia, but before I can even get a word out, she's blabbering on again. I'm expecting her to tell me about some museum she wants to drag me along to (last time I fell asleep for like a second during one of the talks, and everyone gave me dirty looks for ages after I snorted myself awake), but instead she says, 'I've got to go to a meeting this afternoon.'

I look up at her but she's staring down at the spotless frying pan she can't seem to stop scrubbing. Classic sign of a liar. This is my chance to trip her up.

'You seem to be having lots of *meetings* lately. I thought most of your work came through emails?'

'It's just an . . . important client. They're insisting on meeting in person to discuss the details. It's a big one.'

I bet it is.

'Will you be OK on your own?'

Notice how the idea of taking me with her didn't even cross her mind when just a week ago she would've dragged me along, no matter how important the *meeting* was.

206

'Whereabouts is it?' I ask, ignoring her question.

'Oh, just in town. You could invite the girls round if you wanted? There's some popcorn and snacks in the cupboards.'

'We're meeting up later. I can come with you and meet them wherever you're going.'

The pan clatters in the sink. 'No, no. It's fine. I can drop you on the way. Don't want to make them come all this way. What are your plans, anyway? Another support-group meeting?'

My heart jumps, thinking she knows about us organising our weird little sessions, but then I remember that's the line I gave her at the start of all of this. How funny that it's come full circle.

'I can drop you off at the church. Is one-ish OK?'

'Yeah, fine,' I say, realising that she's too good at bullshitting for me to trip her up. At least today. There's no way I'm giving up. I'm going to find out who this home-wrecking bastard is, no matter what.

36. MEHREEN

It's weird to be back where it all started. It's only been a week since we first met at this very grave, but it honestly feels like an entire lifetime ago. Even the weather is the same as it was that day – chilly enough for a jacket but thankfully dry. Still no fog, but I'm glad about that today. I've always used the weather to predict how the day is going to go, and if it were raining or miserable, I would've asked to move our support-group meeting indoors. There's something foreboding about bad weather, as if bad things happen only when it's gloomy. It's a childish thought, I know.

'So how do we start?' Olivia asks.

'Haven't you ever watched American TV?' Cara asks. 'The addiction support groups always start with the serenity prayer.'

'What has serenity got to do with addiction?' Olivia asks.

'I guess it's the idea of peace?' I venture. 'Whenever my Chaos gets too much for me, I look for things that bring me peace. Prayer, music . . . or . . . well yeah . . .' I don't tell them about the self-harm; they'd probably run a mile.

'Peace and addiction,' Olivia says. 'How very apt. Although I wouldn't associate the word *serenity* with Cara.' She laughs.

'Oh, shove off,' Cara says, smacking Olivia's arm.

'Tell us the *serenity prayer* then, Cara,' Olivia says as she folds her legs beneath her.

I cross my legs too. It's like Olivia and I are the kids, sitting on the grass looking up to Cara the teacher, the idea of which is so ludicrous that I can't help but giggle.

'Well, I'm not going to tell you if you're *laughing*,' Cara scolds.

'OK, OK, sorry,' I say. I mime zipping my lips.

She clears her throat. 'God grant me the serenity to accept the things I cannot change; courage to change the things I can; and wisdom to know the difference.'

There's silence for a few seconds as we all absorb the words. Now that Cara's recited them, they sound familiar.

'That's nice,' Olivia says softly.

'Yeah,' I agree. 'Except . . . I thought you didn't believe in God?'

Cara shrugs. 'Who cares? It's just a stupid prayer. Doesn't mean anything.'

'And on that encouraging note, let's get started,' I say. 'I guess we could go round and uh . . . just say how things are going.'

'Be sure to start by saying, "My name is Mehreen and I'm an alcoholic",' Cara laughs.

I roll my eyes, but decide to humour her. 'My name is Mehreen and I'm . . . depressed, I guess. It's been . . . almost a week? Since I last wanted to kill myself, and I'm . . . doing OK.' I turn to look at Cara. 'That's how it goes, right?'

'Sounded good to me,' she replies.

'I feel . . . I feel good,' I continue. 'Optimistic, I guess. I'm trying not to think about how things were, how I used to feel. I'm making an effort to look forward.'

'Cheesy much?' Cara inputs.

I feel my face heat up slightly. 'Sorry,' I say automatically. 'I got carried away, I guess. Um, Olivia, you want to go next?' I turn to her and feel a pang of sadness run through me. I reach over and squeeze her knee. 'How *are* you?'

She rolls her eyes and tuts. 'Please don't do that, Mehreen. I don't want you to treat me differently. I can't stand being pitied.'

'That's not . . . I wasn't . . . trying to . . .' I splutter.

'You don't need to,' Cara butts in. 'That's the thing – people don't seem to be able to help it. Once they know, it's like you're a different person and all they see is that one thing.'

'I don't!' I say defensively. I flick my head between Cara and Olivia. 'That's not it. That's not *all* I think –'

'It's *fine*, Mehreen,' Olivia says with a chuckle. 'Cara's winding you up – aren't you, Cara?' She looks over to Cara and widens her eyes. As if they're communicating in secret.

'Only a bit,' Cara says. 'I'm just saying, I know what it feels like, to have people focus on just one thing. Only mine's super-hard to miss.'

'I just asked her how she was!' I say louder than I meant to. 'What's wrong with that?'

'It's *fine*, Mehreen –'

'No, but it's not, is it?' I say. 'It won't be fine until . . . until we deal with the problem.' I look back at Olivia, trying to wipe any anger off my face and replace it with only concern. Friendly concern.

'I know it seems simple to you,' Olivia says, plucking a blade of grass and playing with it, 'but I can assure you it's anything but. Telling someone would . . . change everything. It would *ruin* everything.'

'What's left to ruin?' Cara scoffs. 'Literally anything that happens after reporting that motherfucker would be better than what's happening now.'

'What if . . . ?' Olivia almost whispers. 'What if Mother doesn't believe me?'

'Of course she'll believe you!' I interject quickly. 'Why wouldn't she? She's your *mother*.'

'She's changed so much since they started dating. It just wouldn't surprise me if she took his side. He could probably talk his way out of it.'

'So – what?' I ask. 'You're really not going to do anything? I mean, if nothing changes, what's to say you won't just be back here with a different set of partners?'

She sighs. 'I . . . I'll do it eventually. Or, I'll be old enough to leave home soon. To be honest, it's not really a problem any more. He's gone, maybe for good. If he doesn't come back, I never have to tell Mother and she'll never start looking at me like I'm . . .' She trails off, trying to think of the word.

'Like you're broken,' Cara finishes.

'Yes, exactly!'

SEE. THEY'RE SO IN SYNC.
YOU'RE THE ODD ONE OUT.

I suck in a little breath. It's back. Of course it's back. Was I stupid enough to believe it had completely gone away? I think about an article Olivia sent me yesterday, about grounding techniques for when you're feeling anxious. I force myself to focus on specific things, one after the other. The symmetry of the print on Cara's T-shirt, the way she fiddles with the hem of it, the way her fingers move, how I'd sketch them. Focus focus focus, until the Chaos drifts away.

'Still, I'm with Mehreen on this,' Cara says softly. 'Even if he doesn't come back, you *need* to tell someone. Either your mother or the police.'

'I will, I promise. I just want a few more good days. For both me and Mother.'

'Whatever you need,' I say, placing my hand on top of hers.

She smiles at me with her slightly watery eyes. 'Thanks,' she whispers.

'OK, Cara, your turn,' I say, swivelling to face her now.

Cara straightens in her chair. 'My name's Cara. I like long walks on the beach and a nice glass of red at dinner. My ideal partner would have a great set of –'

'Cara!' Olivia chides, but she's laughing. We both are.

'OK, fine, spoilsports,' Cara groans. 'I actually *do* have something to report. As it turns out, my mother has been sneaking around getting pounded by some creep.'

'What?!' Olivia and I both exclaim.

'She's got a boyfriend,' Cara explains. 'I heard her whispering to him on the phone yesterday. Having phone sex probably.'

'Wow,' I breathe.

'Good for her,' Olivia says, 'Well, maybe not the phone sex, but –'

'*Good for her?!*' Cara exclaims. 'Her and Dad were together for like *ever* and she's moved on already? It's not fucking right.'

'Ten months is a perfectly acceptable grieving process time,' Olivia says. 'Also, surely this bodes well for you? Maybe she'll become so preoccupied with him that she'll leave you alone, and isn't that ultimately what you wanted? This could be the perfect diversion.'

'I don't *want* her to become obsessed with some random guy. I *want* her to . . . to remember she was married. I just don't buy that you can get over the death of someone you used to love this quickly. Do you think she was cheating on Dad before the accident?'

'I'm sure it wasn't like that,' I say.

'But you can't *know*,' Cara says. 'I need to know. I need to know who this guy is and when they hooked up. I can't stop thinking about that. What if Dad died completely in love with this woman who was . . . screwing someone else? I can't stand it. I just . . . I need to know.'

Olivia and I share a look. I know we should try and make Cara see that she's being irrational, but she's our friend, and she's hurting, so of course rational gets thrown out of the window.

'OK,' I say, nodding. 'So let's find out.'

213

37. CARA

'It's lovely to see you both again,' Mum says to Olivia and Mehreen as I close the front door. 'I'm so glad Cara's managed to finally find some *proper* friends.'

It took her literally three seconds to become the most embarrassing parent again. That must be a new record, even for her. I want to say this out loud, but I've decided I'm giving her the silent treatment. I feel like anything I say either goes completely over her head or just makes her think I'm interested in her sad little life, which I'm not. I'm not talking to her until I find out everything about this bastard she's seeing. I'm surprised she's home to be honest. Maybe her crappy date got cut short. Or maybe they only met up for a quick shag. Gross.

'Nice to see you too,' Olivia says, like the perfect pet she is.

I start going towards my bedroom, wanting to get as far away from Mum as possible. I can't even look at her without picturing her snogging some random, both of them laughing about the fact she's screwing Dad over.

'Wait, wait,' Mum calls as we move out of the hallway into the living room. 'Do you girls want some lunch? I can whip something up quickly. How about –'

'No, honestly, it's fine,' Mehreen says. 'Thank you though.'

'It's no trouble,' Mum says. She walks into the kitchen and starts opening cupboards, still yapping on about what she could make.

'C'mon, let's go,' I tell the others, moving further towards my room.

'But she's going to wonder where we went. It's rude to not finish a conversation,' Olivia says. She stands in the hallway, looking back into the kitchen and then over to us.

'She won't even notice,' I say, angrier than I mean to. I want to storm off, but all I can do is move at a snail's pace to my room. When I look over my shoulder, I see that only Mehreen's followed me in.

'I, uh, don't think it's in her to be rude,' Mehreen explains.

I just roll my eyes and manoeuvre myself onto the sofa. I grab my laptop, mostly just out of habit. After a second, Mehreen comes over and sits next to me.

'So any ideas for a plan?' she asks.

'We need to snoop,' I say, loading up Mum's Facebook profile, the one I've had a pending friend request from for years. 'Do you think they've made it Facebook official?'

'Do adults do that?' Mehreen asks, leaning in.

'Old people are the only ones who even *use* Facebook,' I tell her.

'*Hey.*' She elbows me.

Just then Olivia walks back into the room, closing the door quietly behind her. I stare at her for a second, but she doesn't even look guilty or ashamed. She just comes over and sits on my other side.

'What are you looking for?' she asks.

'Got fed up of cooking with your new best friend?' I ask her.

She doesn't reply so I keep clicking through Mum's page. Her friends list is surprisingly long. I filter it down to people in our town, but there are no men in that batch.

'You said you tried to talk to her about it this morning,' Olivia says. 'If she was that coy with you in person, do you really think she's going to put something about her relationship on the Internet where everyone can see it?'

'She's not exactly smart,' I mutter.

'Olivia's right,' Mehreen says. 'If she's being this secretive, chances are she's being careful too. You said she was rummaging around looking for something yesterday?'

'A form or some letters or something. She ransacked the living room but didn't find anything.'

'Any clue what they were about?'

'Nah. I just heard her say something like "there's no way I'm telling Cara, it's only been ten months blah blah blah."'

'That's it?' Olivia asks. 'How did you come to the conclusion she's dating someone from *that*?'

I clench my fists, ready to punch her in the gob if she doesn't shut up. 'You weren't there!' I shout at her. 'You weren't listening to her phone call. I know what I fucking heard, OK?'

There's a quick knock at the door before Mum barges in. She's carrying three cans of Coke and a multipack of those gross vegetable crisps she keeps buying. It looks like everything's about to fall out of her hands. Olivia rushes over to help her. The suck-up.

'Thanks, dear,' Mum says, smiling down at Olivia, giving her a look like a mother should look at her daughter. When she looks at me, I can tell she sees me as broken. 'I'll make some sandwiches in a bit, but thought you might like some snacks first.'

'Thank you, Diane,' Olivia says, bringing over the drinks to the table in front of us. She looks up at me and I can't tell whether she's trying to say sorry or trying to tell me off for being rude. Either way I just ignore her.

'Let me know if you need anything else,' Mum says as she backs towards the door. But of course she can't leave without asking, 'Everything OK, Cara?'

Sometimes I wonder what she'd do if I told her I could feel my legs again. Maybe I'll try that next April Fool's Day. I don't look at her, don't reply. I can sense her waiting by the door and I know the others probably think I'm being a bitch but I know, if I look up at her, I'll just get pissed off and shout, and I'd rather have some hard evidence before I confront her.

'We're fine, Mrs Saunders,' Mehreen says quickly after a few seconds' pause. I like that she still calls her Mrs Saunders. If that's the only link she has left to Dad, then I'll savour the hell out of it.

Even without looking at her, I know Mum's not satisfied. She wants me to answer, to prove I'm still alive and able to speak. Well, fuck that – I'm not giving her shit. After what feels like an hour of her standing there just staring, she finally fucks off.

'There's really no need –' Olivia starts.

'Don't,' I say. 'Just don't.' I close down Facebook and go looking for her on Twitter and Instagram.

'You're not going to find anything online,' Olivia says, passing me a can of Coke. I take it without looking at her, not because I forgive her but because I'm thirsty. 'We need to search the house.'

'We can't really do that while she's here,' Mehreen points out. 'Unless you've got a good distraction in mind?'

'She seems really intent on feeding us. Could we ask her to pop out to get something special?' Olivia suggests.

'Would that give us long enough?' Mehreen asks, grabbing a packet of crisps.

'We can make her go somewhere far,' I say. 'We'll get some good food out of it too.'

'And we'll be quick,' Olivia says. 'We already know *what* she was looking for and *where* she was looking for it. Three of us, one room – we'll find those letters in no time.'

Mum's humming away in the kitchen when we go in. I hate that she's humming. I hate that she's happy because of this bastard. She's already got the bread out on the table and has her head stuck in the fridge.

'Oh, hi, girls,' she says when she turns around and sees us. 'I'm just about to make those sandwiches.'

Olivia nudges me, but I can't get out any of the lines we rehearsed. All I can do is stare at Mum's smile.

'Um, Cara was just telling us about this great Chinese food you guys had last week,' Mehreen says quickly, nervously.

218

'From Green Garden?' Mum asks. 'Oh yeah, that chow mein was delish.'

'Cara was making fun of the fact I've never actually had chow mein,' Olivia says. She's more casual than Mehreen, who's basically wetting herself.

'Never?' Mum asks. 'How can you have gone this long without trying chow mein?' She laughs.

'Can we get some?' I ask quickly. 'I mean, from Green Garden.'

Mum frowns. 'It's collection only, Cara. And a bit of a trek. How about we go out to the Chinese buffet in town instead?'

'No,' I say forcefully. 'It has to be Green Garden.'

Olivia nudges me again, harder this time.

'I mean, I'm really craving it. Please, Mum.'

She stares at me for ages, and I wait for her to say no.

'Oh, go on then,' she says instead. 'You've twisted my arm.'

She doesn't move though, and I'm scared she's going to try and drag us all along, but thankfully Olivia pipes up again.

'Is there anything you'd like us to do while you're gone?' she asks.

Mum shakes her head slowly. 'No, thank you, dear.' Dear. She's never called me dear. That's a name people use for old people, adults. Sweetie, honey – those are words used on little kids. Kids like me.

'Can you get some chocolate cake too?' I ask. 'Y'know, that one from Costco?'

That'll add some time to her journey. Plus, Costco is next to the graveyard Dad's buried at. Hopefully she'll realise and feel bad about being a cheating skank.

She smirks at me. 'Anything else, madam?'

I just turn around to go back to my room.

A few minutes later I hear the front door open and close. She's gone.

No lectures about not leaving the house or answering the door to strangers. Nothing about making sure I don't fall down in the loo and piss myself again.

She just leaves.

Just like that.

'Nothing in this cupboard either,' Olivia says as she closes the drawer on the TV unit.

'She's going to be back soon,' Mehreen says, looking anxiously at the front door. 'We should just stop now. Maybe we can look when we know she's out for real.'

I roll my eyes, even though I'm worried too. 'Even if she does come in, she's not going to think anything of it. She'll probably believe us if we say we're looking for the remote.'

'What exactly *are* we looking for?' Olivia asks. '"Some letters" isn't very specific. There are lots here: bills, doctors' letters, but nothing romantic.' She rifles through another drawer.

'Oh!' Mehreen says suddenly. 'I think I found something!' She pulls out a pile of white envelopes held together by an elastic band. The top one is addressed to Mum in fancy handwriting. The kind of fancy you'd use to write to your lover. I turn the stack over and see the return address belongs to someone called Owen Gentry.

'So *this* is the bastard she's fucking,' I say, taking the elastic band off. Before I can get it off completely, the front door opens right in front of us.

Mum walks in.

Shit.

'I'd forget my head if it wasn't screwed on,' Mum says, looking down at the mat as she wipes her feet. 'Can you believe I got halfway before realising I didn't have –' She stops talking when she looks up and sees the stack of letters in my hand. I don't even try to hide them; it's about time I exposed her.

'Cara,' she says slowly, 'what are you doing with –'

'With your love letters?' I finish her sentence for her, waving the stack at her. There are about five or six envelopes, which means this has been going on for ages.

'Love letters?' She steps closer, putting down the purse she came back to fetch.

'Just cut the shit, Mum,' I say, moving towards her, into the middle of the room. 'I know everything about Owen Gentry.'

Her head jerks back a bit and her mouth opens slightly. I love that I've got to her, that I've surprised her.

'How could you?!' I say. 'Dad hasn't been gone five minutes and you've already moved on?'

I feel Mehreen and Olivia shuffle slightly behind me. I know they're both probably feeling awkward as hell, but if I don't do this now, if I stop even to just let them leave, Mum will come up with more bullshit – more lies to feed me.

'Cara . . .'

'Were you cheating on Dad?'

'What? No!' She actually sounds sincere. 'How could you even think that?'

'What about these then?' I'm shouting now, and it feels so fucking good. 'If you loved him so much, how have you moved on enough to be getting fucking love letters from some other guy already? It's only been ten months!'

'Cara, what are you talking about? Those aren't *love letters*.'

'What are they then? Oh God, have you been sending each other dirty photos or something?' I throw the envelopes to the floor, disgusted.

She bends down, quick as a flash, to pick up her precious letters.

'Cara, you've got the completely wrong end of the stick,' she says, kneeling on the floor. She's fucking crying now and I can't stand it. Can't stand how she's playing the victim.

'You're a fucking disgrace,' I say, shaking my head at the way she's clutching the letters to her chest.

'Cara!' Olivia warns quietly from behind me. I ignore her.

'Dad used to tell me how he knew as soon as he met you that you were his soulmate,' I say. 'I called bullshit, but he was so convinced that I ended up believing him.' I laugh a little. 'You two made me actually believe in that shit. And now here you are, throwing yourself at other men.'

'Cara!' It's Mum warning me this time. 'How dare you speak to me like that?' She stands up and glares at me with her angry red, tear-filled eyes. But I don't give a shit. There's a fire within me now, anger that I need to pour out.

'How long has it been going on?' I ask. 'How long have you been sleeping with this guy?'

'I'm not sleeping with him!' Mum shouts. 'I'm not sleeping with ANYONE!'

'You're lying! You're a fucking liar. All you do is lie!'

'Cara, stop!' She's sobbing so much she can barely breathe. 'Please!'

'Just tell me who he is! It's not fucking hard!'

'He's no one!'

'He's obviously not no one if you're keeping his letters. Did he break up with you or something? Wouldn't blame him – you're a fucking mess.'

She raises her voice louder than I've ever heard it. 'Cara! You CANNOT talk to me like that! I'm your mother!'

I raise my voice even louder. 'Then why don't you fucking act like it, instead of a cheap slag!'

'CARA!' Her face is red, partly from tears, mostly from anger. I'm so close to breaking her.

'Just fucking stop making excuses and tell me who this prick you've betrayed Dad for is. Tell me! Who the fuck is Owen Gentry?'

'HE'S THE MAN WHO KILLED YOUR FATHER!'

38. CARA

Mum's sitting on the arm of the sofa now, head down, with the letters in her lap. She's crying harder than ever, and all I can do is stare. Olivia squeezes my shoulder and whispers, 'We'll be outside,' before she and Mehreen slip out and I hear the front door click. I'd forgotten they were even here.

'What do you mean?' I ask Mum after a minute of silence. 'That this guy . . . *killed* Dad?'

She doesn't answer. Just keeps weeping.

'Mum!' I say, hard and loud enough for her head to jolt up. 'What the fuck are you talking about? What has this guy got to do with it? We were . . . The car crashed. It was my . . . I . . .'

She shakes her head slowly, looking back at her lap. 'He was the driver of the other car.'

I think back to that night. Me and Dad driving down the dark, winding road, the rain lashing down on the windscreen, Dad's laugh, the smell of popcorn, his last words – *'You're only saying that because you're gay'* – my hand shoving his shoulder and then . . .

'What other car?' I ask. 'It was just us. Dad swerved off the road . . . because . . . because of me. It's . . . it's *my* fault he's dead. No one else's.'

Mum looks at me at last. She frowns and I turn away; I can't bear to see the anger in her eyes. We've never really spoken about the accident; after it happened, I refused to talk to anyone about any of it, still too upset about Dad and my disability – but I know Mum's been silently blaming me this whole time. Neither of us has had the courage to admit it out loud. There's a whole long list of things we've never said to each other.

She leans forward and takes my hand in hers, ducking her head and forcing me to make eye contact. 'Cara, why on earth . . . why would you think it was *your* fault? The other car . . . it crashed right into the front of your dad's. There's nothing you could have done.'

I can't breathe. Can't move. Can't even blink.

Me and Dad driving down a dark, winding road. The rain lashing down on the windscreen. Some headlights appearing up ahead. Dad's laugh, the smell of popcorn, his last words – 'You're only saying that because you're gay' *– the headlights in front getting brighter and brighter, my hand shoving his shoulder and then . . .*

'Honey, why did you never tell me you were feeling like this?' Mum asks, squeezing my hand. 'That you were carrying all this guilt?' She's frowning harder now, her face a big wet mess, but she's stopped crying.

I snatch my hand away. 'Because you never let me fucking talk about it!' I shout. 'You realise this is the first time we've had a proper conversation about any of this? You just kept pretending nothing had happened and I . . . I had to live with . . .' I'm hiccupping, gulping air like there's not enough oxygen in the room, in the world, but there's still so much emotion inside me I need to get out. 'You have no fucking clue, do you?' I shout.

'Cara . . .' She reaches for me again but I move back.

'No!' I shout. 'You . . . knew this the *whole* time? And there was me thinking . . . Do you have any fucking idea how it feels? How *I* feel? What I almost . . .' I laugh a little. 'This *whole* time, I've been blaming myself, wishing I was dead instead of him. And you're keeping letters from the guy who *actually* killed him. Why? Why the hell is this bastard writing to you? None of this makes any sense!'

Mum shakes her head a little. 'Cara, sweetie, please, let's just move on from this –'

'Oh, you'd fucking love that, wouldn't you? Let's just sweep all this under the rug and pretend nothing bad is happening. What is wrong with you? Why are you so hell bent on lying to me about EVERY FUCKING THING?'

'I'm protecting you!'

'I DON'T NEED FUCKING PROTECTING!'

'Cara . . .'

'Mum, I swear to fucking God, if you don't tell me the truth right now, I'm leaving this house forever.'

That does it; she shuts up, not even breathing by the looks of it.

'Tell. Me. Everything,' I say, forcing my voice not to wobble.

She sighs and sits up straight, still on the arm of the sofa. 'Owen Gentry has been trying to make contact for months now. He keeps sending letters asking me to speak to him, to let him speak to you. He says . . . he says he wants to apologise.' She practically spits the last word. 'I've asked your aunt Colleen to try to find some legal way of stopping him. She's sent me some forms to fill in, for an injunction. He's . . . he's relentless, Cara. I only kept these letters because Colleen says they're evidence. She says he's probably only doing it to try to reduce his sentence.'

'Sentence? He's in jail?' My heart jumps.

She shakes her head. 'Community service order. They said it was a *tragic accident*, because of the bad weather.'

'I don't believe you.'

She frowns at me again. 'Cara, your aunt was at the trial, she –'

'I don't believe a word you're saying. You've been lying to me this whole fucking time – why should I believe you now?'

'Why would I lie to you about *this*?'

I shrug and wipe my nose. 'Because you've lied about everything else! You knew this *all* along and didn't fucking tell me. And don't give me that "protection" bullshit. The only person you're protecting is yourself. You don't give a shit about me. If you did, you would have told me about this; you wouldn't have let me . . . go all these months thinking that it was my fault.'

'Cara, honey, if I'd known –'

'Give me the letters,' I say, holding out my hand. 'I want to get the truth from the only other living person who was there that night. Or, was *apparently* there.'

She doesn't even argue, just hands over the stack of envelopes.

I put the pile on my lap and start to leave.

'Cara, please –'

She continues crying, but doesn't finish her sentence. I want to storm out of the front door and slam it in her face, but it takes an age to get my chair over the threshold. The bloody accident took away any chance of having a strop and it's so fucking infuriating right now. When I finally get out, I just leave the door open and zoom down the path as my tears fall freely.

39. MEHREEN

The front door slams open and Cara hurtles out. Her shoulders are heaving and she's sobbing so loud I don't think she hears her mum calling after her. Instead, she speeds off down the street. Olivia and I share a look before rushing to follow.

'Leave me alone!' Cara shouts back at us. She continues pushing herself down the street, towards a little playground in the corner of the cul-de-sac.

'What happened?' I ask. When we left, it seemed like everything was going to be OK – that since Cara's mum was ready to tell the truth, everything would get sorted. But Cara's demeanour says the complete opposite.

'I fucking mean it, just leave me alone,' Cara shouts.

I start to wonder whether maybe we *should* leave her alone, whether this is something she needs to sort out in her head by herself. I imagine being in her position and wonder what I'd prefer, and I realise that if I were alone at a time like this, it would completely break me.

'We're not leaving you,' I assure her. 'Just talk to us.'

Cara has a bit of trouble trying to open the gate to the playground and wheel her chair through it, so Olivia rushes ahead and helps her. Cara speeds in, but the playground is too small to really go anywhere – it's just a patch of tarmac, containing a set of swings, a seesaw and a roundabout. Cara stops in front of the swings and I can see she's still crying. Olivia and I rush around to be in front of her. Seeing Cara's face wet with tears and snot is shocking, sobering almost. She puts on such a tough persona, you almost forget she's capable of being so upset.

'I . . . I don't . . . I can't . . .' Her breaths are coming out as choked sobs, the words getting sucked into each breath. It's like she's hyperventilating.

Olivia kneels down in front of her and puts her hand on Cara's knee. I do the same and reach for Cara's hand. This action seems to flip a switch in Cara and she starts wailing. Her chin touches her chest as her whole body heaves, the tears falling, falling, falling. Olivia and I reach up and wrap an arm around each shoulder. We hug her tight as her body shakes.

'I can't . . .' Cara repeats. 'I need to . . .'

'Need to what?' I ask, pulling back. 'What is it? How can we make this better?'

'I just feel . . .' she sputters. 'I just . . . it's too much. I can't breathe . . . I need to . . . I need to make it go away.'

Olivia looks at me, confused, but I understand. Cara's filled to the brim with emotion – coursing, overwhelming emotion that makes her feel as if her entire body is about to split apart. It's a feeling I know far too well.

'You need a release,' I say. 'A way to get all this emotion out.'

She looks at me, wide-eyed, and nods. 'Is this . . . ? Is this what your Chaos is like?'

I nod.

'How can we fix this?' Olivia asks. 'How do you get rid of it?'

I hesitate, trying to think of a way to put into words the release that comes from the craft knife, but of course I can't. So I roll up my sleeve.

Olivia gasps. Cara just looks at me, eyes wider than ever.

'I don't recommend it,' I say quietly, pulling my sleeve back down. 'That's just how I . . . how it works for me . . .'

'Oh, Mehreen,' Olivia whispers, squeezing my hand.

'What do you do?' I ask her to detract attention from myself. 'When things are just . . . too much?'

Olivia seems to think this over, as if the answer requires a lot of thought. Her face relaxes after a few seconds and she almost smiles as she tells me, 'I scream.'

'Really?' I ask. Olivia somehow doesn't strike me as the screaming type.

'I press my face into a pillow and scream. I scream until my breath is gone, until my voice cracks.'

An idea comes to me. I stand up, throw my arms out to the sides, throw my head back and roar as loud and for as long as I can stand. Until my chest hurts, my throat burns, my face is hot and my body is empty. The sound reverberates around the park, probably loud enough for the people in the nearby houses to hear.

When I open my eyes and look back down at Cara and Olivia, they're both staring at me, part amused, part confused, part shocked.

'It really works,' I say with a laugh.

231

Olivia breaks out into a grin and stands up. She copies my stance and roars too. Hers is higher-pitched than mine, the shrillness of it making me momentarily cringe. When she stops, she lets out a little laugh and turns to me. I smile back and we turn to Cara. She tilts her head back, looks up at the sky and lets out the biggest, longest, loudest roar I've heard. It's guttural and filled with all the anger and pain of what she's been through. I watch her body tense as she continues the sound for as long as she can hold, before she runs out of breath and dissolves into quiet tears again.

Olivia and I wrap our arms around her, comforting her, shielding her, as her breaths become less erratic. There's strength in our embrace, a sense of unity and power. Even though Cara's going through one of the hardest times in her life, our touch tells her that she's not alone, that she'll never be alone. None of us will be.

40. CARA

The letters are all the same. Owen Gentry apologising for killing my father. For driving down that road 'a little too fast'. Him saying over and over again how 'remorseful' he is for his actions and how much he wants to meet with Mum and me 'to talk'. The only thing stopping me from scrunching them all up and throwing them in the dog-shit bin is that Mum said they're the only evidence to get him off our backs.

'I can't believe it,' I say, looking up at Mehreen and Olivia, who are sitting on the swings in front of me. 'How the hell did I not know someone else was involved?'

'Maybe it's what happens with such a big trauma,' Mehreen says. 'Your memory plays tricks. You were so focused on the thought that it was your fault that you probably forgot other stuff.'

'Do you feel better now though?' Olivia asks. 'After finding out the whole truth?'

I look down at the pile of papers in my lap. 'I don't know. Nothing's really changed. Dad's still dead. But now there's this guy who's responsible. And he's . . . he got away basically scot-free. No jail time or anything. He just has to pick up rubbish or some shit. He gets to *live*.'

'But . . . do you feel relieved at least?' Olivia persists,

swinging slowly. 'Now that you know it wasn't your fault? After living with that guilt for so long, don't you feel . . . at peace?'

I shrug. 'I . . . I don't think I know what peace feels like any more.'

'Would you want to meet him?' Mehreen asks.

'Fuck no,' I say, pissed off that she would even suggest that. 'This guy *killed* my dad, Mehreen.' I look back at one of the letters – the one he addressed to me directly. 'He seems like an absolute arse. Listen to this – "I feel so terrible that I caused your disability; that I've ruined your life." What a prick. He talks about what happened to me more than about the fact he fucking killed my dad. There's no way I'm meeting him.'

'Did your mum say whether she will?' Mehreen asks. 'Do you think she already has?'

I roll my eyes. 'Don't even talk about her. I'm more pissed at her than at this bastard. He's at least owning up to his shit, feels bad about what he did. She's been lying to me for months. But why am I surprised? She's a fucking mess.'

'She lost her husband, Cara,' Olivia snipes in her snooty voice. 'She was grieving too. Also, she didn't know you thought it was your fault. If she did –'

'Why do you always take her side?!' I ask, glaring at Olivia. 'You're supposed to be *my* friend.'

'I'm not taking sides!' she replies, annoyingly high-pitched. 'I'm just saying you should talk to her. You've both been so wrapped up in your own grief that you haven't spoken to each other properly. If you just had an open and honest conversation –'

'Oh, you're one to talk!' I almost shout back at her. 'Told your mum about your rapist yet?'

Olivia gasps and stops swinging immediately. Good. That'll teach her to be such a hypocrite.

'Cara, that's not fair,' Mehreen says harshly. 'Olivia's only trying to help.'

I look over and Olivia's just staring at me. I thought she'd start crying, but instead her eyes are locked on mine – it's kinda creepy, so I just turn away and look at the seesaw instead. I expect her to say something, to carry on cussing me out, but both of them go silent. For a long while no one speaks. I'm worried I've annoyed them, pissed Olivia off so much that they'll both leave; there's no way I can be on my own right now. So I just blurt out the first thing that comes into my head.

'My dad used to bring me to this playground all the time,' I say. I don't look to see if they're listening, just keep babbling. 'I haven't been here since I was, like, twelve, and now that I'm here, it's weird. All I can think about is Dad.'

'Tell us about him,' Mehreen says. 'It seems like you had a really good relationship. I can't imagine being that close with my dad.'

I relax and smile. I think about the first time he brought me here – how we got on the seesaw together and he wouldn't let my feet touch the ground until I'd admitted to hiding sweets in my bedroom.

'He was an accountant,' I tell the girls. 'But like a *cool* one. He used to always wear these bright, ugly socks. They looked ridiculous with his suits, but we had a competition between us, guessing how long it would take someone to comment on it. He played it so cool that no one ever did. He used to take me on these daddy–daughter dates – that's what we were doing on . . . the night of the accident. He always bought us a bag of popcorn each – sweet for him, salted for me. But by the end of the film we'd have swapped.'

I picture him in the car, turning to me and laughing. I see the flash of headlights shining across his face. My eyes start burning and I blink hard to try to stop what's coming.

'He used to . . . He was . . . He was just the best. Not even just the best dad. He was the best person, the best . . . everything.' The tears begin to fall, hard and fast. 'I miss him so fucking much.'

I hear the others slip off the swings and next thing I know they're hugging me again. I swear I've had more hugs since meeting these two than in the past five years. I start to regret being mean to Olivia.

'Try to focus on the positive memories,' Mehreen says when she pulls away. 'Remember him the way he was, focus on the good he left behind. The smile he brings to your face whenever you think of him.'

I nod. She's right. It feels good to think about him, about *before*.

'You should share these memories with your mother,' Olivia says.

I roll my eyes and am about to nicely tell her to fuck off, but before I can say anything, she raises her hand, stopping me.

'No, wait, just listen. Yes, she did a terrible thing by not

236

telling you. But even you can't believe it was with malicious intent. Your mother just isn't like that. You saw how emotional she got earlier. Just go and talk to her, tell her about these wonderful memories you have of your father. Tell her how you feel, how you blamed yourself, how bad things got. Have your own little support-group meeting.'

I know she's right, that there's nothing to do *but* talk to Mum about it, but the thought of it fucking terrifies me.

Olivia looks like a little puppy though, begging me to do what she's asking, and I realise I can use this to my advantage.

'OK, right. Do me a solid,' I say to her. She looks confused and it makes me laugh. 'I mean, let's make a pact.'

'Because the last one worked so well?' She raises an eyebrow.

I don't let her distract me with jokes – instead I put on a serious face. Or at least what I think is a serious face. 'I'll talk to Mum about this, like, have a proper chat. If you tell your mum everything about . . . about that bastard.'

41. OLIVIA

'I'll talk to Mum about this.
Have a proper chat . . .

if

you tell your mum **everything**.'

Tell
your
mum
everything

everything

everything.

I think back to these past few days,
the quantity of baked goods Mother and I have created
TOGETHER.
The outings we've had
TOGETHER.

Just her and me.

The fact she hasn't mentioned *him*
once.
But I also think about the crying I hear from her bedroom
every night,
the way her body seems to lack
energy.

I want to tell Cara that it's not the **right time**,
that Mother needs to *heal*,
               needs to excise all loving feelings for him

        first.
But Cara's looking at me
as if she's **challenging** me,
daring me to say **no,**
because she knows then she'll have an **excuse** too.

'I will,'
I promise.
And I actually mean it.
'I just need a couple of days to . . .
to
prepare myself.'
'Maybe the day after tomorrow?'
'I'd like you both there, if that's OK?'

'Of course.'
That's Mehreen.
Cara just smiles.
'You've got yourself a deal.'

42. CARA

Mum's still sitting on the arm of the sofa when I get back in; her back is to me, but I can tell she's just staring off into space. She doesn't move, even when the door clicks shut. Through the window I can see Olivia and Mehreen walking away down the street, and there's a twinge in my chest; I'm just so bloody thankful they exist, that they were here today. They offered to come back in, but I know I have to do this alone.

'Well?' I ask Mum. She jumps off the sofa and turns around – her face is still a mess of tears and snot, her eyeliner all smudged and panda-eyed.

'Cara, sweetheart, can we just . . . talk about this?'

I force myself to be calm, to cut her some slack, like I promised Olivia I would. 'I'm listening,' I say, transferring off my chair and onto the sofa.

She sits down on the table in front of me, so we're face to face. This feels way too close. She tries to take my hand, but I don't let her.

'I'm sorry,' she says, looking down at the floor and fiddling with her ring. 'I guess I can't say anything more than that. If I'd known about you blaming yourself . . .' She pauses and shakes her head a little. 'I . . . I genuinely thought I was protecting you by not telling you about him contacting us, by just not talking about the trial at all. You were going through so much, I didn't want to pile more stuff onto you.'

'When are you going to get it into your head that I'm not a little kid?!' I'm shocked at how loud it comes out. 'I don't *need* protecting. I don't need you to keep secrets from me. This was the most important thing that's happened in our lives, the saddest thing. I can't . . . I can't even begin to explain how much us not talking about the accident made it harder, Mum. Don't pretend you did this for me. If you were thinking of me, you'd have told me the truth about this guy – I deserved at least that.'

I'm crying again and it's so fucking annoying. I hate crying. I've probably done more crying today than my entire life. Mum's crying too, but quietly, like a normal person. She takes a deep breath and looks right at me; her eyes are the saddest I've ever seen them. 'You're right,' she says quietly. 'It was the wrong decision, but I honestly thought it was for the best.' She takes my hands again and this time I don't pull away. 'When I got the call that day, it was like . . . like my world had ended. I can't even remember how I got to the hospital. And then there was a decision to make – which of you to find first. They'd separated you and your dad and none of the receptionists seemed to know where either of you were. When I finally got some information, I ran to you. I didn't hear about your father until . . . just before they took you in for surgery. I remember sitting in the waiting room and forcing myself not to think about him, forcing myself to focus my attention on you, on what they were doing to save

242

you. When you came out after your operation, I forced myself still not to think about him. I knew that if I thought about him . . . that if I thought about the fact he was . . .' She takes a huge shuddering breath.

'It was the only way I could cope, not letting myself think about him, or what had happened. When the doctors told me about your paraplegia, in a way I was . . . glad. It gave me something to focus on, something to manage. I didn't have to think about the fact your dad was gone and that there was a man to blame, because I had a job to do. I needed to get you to all these different appointments, keep track of which medicines you were taking, and when. And that, I guess, was *my* way of coping. I didn't want to have to grieve for your father, so I blocked it out. I tried to convince myself none of it happened, forced myself not to think about him . . . tried to . . . erase him from my head.'

She breaks down for real now, hands over her face as she wails. The room around us is so empty and quiet that the sound of her crying echoes from everywhere, making it sound like it's coming from all different directions and not just in front of me.

'I . . . h-hate myself for it . . .' she sobs. 'I d-didn't know what t-to do. They don't . . . train you for this. No one p-prepares you to be a parent. Or a w-w-widow.'

I feel like shit. I had no clue she was suffering this much. To be honest, I didn't even think about how she was feeling, how Dad's death had affected her. I had only thought about me. I grab her hand from her lap. She doesn't look up at me, or even stop crying, but she does squeeze my fingers.

'Shit, I'm sorry, Mum. I didn't . . . I didn't think about it like that. I didn't think of you. I've been so self-obsessed . . . I'm . . . I'm sorry.'

Mum and Dad had been married for five years before I was born. She'd spent most of her life with him; they were childhood sweethearts. They were the gross PDA type of parents who would embarrass the fuck out of me in public. They were . . . in love. So over-the-top in love. The kind of love they show in films. I never once considered that Mum was probably hurting way more than me. I never saw her crying, she never moped around in her pyjamas or stayed in bed. She didn't become an alcoholic or anything like that. I realise now how much she kept inside her, how much she hid.

I pull on her hand until she gets the hint and moves onto the sofa too. I rest my head on her shoulder and wrap an arm around her. 'I'm sorry,' I say again.

'I'm sorry too,' she sniffles, leaning her head down on top of mine.

'God, what a pair of saps we are,' I say, wiping the snot off my face.

I feel her body shake as she laughs.

'At least we have each other though, right?' I add, lifting my head up and looking at her.

'Always.' She smiles through her tears.

43. CARA

14th April
(4 days until Date of Termination)

There have been many times I've regretted putting *Supernova* by Ansel Elgort as my ringtone – that time my phone went off during Aunt Caroline's funeral, that time it started playing just as I was about to kiss Eva Hamdeh for the first time. But never have I regretted having such a heavy bass ringtone as much as right now, when it's going off in the middle of the fucking night. I want to wrap my pillow around my head and wait for it to shut up, but you know it's got to be serious if someone's calling at this time. I yank the duvet off my face and am surprised to see the sun shining rather than it being pitch black. I pick up my phone from the side table; it's an unknown number, of fucking course. I check the time and it's seven a.m., not three, which is what it feels like. I don't normally answer calls from numbers I don't know, because duh, that's how serial killers work, but I'm half asleep and not really thinking.

'Hello?' I croak, my voice sore from snoring (not ashamed to admit it).

The person doesn't answer. I can't even hear breathing. I

pull the phone away to check the screen, but it hasn't cut off.

'Helloooooooooo?'

Nothing.

'Thanks for waking me up, fucktard,' I say before ending the call.

I wait for it to ring again, but it doesn't. I do have a whole bunch of notifications though. Including an email from, you guessed it, MementoMori.com. God, when are these idiots going to get the point? I delete the email without even opening it and go to check Twitter, but before I can even click on the app, the icon disappears. Just flat out vanishes from my home screen. I scroll through the pages, to see if I just accidentally moved it or something, but no, it's literally just vanished. I go to click on Snapchat, but as soon as I do, that icon disappears too. What the fuck? Before I can do anything else, more apps start disappearing from my home screen one by one. First all the social media, then my games, then even the basic iPhone ones I thought you couldn't delete. I try clicking all over the screen, swiping around, but it's like the phone's possessed. When it finally stops freaking out, the only thing left is the picture I've used as the background, a photo of me and Dad.

I turn the phone off and restart it, but nothing comes back, so I grab my laptop and connect my phone to it. I start restoring the phone from backup. The progress bar starts moving and all of a sudden the green webcam light flicks on. I guess it's all part of this stupid process. I sit watching the stupid bar on the screen moving at the pace of a snail towards the end.

One hour and seventeen YouTube videos later, the restoration isn't even halfway complete. I feel like slamming the laptop shut and throwing it against the wall, but instead I just take out the SIM card from my phone and put it into an old crappy one. There's no way I'm going without a phone for even a day.

Mum knocks on the door, telling me breakfast is ready. She doesn't come in, like she normally would, and I can't help but wonder if she's pissed at me for accusing her yesterday, even after our little heart-to-heart.

She's not in the kitchen when I get there, but she's left the cereal boxes and milk out. Yep. Definitely pissed. I should do something to cheer her up, right? Maybe I could wash the dishes, although I wouldn't be able to reach the drying rack to put things on properly.

Or I could just enjoy the peace . . .

I tuck into a bowl of Shreddies, thinking about how to cheer Mum up. I thought we'd left things at an OK place last night, with us both agreeing not to keep secrets any more (not that I'm EVER going to tell her how I really met Mehreen and Olivia). But maybe she's less OK about everything than I'd thought.

'Morning, sweetheart,' Mum says from behind me.

I turn to find her walking in with a stacked laundry basket in her arms. She seems to be smiling, so that's good . . . right?

'Hi, Mum . . .' I say, waiting for her to show what she's feeling.

She comes over and kisses me on the head before walking into the utility room.

247

So maybe she's not pissed.

'Everything OK?' I ask.

She smiles as she places the now empty laundry basket to the side. 'Everything's great,' she says.

I squint at her, trying to figure out what's different, and then I spot it. She's wearing something new today. But it's not new. It's one of Dad's shirts. It's blue and checked and the front pocket is ripped so that it's hanging half off. He used to wear it whenever there was DIY to be done. I remember there being holes in the bottom of it, just like the holes I poke into the bottom of my T-shirts sometimes.

'Is that . . . ?' I ask.

'Yeah,' she says quietly. 'Is that OK? I just . . . I wanted to be close to him today.'

I nod, but slowly, not able to say anything. I kinda want to cry, but I don't know why. As if Mum senses this, she comes over and wraps an arm around me. I bury my face into her chest and take a deep breath. I want to be able to smell Dad, but there's nothing. This makes the tears come for real. Mum hugs me harder and then we're properly hugging, not just the one-armed thing we had going earlier.

'I know, sweetheart,' Mum says, her voice also full of tears. 'Hey, I have an idea!' She pulls away from me and I'm annoyed cos it was warm.

I wipe my eyes without her seeing and ask, 'What?'

'How about we go and visit your dad?'

'When did scientists figure out how to get to heaven?' (Not that I believe in that shit.)

Mum rolls her eyes. 'Very funny – I meant his grave. We

haven't been together in . . . in a really long time. He might start to think we've forgotten him.'

She says this as a joke but it hurts. It's true; I've only been to his grave twice. I don't see the point; it's just a piece of stone sticking out of the ground. He's not there. It's not how I want to remember him. I want to tell Mum all of this, but she already looks so sad. If spending time with his decaying corpse brings her peace, then who am I to stand in the way of that? She hasn't had any time to go and 'see him' because of me, so it's only fair I start to pay that back to her.

'Sounds good,' I tell her. 'I'll go get changed.'

44. MEHREEN

Now that the pact is over, I realise I should probably actually revise for my GCSEs. I hadn't completely discounted taking them (maybe part of my brain always knew I wouldn't be able to actually go through with everything), but when death was the only thing on my mind, it was easy to forget about how terrible I am at school as a whole. And how much of my homework I'd just shoved to the back of my consciousness, and to the bottom of my backpack.

I load up the school website and log into the student portal. My laptop pings with a new email alert and my heart sinks when I see who it's from. I don't even open it to see whether it's a reminder or a new task. I immediately delete it from my inbox and then from my trash bin. My heart's pounding, but I just repeat what Cara said the other day: there are only four days left until their deadline. The emails, the reminders, everything will stop after that. My hands are still shaking though, so I add @mementomori.com to my blocked senders list. There. That should do it.

I distract myself by downloading a maths worksheet and starting on it. I read through the instructions, groan at how hard even the first question seems, and pull out my school-book, placing it right next to my laptop. I turn to a fresh page and start working out the answers, while my laptop plays the new episode of *Dear Hank and John*. After a few minutes I get distracted, as per usual, and start doodling. I've had an idea for a comic book that I haven't been able to get out of my head. Cara was so impressed by her character in my comic about our pact that she started ranting on about how there aren't any disabled superheroes. So, I've started writing one. It's early stages at the minute, obviously, but I'm excited by it. I'm planning on getting it done in time for Cara's birthday in August.

The podcast comes to an end, so I swap from my now heavily doodled book to the laptop again, only to find the green webcam light on. Huh, that's weird. I close the laptop lid, thinking it's just a glitch. I wait for a few seconds for it to go to sleep, then open it up again. Fixed! I log in, but as I do, the light pops up again. It's unnerving me now. I look at the bottom of my screen, at all the programs. The FaceTime app is open, despite my never having used FaceTime on my laptop. I click on it, and the window pops up, my own face staring back at me, waiting for me to call someone. I close the app completely, and the light disappears. Huh. I guess I must have accidentally opened it when I downloaded the worksheet. I click over to iTunes to find another podcast to listen to.

I give myself a half-hour of concentrated maths time, during which I feel like throwing my book out of the window on countless occasions. When my timer rings out, I immediately close my book and push my chair back. I need to physically remove myself from my desk, otherwise I genuinely think I will cry. I go downstairs in search of a snack. Post lies scattered on our doormat. I pick up the small stash of envelopes and catalogues and leave them on the side table before walking into the kitchen, where Imran is kneeling in front of the washing machine, pulling damp clothes into the laundry basket. I stop in my tracks.

'Since when do *you* do any washing?' I blurt.

He turns to look up at me but doesn't maintain eye contact as he mumbles, 'Mum washed the top I need, so now I have to dry and iron it before tonight.'

My instinct is to offer to do it for him. I know he doesn't have a clue how to use the dryer or even the iron. And since Mum's not back from Aunt Nadiya's till late tonight, there's no way it's going to get done right. But I resist. I resist because I'm actively trying to stop being a pushover. Imran is a grown bloody man. If I'm the only one in this world who'll give him a reality check, then so be it.

'You know you want to start the dryer,' Imran whines as I pull out a pack of chocolate bourbons.

'Nope.' I don't even turn to look at him.

'Oh, c'mon,' he says. 'You know how to do all this girly shit.'

'Since when was washing exclusively a female task?' I ask, separating the halves of my bourbon and licking the filling.

'You know what I mean – girls like doing this stuff,' he rebuts, closing the washing machine door and standing up.

I cock an eyebrow at him. 'I can't think of a single person, regardless of sex, who would admit to liking doing laundry.'

'I don't have time for this,' he says, picking up the basket and placing it on the empty dinner table. 'Shove this lot in the dryer, would ya?'

I try and quickly swallow the biscuit in my mouth to snap back at him, but he's already out of the room. Ugh, that idiot. I put the biscuit packet back into the cupboard and curse him under my breath as I take the basket over to the dryer. I shove the clothes into the machine and contemplate putting it on the wrong setting – shrinking his clothes or leaving them damp – but I'm anxious about the ways he would get back at me. As kids, whenever I'd dare to play a prank on him, he'd always repay me with something ten times worse. It instilled a fear in me that I still can't shake. So of course I put his clothes in the dryer and switch it on, like the good little sister I am.

The pile of post catches my eye again as I'm about to go back up to my room. On the top is a letter addressed to Imran, with the address of the local police station at the top. The police! I pick up the brown envelope and try to shake the paper inside a bit so I can read it through the little window. No luck though. The envelope looks similar to the speeding ticket Imran got a few months back. Dad was so mad at him over that. If I just leave it slightly hidden from obvious view, Imran won't find it, but Dad will. I grin, thinking about how much trouble he's going to get in. I grab all the letters and fan them out slightly. As I do, I find an envelope addressed to me. There's a logo in the top corner for LunarLlama, one of those websites where you can create and send custom cards online. I carefully open the envelope and pull out the card. On the front is a photo of Bossfort Beach, with the words 'Sorry for your loss' in white script across it. My heart leaps into my throat as I open the card and read the message inside.

Mum, Dad, Imran,
I guess if you're reading this, then I'm gone.

No. No way. It can't be . . .

You probably haven't noticed, but I'm miserable. I have been for a long time.

I scan through the rest of the message quickly, my hand now trembling, heart pounding. It seems to be verbatim my suicide note. How is this here? Why is it here? And why the hell is it written on a condolences card? I check the envelope and letter to see if there's a sender name, but there's nothing except the generic company details. I can feel my head going fuzzy, my breaths becoming laboured. This has to be MementoMori. They're the only ones who had access to my note; I remember uploading a photo of it to the site before we all threw our paper copies into the sea. But why would they do this? What are they hoping to achieve?

My legs are quivering now, and I know I'm about to have a full-blown panic attack. I scrunch the card up in my fist and drag myself upstairs; I have to hold on to the banister and occasionally place my hand on a higher step to stop myself from falling down. I manage to stumble into my bedroom without Imran seeing me. I shut the door and lean against it before sliding down to the floor. I wrap my arms around my knees and ride out the panic attack, trying to breathe through it, but feeling like the world is about to crumble right beneath me.

You should never have broken the pact.
THERE'S STILL TIME TO GO BACK.
You won't have to feel like this ever again.

45. OLIVIA

I often think about the **last day**
Mother and **Daddy**
spent under the same roof.

We were having lunch
                    (salmon en croute),
and they were both silent,
exhausted from the **arguing**
that had been polluting the house
                    all morning,
                    all week,
                    all month.

I was only ten.
Didn't understand.
Thought the silence was **good**.
<u>Anything</u> was better than the **shouting,**
the **SCREAMING,**
the crashing of crockery.

I didn't *know* it was going to be the **last** time,
that the next morning,

Daddy would take all his belongings and

L E A V E.

That I'd only see him on weekends after that,
then eventually only during holidays,
and now only when he has time . . .
when he can *tear himself away* from his **new** wife/life.

I used to **wonder** whether I would have done anything *differently*
had I known it was the
last time
we'd all be **together**.

Would I have *begged* him to stay?
Tried to **force** them back together?
Would it have worked?
Would things have turned out

differently
if only I had known?
Would things be **good** now?

For **years** I **wondered** about these things incessantly,
so now that it's my **last day** with Mother
before

EVERYTHING
changes,

I make sure to do it *right*.
So that I'll have **no regrets.**

I've downloaded her **favourite** film
for us to watch together,
cuddled up on the sofa,
and have told Maria to cook her **favourite** meals for lunch
<u>and</u> supper.

As I'm dressing for lunch,
there's a
ping
from my laptop, which sits open on my desk.
I adjust the angle of the screen to check the alert
and am instead
dis   trac   ted
by the little green light
right next to the camera.
I look at the bottom of the screen.
The Skype app is loaded, but when I open the window
          there's **no one** calling,
          there's **no** notification,
and yet the green light
                    stays on.
I close the app completely,
   but the light   *stays on.*

Another *ping.*
And this time I see the alert: an iMessage from Mehreen.

A succession of *pings*.

Mehreen: GUYS, are you there? I'm freaking out!!
Mehreen: A copy of my suicide note just came through
the post inside a weird 'sorry for your loss' card.
Mehreen: HOW IS THIS HAPPENING? Did you get the
same?

A copy of her suicide note?
I'd forgotten we even wrote those . . .
A lifetime ago.

Cara: WHAT?! Inside a card?!
Cara: Just checked the post here - nothing
Cara: ???

I breathe a *sigh* of relief
that the post for us today
was just an invoice for school fees.

Olivia: Did your parents see it?
Mehreen: NO. Thankfully they're not home. But I'm so
confused. This has to be MementoMori, right?
Olivia: They must have taken it from the photo you
uploaded.
Mehreen: But WHY?! Why are they doing this?
Cara: They're probably just tryna freak us out,
since we haven't been doing the tasks. Just ignore

it. The deadline's in a few days. Everything will
stop then.
Mehreen: You really think that?
Cara: Deffo. Bastards are just trying to be scary.
Ignore them.
Olivia: Try not to worry about it. It'll all be
fine.

It'll all be *fine*.
Do I **believe** that?
Or am I turning into *everyone else?*
Using *empty* phrases
to console?

I cannot fathom how the note would get back to Mehreen,
but have no trouble
believing MementoMori
THRIVE
on instilling fear into us.

But really,
how much damage can a website do?

I **close** the laptop,
close out Mehreen and Cara
and go down to my mother.

Tomorrow.
   Tomorrow and tomorrow and tomorrow.

Everything will **change**.
I will become the girl
everyone *whispers* about.
People will see me as

damaged.

Even Mother will have a hard time looking at me,
blaming me for
driving
her boyfriend away.

But there's still **today**.
Today we can be a normal family.

46. CARA

Dad's graveyard is much nicer than the one Mehreen, Olivia and I meet at. There are men trimming the hedges, no litter on the grass and beautiful statues dotted around. I follow Mum up a path towards a patch over to the left. I don't even remember where Dad's grave is. That does make me feel a bit guilty, but I remind myself that it's not him here, just bones.

We stop at his grave. He's got an average-sized headstone, not a ridiculous huge one like some others here, or one with his photo on (those creep me out). It's not plain, but it's also not over the top. Just like Dad. Mum bends down and takes away the bunch of dead flowers that have crumpled to pieces.

'Sorry it's been a while, Joel,' she whispers as she cleans. There's a metal pot sunk into the ground as part of his headstone and she sticks her new flowers – a bunch of white roses – into it and fluffs them out. She runs her hand over the top of the stone as she stands up.

'Look who's here,' she says to the headstone. She looks at me, waiting.

'Um . . . hi . . . Dad,' I say, waving a little and then feeling like an idiot for waving to a stone.

Mum sits cross-legged on one side of his grave while I stay on the other side, sort of just watching her talk to him. She catches him up on her life, as if he's just been away on a business trip. I notice she doesn't mention anything about Owen Gentry or our fight yesterday. She doesn't tell him I thought I killed him or that she forced herself not to even think about him. She's acting as if he's really alive, and it makes me even more scared that maybe she's had a break-down.

'Right, Cara?' she says all of a sudden.

'What?' I ask, realising I'd completely tuned out.

She frowns and stares at me for a second. I fiddle with the hem of my top, avoiding looking at her sad eyes.

'You should talk to him,' she says. 'I'll leave you alone for a bit.'

'No, it's fine,' I tell her, finally looking up. 'You can stay with . . . him. I can wait at the car.'

'Cara, what's wrong? Was this a mistake? Is it too soon?'

'No, no, it's fine. It's just . . . I don't know what to say. That's not . . . You know that's not him, right? That he's not listening to any of what you say?'

I expect her to be mad, tell me I'm disrespecting Dad or something, but she smiles.

'How do you know he's not listening?' she asks. Not in a mean way, but as if she really wants to know why I think that.

'Um, cos he's dead? Pretty sure you lose the ability to hear when your heart stops beating.'

'I know you're not religious, and neither were me and your

dad, to be honest. But . . . I believe that there's some part of him somewhere, watching over us. It gives me peace to think that. So even if I'm wrong, it makes me feel better to talk to him and believe he's listening to me. It makes it feel like he's still here.'

I want to argue with her, to tell her that that's bull, but I remember a conversation I had with Mehreen about her faith. She told me it wasn't fair for me to diss other people's beliefs, since it didn't impact my own. Mum's just told me *she* believes all of this; she didn't say I have to or that I *should*. I guess if it brings her comfort then I should keep quiet.

'Right, OK,' I say, trying to finish the conversation without agreeing with her.

'Really, you should try it.' She gets up off the ground and brushes herself down. 'I promise, you'll feel better.'

'I doubt it.'

'I really feel like it might benefit you, after everything,' she says. 'But of course I'm not going to try to force you to do anything you don't want to.'

That'd be a first.

'Mum I don't –'

'I didn't realise I could drive right up here,' she says quickly, looking at the paths behind us. 'I'm going to go and fetch the car. You can do whatever you want while you wait.' She hesitates before kissing the top of the stone and whispering something to it. 'I'll be back in a few minutes,' she says to me.

I roll my eyes as she leaves, then look back at the stone.

264

The text reads: 'Joel Saunders, Beloved father and husband'. He should have a better inscription. He was more than just a father and a husband. He was the biggest *Neighbours* fan I've ever known. He could shove his entire fist in his mouth. He was kind. Understanding. Sweet. He was so much more than just those two roles. All of a sudden it's like I can hear his real voice in my head.

'Stop being such a sap, kid,' he laughs.

I smile; that's totally what he'd say. He'd tell me that this stone, these words, mean nothing as long as I remember him the way he was.

'I watched that film again the other day,' I say out loud, but quietly enough that if someone caught me, they'd think I was praying. 'That one we watched on the last day. You were right; it was pretty good. I forced myself to watch it as just a film rather than social commentary, even though you know I live for that shit.'

I sigh, looking around to make sure I'm alone. Might as well give this a try . . . for Mum, I mean.

'I miss you,' I say. 'So much. It's . . . I know I'm supposed to be over it by now, but I don't see how I'll ever *not* miss you. When does it go away? Everyone says there'll be a time when I'll think about you and smile rather than cry. Can we fast-forward to that bit, please?'

'No shortcuts,' he says in my head. 'They're never worth it in the long run.'

'You obviously never used the alleyway on Blake Road. Cuts a whole five minutes off the journey to school,' I say in my head.

I take a deep breath. Mum's going to be back any second and I don't want her to see me doing this.

'If you're watching, or up there, or whatever . . . if you've got any superpowers, just . . . look out for Mum. This . . . Everything's been hard on her, and I know, I know, I haven't helped that at all. But I'm trying now. If you've got the power, pull some strings to make her happy, yeah?'

I hear the car pulling up behind me.

'Right, yeah. Peace out, Dad. I promise I'll come more often. Not sure about this talking thing though.'

'I love you, Cara.'

'Love you too, Dad.'

Mum hums all the way home, tapping away on the steering wheel. I take that as a good sign. I expect it to get annoying, the constant tap-tap-tapping, but somehow I put up with it. I look at my phone, expecting Mehreen to still be freaking out about her note arriving in the post, but my phone's blank. I shoot a quick message to her, just checking in.

Cara: Mehreen, you doing OK?

She replies almost immediately.

Mehreen: Can't talk. Don't contact me for a while.

The message is shorter than her texts normally are, and there's no kiss at the end. She must be really freaked out. I know she said not to, but I can't help but try calling her; she doesn't answer – probably just needs some space.

'Feel like going out for dinner?' Mum asks.

I turn to her and smile, putting my phone back in my pocket. 'Sure, Mum. You can choose where we go.'

47. OLIVIA

15th April
(3 days until Date of Termination)

Mornings in the Castleton household,
during weekends and holidays,
normally
start **precisely** at 10 a.m.
Normally
I'll come downstairs to find Maria in the kitchen and
             Mother at the table with a newspaper/
                              her tablet/
                              some sketches for work.

But today
Mother is **nowhere** to be seen.
I look at Maria questioningly,
but she just *shrugs*.

I search for Mother in the living room
                      her bedroom
                      her office
                      the bathroom.

Search, search, search
until I find her
    sitting on the floor
        of the guest bedroom,
           surrounded by *his* possessions,
           sitting in the middle of an

EXPLOSION
of photographs.
The frame from the mantelpiece lies by her knee.
She's crying freely,
the tears drop
             p
                 ing into the wineglass glued to her hand.
I expect her to <u>compose</u> herself when she sees me.
                       Castletons never show emotions this openly.
But instead she reaches out with her free hand.
Her face *contorts* further when I take it
and I fall to the ground too,
wrapping my arms around her.

I can see *his* eyes **staring out** at me from dozens of images
on the floor,
can smell *his* aftershave on the shirt in her lap,
but I force myself to **PUSH** him away
and <u>focus</u> on my devastated mother.

                            'I miss him.'
                         That's Mother.

'I miss him so much.'

I don't reply.
Just stroke her hair.
Angle my face so the stench of wine d r i f t s away.

'Why won't he answer my calls any more?'
She's *slurrrrrring*
and seems unsteady
when she pulls away from me to sip her wine.
Or should I say gulp?
It's evident she won't **remember** this conversation.

'Did I do something wrong?'
I don't reply.

'I should apologise, shouldn't I?'
I don't look at her.

'He's a good man, isn't he, Olivia?'
I hold back the bile jumping up my throat.
'He's always been friendly towards you, hasn't he?'
I can hear Mehreen and Cara in my head
telling me this is the
PERFECT TIME
to tell her the truth.
TODAY'S THE DAY, after all.
I **promised** I'd do it . . .
But . . .
But right now,

I can *barely breathe*,
let alone form coherent thoughts.

'Are you the reason he left?'

Tears **spring** from my eyes
as I snap my head towards her.
My heart,
lungs,
brain,
have all STOPPED.

My entire life is

perched

on this moment.

'Taking on a teenager is a big ask.
Do you think he became overwhelmed?'

Mother twists her body,
so suddenly,
it makes me **gasp**.
She puts her hand on my arm.

'You two are close.
Will you talk to him?
Will you convince him to **COME BACK?**'

I jump up,
almost spilling Mother's wine in the process.
'I have to go.
I made plans with friends.
I have to leave now.'

Lying comes so naturally to the Castletons.

She doesn't even call after me as I **run**
to the bathroom.
Doesn't come to stroke my hair as I **vomit**.
She's too busy with her photographs, wine and
fake memories.

48. MEHREEN

The letter box clatters. I shoot up off my bed and down the stairs faster than I ever have before. I'm at the door barely after the letters have touched the ground; I can see the postman walking away down the path. There's a white envelope similar to yesterday's. It's happening again. Without checking who it's addressed to, or whether there's a logo, I rip the envelope open.

Mr Miah,
    Find enclosed your electricity bill for this period.

I deflate and examine the envelope. Sure enough, the electricity company's logo is staring out at me. I stuff the letter back inside and place it on the table. The other envelopes are also addressed to Dad and have recognisable logos, so I resist tearing them open.

WHAT DOES IT MATTER ANYWAY?
*No one would care even if they
    did read your suicide note.*
**THEY'D PROBABLY LAUGH AND WISH
YOU HAD GONE THROUGH WITH IT.**

I pour some Shreddies into my bowl and sit down at one end of the table. Dad's phone chirps at my elbow. An email alert. That tone has instilled so much fear in me that my hand flies out to snatch the phone without even thinking about it. Dad turns to stare at me, his teacup poised mid-air in one hand, the other reaching for the phone that I'm now holding. His brow creases as he looks at me.

'Um, sorry,' I say, quickly pressing the button on the side of the phone so the screen lights up again. 'I thought it was mine.' I take a quick glance at the notification, but it's not from MementoMori. Of course it's not. Stupid to even think that. The website knew our address from when I signed up, the note was taken from the photo we uploaded. They have *my* email address, but they wouldn't be able to get to my parents. I just need to ignore them, like Cara said. Everything will be fine. Nothing else will happen.

Dad's frown deepens and I feel like he's going to say something, but he just shakes his head slightly and takes his phone from me. He sips his tea as he glances at and deletes an email from a Nigerian prince. Mum chatters on about how crazy Aunt Nadiya has gone with organising her daughter's wedding. Something about last-minute guest additions and how it looks like it's going to rain on the day. I don't think anyone in the room is paying attention, but that never usually stops her.

I take my bowl to the sink and drop it in. 'I'm going out today, remember?' I say to Mum.

'Out, again?' she asks, not even looking at me. 'Enjoy it while it lasts. School opens again soon and you need to improve your grades.'

'Yeah, OK,' I mumble, though I know she's not really listening. I slink back up to my room.

I open my laptop and scroll through Facebook and Twitter for a while, ignoring all the snap-happy group photos from everyone at school. The green light suddenly turns on again and my heart jumps. What on earth is wrong with this stupid laptop? I check the FaceTime app, but even that's not open this time. I check my settings for the camera and microphone, but that's no help either. Suddenly, the Skype icon starts bobbing up and down at the bottom of my screen. I click on it, expecting to find another blank window, but this time there actually is an incoming video chat. From Cara. I guess the reboot I did yesterday did the trick. I click the accept button, and after a few seconds Cara's face appears.

'Hey!' she says enthusiastically.

'Hey! I thought we were meeting at Olivia's?' I ask, checking my watch to make sure I haven't completely lost track of time over the whole post freak-out.

'Slight change of plan. What's up with your phone, Mehreen?'

'What do you mean?' I take out my phone and unlock it.

'I know you told me not to contact you, but I just wanted to make sure you were OK. I've been trying to call you since yesterday. Didn't you get my texts?'

'What? No!' I feverishly check my phone signal, that it isn't on silent. Everything seems fine. I check my texts and call log, but there's nothing from Cara.

'Anyway, I guess it doesn't matter. I've got something more

important to show you.' She twists her laptop to the side to show Olivia sitting on the sofa.

Olivia?

There's a pile of snacks on the table too, as if they've been there for hours.

They probably hang out without you all the time.

'Seriously?' Olivia screeches, jumping to her feet. 'You're really making the most of this, aren't you?' She's laughing as she walks towards the screen.

'Hi, Mehreen,' Olivia says, bending slightly to wave into the camera.

I slowly raise my hand to wave back. 'Making the most of what?' I ask. 'What's going on?' My voice almost betrays my desperation.

'Look at what she's wearing!' Cara giggles from off-screen.

Olivia rolls her eyes and steps back to show me her outfit. Only it's not hers. I recognise the black T-shirt with skeletons spelling out the alphabet.

'Are you wearing Cara's clothes?'

'Borrowing them,' Olivia clarifies.

'She pissed herself!' Cara shouts from off-screen.

'I did not!' Olivia shrieks. She shoves Cara and I can hear their laughter echo around the room.

Look how much fun they have without you.

'I got caught in the rain on the way here,' Olivia explains. 'I'm wearing this until my clothes dry. Do I look horrible?' She scrunches up her nose.

'No, you look fine,' I say. 'But, uh, what are you doing at Cara's? I thought we were all going to yours to tell your mum about . . . y'know. Did something happen?'

Olivia tucks a strand of her hair behind her ear. 'Mum was in a bad way this morning. I had to get out of there and didn't know where else to go.'

'Oh, I'm sorry,' I say, desperately wanting to ask for more information, but getting the sense that she's being evasive on purpose.

The laptop swings around so now Cara's back in the frame too.

'So we're gonna cancel today,' Cara says. 'Olivia's breaking *another* pact. She owes me one.' She turns to smirk at Olivia, who rolls her eyes.

'Oh. OK,' I say, trying not to show my deflation. I *need* to get out of the house. I can just tell it's going to be a bad day. 'Did you guys still want to hang out?'

'Sure, can do. Whatcha wanna do?'

'Oh, I have an idea!' Olivia says, pushing herself into the frame more. 'I was looking up ways to help with your anxiety, Mehreen. And everyone seems to suggest yoga as a great coping mechanism.'

I smile at the thoughtfulness of Olivia doing this research on her own. 'That sounds great! I've never done yoga before. Is it hard?'

'Um, I think you're both ignoring the elephant in the room,' Cara says. 'The elephant being my freaking chair.'

'I checked ahead – there's a class at the leisure centre that does wheelchair-friendly classes,' Olivia says. 'There's

277

one at eleven. I asked if we could come, and they said it was fine.'

'Ugh, still, pretty sure I'll suck at downward-facing dog in this thing.' Cara gestures to her chair.

Olivia elbows her. 'What makes you think it's the chair that would be the problem? Yoga requires grace. I don't think you have an ounce of that.' She laughs.

Cara rolls her eyes. 'At least I didn't piss myself.'

'Stop saying that!'

They start shoving each other, all the while laughing away. Laughing harder than I've seen them laugh before. All I can do is sit and wait for them to finish, wait for them to remember I'm even here. I can feel my heart pounding and hear the growl of my Chaos getting ready to pounce.

YOU COULD LOG OFF AND THEY WOULDN'T EVEN NOTICE.

'Um, so, meet in an hour?' I almost shout at the screen, desperate to be back in the conversation, desperate to not be pushed out, desperate to hold the Chaos at bay.

'Yeah, we'll meet you by the bus stop in town,' Cara says.

The screen goes black without even a goodbye.

49. MEHREEN

'How on earth was that meant to be good for my mental health?' I say as I take my tray from the McDonalds cashier. I feel a twinge in my side as I reach across. 'I thought yoga was supposed to be relaxing but I swear I'm more stressed. Plus, I'm sure I pulled a muscle.'

Olivia laughs, carrying her own tray over to the table Cara's saving for us. 'Well, I enjoyed it. It really took my mind off everything.'

'In which case, it was definitely worth it,' I say, smiling at her. She explained what happened at home this morning and why she changed her mind about telling her mother the truth. It's nice to see a smile on her face after that.

'I enjoyed it too,' Cara says, surprising me. 'Enjoyed watching you fall over a million times, Mehreen.' She takes a bite of her burger.

'Oh, shove off,' I reply, throwing a chip at her. 'Balancing on one leg is *hard*.'

'I would insert a paraplegic joke here, but I'm too hungry.' Cara shoves more of her burger into her mouth.

My phone chimes on the table. I wipe my fingers on a napkin and pick it up. It's an email alert from MementoMori.

'What the hell?'

'What is it?' Olivia asks.

'I blocked them,' I say. 'I blocked the email address and the entire domain – how on earth are they still emailing me?'

Cara's phone chimes before anyone else can say anything, and then a split second later so does Olivia's. I open the email up and begin reading.

From: Administrator (admin@mementomori.com)
To: Mehreen Miah (mehreenmiah@hotmail.co.uk)
Subject: Missed deadline

You have missed the deadline to complete and submit photographic evidence of having completed Task 3. As mentioned in previous communications, failure to complete tasks in a timely manner contravenes our terms and conditions. Since this is your first missed deadline, we will extend the allocated time to complete this task. However, your meeting today at 8 p.m. will still go ahead and you will receive an additional task. The tasks must now be completed concurrently and photographic evidence of both provided by 17th April.

Next meeting: 17th April, 12 p.m.
Location: Bridgeport Swim Centre, Bridgeport BP7 2NF

Failure to adhere to this new deadline will oblige us to take further action against you.

'Why won't they just stop?' I say. I can feel tears coming on, my heart already pounding. 'I *swear* I blocked everything. I don't get why this is happening.'

'They're just trying to scare us,' Cara repeats calmly, stowing her phone in her pocket and picking up her burger again. 'Waving their dicks around, showing us what they can do. It'll stop after the deadline.'

'What if it doesn't?' I ask. 'They keep going on about these terms and conditions, further action and whatever. What does it even mean?'

'It seems like they're clutching at straws,' Olivia says. 'Have you noticed how they keep using the same threat but never acting upon it, or even expanding on what "further action" means?'

'Exactly!' Cara says. 'They're bullshitting.'

'I tried looking for the terms and conditions on their website,' Olivia says. 'But there's nothing there. I remember a tick box when I first signed up – I guess I should have read that.'

'Who the fuck reads the terms and conditions?' Cara asks.

'This whole thing is like a contract though, isn't it?' I say. 'Those are hard to get out of, right? Maybe we should ask your lawyer aunt for help, Cara.'

'You need to stop freaking out,' Cara says with a tinge of annoyance in her voice. 'Nothing is going to happen. There's only three days left. We can just ride it out.'

STOP BEING A WUSS - THAT'S WHAT SHE MEANS.
Look how calmly they're taking it.
WHY CAN'T YOU BE MORE LIKE THEM?

'I still really want to know who's running this website,' Olivia says, flicking through on her phone. 'I shudder to think what kind of person would even think of creating something like this.'

Cara shrugs. 'It worked, didn't it? We wouldn't be here if it hadn't.'

'Yes, but what do *they* get out of it? People sign up, go through with it, then what? What satisfaction do they get? Why are they so obsessed with us sticking to their rules? And why the obsession with photographic evidence?'

'There are some sick people in this world,' Cara says nonchalantly. She takes another sip of her drink. 'They probably get a kick out of knowing they had some part in people dying. In watching people like you two panic. And the photos are part of that – look how they used it against Mehreen.'

'Did either of you end up getting your notes in the post?' I ask, hopeful. It feels weird to be the only one who had that happen. As if I'm the worst one in this trio, the weakest link.

They both shake their heads.

YOU ARE THE WEAKEST ONE.

'It doesn't matter now anyway,' Cara continues. 'The only other thing they have of us is selfies from the graveyard and the dressing rooms. Not like they can do much with that.'

'Well, we also didn't think they'd do anything with the photograph of our notes,' Olivia points out. 'So who knows?'

My heart sinks. The fact that Olivia and Cara seemed unconcerned was the only thing getting me through, the only thing stopping me from totally freaking out about that note. But now that Olivia, the most sensible one of us all, is questioning things, it feels as if the foundations are shaking, letting my doubts and fears creep back in.

You should've ended it when you had the chance.

50. OLIVIA

When I get home,
Mother is in the living room,
TV on, with a glass of . . .
water!
in her hand.
She seems to be in a **good** mood,
she's *smiling* at the screen,
no sign of tears,
the photos, letters and clothes packed away.
She seems to have recovered from this morning.
Although her red rimmed eyes
and *exaggerated* make-up
tell me
she's most likely just
PRETENDING
it **never happened**.

                    Castletons never show emotions openly.

I decide to try to
distract her,
pamper her,
to show her it's OK

when it's just
US.
Better, even.

I tell her to pick her **favourite** restaurant for dinner
and that it will be
my treat.
She smiles,
almost
a **real** smile,
and tells me that her favourite restaurant is out of my budget.
She seems *touched* by the sentiment though,
and tells me to pick *my* favourite restaurant instead.

I don't have *favourites*.
No one thing I like **better** than the rest.
I've learned that when there's something you **value,**
it *hurts* when it's taken away.
And the way to **avoid** that?
Avoid *favourites*.
Avoid showing *passion* for anything.
Avoid letting anyone know what you *value*.

Mother is different though.

I want to *impress* her with my choice.
I want to show her I'm like her.

You look just like your mother; sorry I thought you were her.

No. No. No.

I go up to my room and use my laptop to search for a
respectable
beautiful
fancy
restaurant.

Mehreen and Cara pop up in the group chat,
and I get
distracted
arranging a support group meeting for the 17th.

'Olivia?'
Mother calls after a while.
'Are you ready to go, dear?'
Dear.
Dear.
<u>Dear.</u>

A flutter in my chest.

'I'm so glad you suggested this,'
Mother says, wiping caramel sauce off her lips.
Her smile has returned **full force**.
'It's been lovely spending time **with you** these past few days.'
She places her hand over mine.

**This is how it could be,
how it should be.**

Mother has always been so
preoccupied
    with work
    with her romantic partners
    with herself
that I assumed she had no time for me.
But now I realise . . .
I just had to make some effort myself.

        'I've seen a real change in you recently.
                You seem . . . happier.'

      Mother . . . noticed?
                'Is there a reason why?'
        She cocks her eyebrow, with a smirk,
           wine glass poised by her lips.

        **This is it.
        The perfect time.**

But before I can form the words,
my phone lights up on the table
and lets out a

SHRIEK

louder than *anything* I've ever heard.

I jump.
Mother jumps,
splashing wine all down her dress
and **cursing**.
She grabs her napkin to clean herself up
as I try to **quell**
the **SHRIEK.**

The phone itself looks **normal.**
There's no alert for an alarm
or an incoming call.
I put it on *silent,*
but pressing the button is futile.
The **SHRIEK** gets an octave higher
and I *hunch* my shoulders to try to **cover** my ears
as I *swipe* and **tap** all over the screen.

The other patrons are irritated now.
Everyone is turning to **STARE**
and I can feel my face **heat up**.

Suddenly
the screen of my phone turns **RED**
blood red.
Red and **SHRIEKING**.
I hold the power switch
until the whole thing turns **OFF**.

The *echo* of the noise   r e v e r b e r a t e s   around
the restaurant
and inside my eardrum.
But then a wave of silence spreads,
as people stare intently.

Mother gives everyone an apologetic smile,
then turns to me,
face BLAZING
from the <u>embarrassment</u>.
'What on *earth* was that?'

'I honestly don't know,' I reply.
When I try to switch the phone back on,
Nothing loads.
Instead, the screen is

D O M I N A T E D

by a clock face
that reads 8 p.m.

The time Mehreen, Cara and I were supposed to
upload evidence of having
inflicted pain on each other.
And I realise what caused that racket.
Or should I say *who*?

51. MEHREEN

16th April
(2 days until Date of Termination)

Wedding prep for cousin Sabrina's big day has reached
feverish levels. It has leaked out of Aunt Nadiya's house and
travelled a whole ten miles into our kitchen, where she and
Mum sit at the table making samosas. Sabrina and Wasim are
here too. Wasim's with Imran upstairs being unproductive,
and Sabrina's tapping away on her phone in the living room,
sitting with her feet up on the sofa. God forbid the bride do
any work.

There's a whole production line in the kitchen. Mum rips
off strips of pastry and forms it into triangular pockets, gluing
the seams with a concoction of flour and water. I take these
and stuff them with a lentil mixture, before passing them on
to Aunt Nadiya, who uses the same flour/water mixture to
seal the samosas and places them neatly on a tray, ready to
be fried later.

Being in the middle is awful. It's like being in school with
Calliope and Pascha – when they have one of their endless
conversations about things I have literally no interest in but
can't escape. Mum and Aunt Nadiya seem OK with me not

chipping in though; I can tell they wish I was hanging around with Sabrina, asking her for make-up tips and how to snag a husband. I can't decide if I'd rather do that than be sitting here. I can't even eat the lentil mixture like I normally would, because Aunt Nadiya would make some comment about me stealing the food and effectively ruining her daughter's wedding.

'I tried to tell her,' Aunt Nadiya blabbers on. 'I said to her, "You need to learn what to do in the kitchen – you can't expect your mother-in-law to do all the work." But does she listen to me? Of course not!'

I sneak a look at Mum and she rolls her eyes at me secretly, which makes me smile.

'It's not like in our day though,' Mum says. 'Sabrina probably won't even be living with her in-laws for very long. Mikail and her will want to get their own space. There's already too many people living in that house.'

'The more people, the better, I say,' replies Aunt Nadiya in a haughty tone. 'The daughter-in-law is supposed to serve the family, so why would she live separately? Makes no sense. All these modern girls.' I swear she gives me a look filled with contempt at this point.

'No, Mehreen.' She takes the spoon from my hand. 'You need to pat it down like this – it gets more filling that way.' She uses the back of the spoon to squish the lentils in.

You can't even stuff a samosa properly.

'OK,' I say, taking back the spoon. I want to keep doing it my way, because overstuffed samosas always split apart later, but of course her eagle eyes are watching me so I have to do it her way.

My phone pings in my pocket. The email alert I've now come to dread. Even though I've blocked MementoMori, each time I hear an email notification, I'm convinced it's them. Every time I ignore their email, I keep expecting another copy of my note through the door, or worse. I'm on constant alert for something to go tremendously wrong.

THINGS ALWAYS GO WRONG FOR YOU. THIS IS GOING TO BLOW UP IN YOUR FACE.

I could ignore the message, just pretend it's not there, but it'll niggle in my brain until I go crazy. I wipe my hand on a tissue and pull my phone out from my pocket. Mum and Aunt Nadiya are engrossed in conversation so don't even notice.

The email isn't from MementoMori though – it's from Olivia, which is odd considering we usually text. There's an attachment to the otherwise empty email so I open it up. A photograph dominates my entire screen and as soon as it loads completely, I drop my phone. It clatters against the tiled floor and skitters away under the table. I shove my chair back with a loud scrape and get on my hands and knees to retrieve it.

'What are you doing?' Aunt Nadiya asks, bending over to look under the table.

Oh God – if she sees the photo, I'm dead. She's going to get the completely wrong idea. I quickly put my phone to sleep and scramble back out.

'Oh, um, I just need to . . . use the bathroom,' I say.

Aunt Nadiya looks at me quizzically and I can tell she wants to tell me how weird I am and how that won't go down well with my future in-laws. I turn to Mum and she nods, though looks just as confused, but that's all I need. I run upstairs to the bathroom and lock myself in. My hand's shaking as I unlock my phone.

The photograph is of Olivia. Olivia in her underwear. She's standing with her body towards the camera, her thumbs hooked into the sides of her knickers, as if about to pull them down. She's looking to the ground, her wet hair falling around her face. Through the curtain of blonde though, you can see she's smiling.

It looks like she's posing for the photo, like one of the photos Pascha casually sends to her boyfriend every now and then. But surely Olivia wouldn't? She's not that kind of girl.

I call Olivia. Her phone doesn't even ring, just asks me to leave a message. I don't. What would I say? I try again and again and again, but I'm guessing she's turned it off.

I examine the photo more closely. The wall behind her is wallpapered in a black and white floral pattern that looks oddly familiar. I zoom in close to her face, looking for signs of . . . what? What other story could this photograph tell? There's willingness in her body language and written all over her face. I move the image around to zoom in on the photo frame hanging on the wall behind her. A small square frame with three heads in it. Cara, her mother and a man that must be her father. Why on earth is there a picture of

294

Cara . . . ? Hang on – it's Cara's house! Cara's room, in fact. Why would Olivia be dressed like this in Cara's room? And it's not a selfie – why would she let someone take a photo of her this way? Wait . . . Could it be? Are they . . . *together*?

They've preferred each other since you met.
YOU'RE ALWAYS THE ODD ONE OUT.

I call Cara. Her phone doesn't ring either; there's just some automated message about her phone being unreachable. I don't know whether that means she doesn't have signal or she's turned it off or what. I keep trying though. I alternate between her and Olivia over and over, the Chaos reaching deafening levels in my head for the first time in a long time.

THEY WERE NEVER YOUR FRIENDS.

I stand up off the loo on shaky legs.

EVERYTHING THEY TOLD YOU WAS A LIE.

I walk over to the sink and, as if I'm not even in control of my body, I open the cabinet above it.

THEY'RE PROBABLY TOGETHER RIGHT NOW. LAUGHING ABOUT WHAT AN IDIOT YOU ARE.

I find Dad's razor in my trembling hands.

You're always in the way.
THE WORLD WOULD BE
        BETTER OFF WITHOUT YOU.
  No one would even notice...

52. OLIVIA

SLUT

noun

A woman who has many casual sexual partners.

I receive fifteen different text messages
with variations of this word
        this **name**
        this <u>label</u>.
Messages from people I thought were my **friends.**
People I've **shared** classes with,
       shared assignments with,
       shared food with.
People I barely know.
And people I don't know **at all**.

I also get messages *propositioning* me
in graphic, vulgar terms.

At first I'm
terrified
that everyone has <u>found out</u>
about *him*.

But that's impossible.
The only people who know are Cara and Mehreen . . .
  and they wouldn't tell . . .

I try to **ignore** the messages,
try to <u>clear</u> all the notifications on my phone.
I load up Instagram just to get rid of the little red circle.

My phone
        almost
                S M A S H E S
                        to the ground
                                when I see it.

                See <u>me</u>.
          Only it can't be me . . .
                I **didn't** . . .
                I *wouldn't* . . .

            I **zoom** in on the face,
                on *this girl's* face.
          There's no denying it's **me** . . .
                    But

WHERE DID THIS COME FROM?

              I look like I'm . . .
          like I'm about to . . .
        like I'm doing it on purpose.

This photo was
NOT
taken with my
CONSENT.

Everyone thinks it was.
That I *am* the names they're calling me.
No one will
        believe
                that I have no idea
                                how
                                when
                                where
                                        this was taken.

Except . . .
I can identify **WHERE** . . .
I made a comment
about that eyesore of a wallpaper design
the first time I saw it.

Cara?

Cara . . .

CARA!

Why would Cara *take* this?

Why would she *share* it?

I load up her Instagram profile,
But it's not there . . .
All the likes
and
comments
are coming from

MY profile.

The photo was shared from
. . . my profile?
No caption.
No filter.
Just the image.

No one has access to my account,
   an account I barely use
   an account I used to only have a handful of followers on,
but now have over one thousand.

Why would Cara do this?

A new comment on the photo pops up.

     U know she's askin for it ;)

ASKING FOR IT.

That's what they'll think.
If I tell Mother . . .
if I tell ANYONE
about *him*,
they'll see this and say that
I was asking for it.

He'll say I was
asking for it.

They'll blame me.

53. CARA

17th April
(1 day until Date of Termination)

I haven't heard from Mehreen or Olivia, and they're not replying to my texts, so I assume the support-group meeting we arranged for today is still on. The Wi-Fi at home stopped working yesterday, and I've run out of data on my phone, so I hope they haven't been trying to get in touch by email or whatever. I've been going out of my mind without the Internet – no Twitter, YouTube or Instagram. I had to spend last night watching some weird French film with Mum – the subtitles flashed past way too quickly to follow what the hell was even happening. That's why I NEED this meeting today, need some decent human contact.

Timothy Linnighan's grave has become our home base. I hang out with him and play on my phone as I wait, telling myself I'll give up and go home if they don't come before I beat the next level of Candy Crush. I still haven't managed to fix my normal phone after everything disappeared from it the other day, and this old crappy one doesn't have my old high scores on it, which is annoying.

A few minutes later, I look up after losing another life and, thank fuck, Olivia's heading this way. She's looking around the graveyard and walking slowly, as if she's lost. Don't blame her – all the rows look the same. The only reason I'm here on time is because I memorised the route.

'Olivia!' I call out, waving like an idiot before I realise I'm waving like an idiot.

It works though; she lifts her head, then stops on the spot for a few seconds. I wave again in case she didn't see me properly, but she still doesn't come any closer. She looks around again so I move towards her. When she sees me coming, she wipes her nose with the tissue in her hand and slowly comes to meet me.

'Hey!' I say. 'How're y— Wait, are you crying? What's wrong?'

She wipes her nose again and I notice her eyes are already red and puffy. 'Oh, as if you don't know,' she says.

'What're you on about? Did you end up telling your mum or something?'

'No, I didn't talk to Mother, how could I? She won't take me seriously after . . . after everything.' She starts properly crying again, ducking her head so her hair falls over her face.

I reach out to touch her on the arm, to comfort her like she always tries to do with us, but Olivia snatches her arm away.

'This is all *your* fault,' she spits, stepping in close now, jabbing her finger at my chest.

'I have literally no clue what you're on about,' I tell her, cringing back in my chair. This new Olivia looks ready to cut a bitch.

She roots around in her huge handbag and pulls out her phone. After a few taps and swipes, she throws it at me. I catch it in my lap and turn it over. It's a photo of Olivia in her bra and knickers. I feel my face go hot and shove the phone back at her.

'Why are you showing me this?' I ask. 'Why would you even take –'

'I *didn't*,' she says, angry crying. 'This was taken at *your* house. From *your* laptop, judging by the angle and quality. I don't know how it happened, but it's *everywhere* . . . so many people have . . . seen it, shared it. I keep reporting it, but there's just so many . . .' She breaks down completely, crying in that way where she can't even breathe properly.

'You think *I* did it?!' I know I should be trying to comfort her, but does she really believe I took a photo of her in her pants and shared it online?

'It was at YOUR house!' she screams. 'That day I had to wear your clothes because mine got wet. It's your fucking room!'

I can't help but suck in a breath. You know it's serious when Olivia swears.

'What, you think that just cos I'm gay, I want to take photos of you in your knickers? So I can . . . so I can what? Sorry to burst your bubble, but I'm not into you like that!'

'How else do you explain it?!'

'I left the fucking room when you changed. Are you calling me a perv? You're really fucking full of yourself, you know that?'

'I don't know what I'm saying!' She cries harder. 'I just don't understand how this all happened.'

'Oh, so of course it must be *my* fault, right? You think if I wanted to take photos of you, I'd go and post them online where you can see it? On YOUR account too? And then come and meet you? You really think I'm that shitty a person?'

She starts to stutter something – I can't tell whether she's apologising or accusing me again.

She takes a deep shuddering breath. 'How else could it have happened?' she asks. 'I'd never take a photo of myself like that.'

I think back to that day, trying to remember what exactly we did, whether Mum came into the room at all. I think back to my laptop and how it's been weird recently, with the webcam switching on by itself.

'Oh shit,' I say. 'Do you think . . . ? Do you think MementoMori's behind this?'

Olivia looks at me and I wait for the words to hit, for her to realise how much sense I'm making. But she doesn't. She's still looking at me like she wants to kill me.

'*That's* your excuse? You think a faceless *website* took a photo of me without my knowledge and posted it online?'

'Think about it. The emails, the calls. Mehreen's note? And unless *you* did it, I can't fucking figure out who else it could've been. Or are you gonna blame my mum next?'

She doesn't say anything.

'Are you fucking serious? Now you're calling my mum a perv too?'

'I'm not saying that! I'm just . . . so confused. The emails and calls make sense – they have our email addresses and numbers from when we signed up. Mehreen's note was uploaded to the website. But this is different. This . . . this photo isn't linked to any of the tasks, to the pact at all.'

I'm so fucking pissed I want to deck her in the gob. Just then I see Mehreen coming towards us.

'Don't tell her, please,' Olivia begs. 'I can't . . . I couldn't bear her seeing it too.'

'Fine. But for Mehreen, not you. She'll get all worried about it. You, on the other hand, can go fuck yourself.'

I turn around and move back towards Timothy Linnighan's grave without even checking whether Olivia is following me. For all I care, she can fucking drop dead right next to Timothy.

54. MEHREEN

Cara and Olivia are already at our regular spot as I walk up the path. They're very close to each other, having an intense conversation. If a stranger saw them, they might assume they were about to kiss.

MAYBE THEY ARE TOGETHER.
You're interrupting their couple time.
THIRD WHEEL. AS ALWAYS.

I'm relieved they're both here – I didn't know whether they would be, considering neither of them were answering their phones or my messages yesterday. Or maybe their phones are playing up the way mine did the other day. I was tempted to go round and see Olivia after everything with the photo leaking, to make sure she was OK, but I thought that maybe the incident would have prompted a discussion between her and her mother, and that she'd have found the guts to tell her everything. I'm hoping something good can come of that photo debacle. It just keeps spreading; I saw it on the accounts of multiple people from my school today. People who don't even know Olivia have it, are sharing it, are writing horrible things about her. I report every post I see, but it makes no difference. I'm dying to know why she shared the photo, why she even took it, whether she knows how widely it's been shared.

Cara and I make eye contact when I'm just a few metres away. I smile at her, but her face morphs into a scowl. Olivia catches my eye too but quickly turns to Cara to say something I can't make out. Cara replies, then wheels herself towards the grave we always meet at.

You just ruined their conversation.
YOU RUIN EVERYTHING.
YOU SHOULD JUST DISAPPEAR.
Everyone's better off without you.

'Hi,' I say as I join them both.

Olivia sniffles and raises a tissue to her nose.

'Olivia, are you . . . OK?' I ask, ducking to try and see her face.

She looks up sharply, her eyes stabbing me. Her bloodshot, puffy eyes are streaming. 'You've . . . you've seen it, haven't you?' she asks.

I don't ask her to clarify what she means. I just nod. 'Why . . . why would you post something like that online?'

She laughs once, exasperated, sarcastic, bitter, angry. 'You really think I'd do something like that? You . . . you know *everything* about me, Mehreen, and still you . . .' She dissolves into tears.

'No, sorry . . . Olivia, I didn't . . . I'm sorry, I didn't mean it like that,' I blabber.

She's still crying and I want to reach over and wrap her into a hug but I'm scared she'll push me away.

'I did think it was strange,' I admit. 'What . . . what happened? Who posted it?'

Olivia shakes her head.

'Oh, didn't you hear?' Cara butts in. 'I'm the sicko who apparently gets a kick out of taking photos of people in their pants, without even being in the room, and then sharing that shit online. Didn't you know that all us lesbians can't resist a straight girl in her knickers?'

'That's not what I said!' Olivia protests, actually stamping her foot.

I'm desperate to ask her more about what happened, but I feel like if I do she'll storm off and it'll all be my fault. I need to fix this, need to calm them both down.

'Guys, stop fighting! Please,' I beg. 'Just calm down.'

Somehow my words get through. They both stop glaring at each other and seem to visibly relax. But now we've descended into silence, and I know if this goes on too long, it could have disastrous results.

'Olivia,' I say, 'I know things are . . .' I can't think of a word big enough to contain the feeling of what's happening to her.

She looks up at me though, cocking her eyebrow as if waiting to see if I can attach a word to her feelings that won't make this ten times worse.

YOU HAVE NO IDEA WHAT SHE'S GOING THROUGH.
Don't try and pretend you do.

'It'll pass,' Cara says. 'Shit like this soon dies down. You've just got to wait it out, that's all.'

'That's *all?*' Olivia scoffs.

'Mehreen got over the note. You'll get over this.'

'The note?' I ask. I turn to Olivia. 'Wait, this was MementoMori?!'

My heart's pounding, pounding, pounding.

'No,' Olivia says firmly. 'Or . . . maybe. I don't know.'

'Nah, Olivia would rather believe it was *me* who did this rather than the crazy fucking website that's determined to make us kill ourselves.'

Of course! Of *course* it was them. Between the constant emails and the card through the post, they've left me a nervous wreck. I should have guessed they'd target the others soon enough. They're not going to let up and it's terrifying me.

THEY'RE NOT GOING TO GIVE UP UNTIL YOU'RE DEAD.

You made a promise – you have to keep it.

Olivia's eyes are daggers. She uncrosses her arms and points at Cara. 'You're only acting so cavalier because your life is back on track. You don't have anything to worry about, now you've made up with your mother, now that you finally realise the accident wasn't your fault.'

'What?!' Cara shrieks.

'Guys, c'mon.' I try to play peacemaker again but it's no use.

'Why are you even still here?' Olivia asks Cara. 'This was supposed to be a *support* group. You don't have anything you even need *support* with. Your life is perfect. Just . . . leave.'

I expect Cara to shout back, to give as much as Olivia's just handed out, but her face is pinched; I swear she's about to cry.

'You know what?' Cara says eventually. She's quiet and it seems like she's forcing her words out. 'You're right. Fuck this all. Fuck you both.' She doesn't even look at me before speeding off, her hands pushing her wheelchair faster than I've ever seen. I turn to Olivia and she breaks out into a new wave of tears.

Everything is falling apart all over again.

55. OLIVIA

Mehreen and I walk home together
side   by   side.

Wordless.

I can't get Cara off my mind.
Her reasoning makes **sense;**
if **MementoMori** can post Mehreen's note then . . .
could they have <u>hacked</u> Cara's computer?
Mehreen tells me she's having **issues** with her laptop,
so it seems *plausible*.

But this **rift** between Cara and me
has become **too big** now
                         to solve
                         to reconcile.
I should *apologise.*
                    I said some terrible things . . .
But right now
apologising is the **last thing** on my mind.

A thought **pops** into my head

gro**w**S

E X P A N D S

takes over

and before I can **process** it

I <u>blurt</u> to Mehreen,

'Do you ever get the urge to go back

to the plan? The pact?'

Her head jerks up and she slightly

stum

bles

as she walks

'It'll get better,'

she says after a few seconds.

She doesn't sound **convinced** though.

So I take her answer as a **YES**.

'There's only one day left . . .

Like Cara says,

they'll

STOP

after that.'

'The website may stop,

but you and I both know these

FEELINGS

won't.'

She doesn't **reply** straight away.

Her head is still **down** as she walks.

Would it be the **same**

if it were just the *two* of us
instead of *three*?

'Should we **tell** someone?'
That's Mehreen.
'About the website.
If it's getting worse, maybe we need to tell someone
so they can
STOP
it.'

If we told, we'd have to **admit** what we were planning.
We'd have to explain *why*.
Everyone would know.
Asking for it.

I want to tell her
there's no point
I want to tell her
no one can help us
I want to tell her
I feel utterly helpless right now.
But I can see
that my feelings
my questions
are causing her discomfort
so to **save** *her*
I just say,

'Cara's probably right. It'll all stop after tomorrow.'

56. MEHREEN

18th April
(Date of Termination)

Aunt Nadiya's place is a zoo. Sabrina's mehndi ceremony is tonight and the entire extended family is crammed into this three-bed house. Normal families would just go straight to the venue, but of course, because we're Asian, if we don't show our face at the house beforehand, we're basically the worst, most selfish humans on earth. Mum skitters off to the kitchen as soon as we step in, to join all the aunties and distant grandmas. Dad shakes the hand of every man in the living room before sitting down and lighting a cigarette. Imran's just as pissed as me for having to come, but he's already gone up to Wasim's bedroom. That just leaves me. I'm expected to go and join my cousins upstairs as they do their hair and make-up. I'm supposed to *want* to talk about who's got the best outfit, what design I want for my mehndi. But that's just another part of my life where I don't fit in.

YOU'D NEVER FIT IN ANYWHERE. IT'S POINTLESS EVEN TRYING.

I step into the kitchen, hoping I can volunteer for some menial task that will keep me occupied. The rush of heat hits me, the smell of fried snacks overwhelming. The grannies are all sat at the dining table, folding paan into intricate designs to place with the chopped betel nuts on the trays. Mum and my aunts are stationed around the kitchen – mixing, cooking, packing the food for transport.

'Can you believe little Sabrina's getting married?' Aunt Alisha asks as she mixes the paste for onion bhajis.

'Little?' Aunt Nadiya exclaims. 'That girl's well past her sell-by date. We're lucky that Mr and Mrs Khan didn't mind her age.'

Sabrina's twenty-nine. Thirteen years older than me. I've only got thirteen years before I become out of date.

As if anyone would WANT to marry you anyway.
HAVE YOU SEEN YOURSELF
IN THE MIRROR?

'Is there anything I can do to help?' I say loudly to the room, trying to quieten the Chaos.

Only Aunt Zoya turns to look at me. 'What are you doing down here? You should be upstairs with the girls, getting ready.'

'Who knows,' Aunt Nadiya says, 'maybe we'll find *you* a husband tonight. It's time, na, Ambreen?'

'Mehreen's only sixteen,' Mum says without looking up from peeling carrots. 'She needs to focus on her studies.'

I smile at her back.

'Oh, who cares about studying?' Aunt Nadiya says. 'What's the point in getting all these qualifications? None of that matters after you're married.'

Aunt Alisha joins in. 'She's right; you might as well get in here and learn to make some bhajis. It's good for girls to get a head start. I wish my Jameela would show more interest in the kitchen and less in that camera of hers. That girl's always taking photos of nothing – it's so silly.'

SO SILLY. *Like your stupid comics.*
It won't get you anywhere.
Just go and learn to make bhajis.

I expect Mum to butt in again, to back me up. To tell them how she wants me to live out the dreams she couldn't accomplish, but she just continues peeling, whispering something to Aunt Nadiya as she does.

'Don't listen to any of them,' Aunt Zoya says. Her voice is quieter and calmer than everyone else's and part of me expects her to soothe me further, but she just ends with, 'Go upstairs and get dressed with your cousins. They'll be wondering where you are.' She pats me on the back, like a little child, then jumps into conversation with the rest of them. I'm left standing in the middle of the room like a piece of driftwood in the sea.

YOU DON'T BELONG HERE.
YOU DON'T BELONG ANYWHERE.
No one would even notice if you were gone.

As I climb the stairs I can hear the laughter from Sabrina's room. I stop a few steps from the top and linger. I can't decipher exactly what they're saying, but my body is begging me not to go in.

THIS DAY IS GOING TO END BADLY.
JUST GIVE UP. Nothing's ever going to get better.
Maybe you should listen to Olivia and go back to the pact.
THERE'S STILL TIME.

Sabrina's bedroom door is open, but I hesitate on the landing, watching all my cousins crowd around mirrors as they put on their make-up and style their hair. I knock on the door, feeling weird about just walking in without announcing myself, but there's too much noise for anyone to hear it. After standing there like a loser for a couple of seconds, I step inside.

No one looks up.

No one says anything.

I perch on the ottoman at the foot of the bed, right next to a wall. Definition of a wallflower, I am.

'Oh!' my cousin Riya says as she turns away from the mirror she's kneeling in front of. She almost jumps at the sight of me. 'When did you get here, Mez?'

Mez. Mez. Mez.

'Um, just now. How're you?'

She doesn't answer me, just turns around and continues applying foundation. I watch her reflection as she focuses on one cheek in particular, trying to cover a smattering of acne.

She catches me looking and we make eye contact in the mirror.

'Do you want some?' she asks. 'I can do yours after I've finished?'

'Oh yeah, that's a great idea!' Tahereh chimes in, crawling across the bed to come up behind me. She looks into the mirror too. 'We could totally give you a makeover! Wanna take your scarf off?' Her chin is resting on my shoulder now, her hand fiddling with my scarf on the other shoulder.

'Oh, um, no. Thanks.'

'Oh, c'mon,' Riya pleads. 'I won't do much. Real subtle like.'

JUST SAY YES.
THAT'S THE ONLY WAY YOU'LL FIT IN.
Be more like them and people might start to like you.

'Yeah, OK,' I say. My voice sounds unsure, and I hope they can't hear the quiver.

Riya stands up and hovers over me, beginning to poke and prod my face with sponges and brushes and pencils. I close my eyes.

No amount of make-up is enough to cover up what a freak you are.

'There! All done,' Riya says after what feels like forever. She moves away and I look at my reflection.

'Wow,' I say, strangled. 'Thanks, Riya.'

YOU LOOK RIDICULOUS.
LIKE A KID PLAYING DRESS-UP.

'You look great,' Tahereh says. 'You should totes lose the scarf though. There won't even be any guys there.'

Thankfully, before I have to think up a response, Sabrina turns up in the doorway, her make-up artist and photographer in tow.

'Well?' the make-up artist says. 'What do we think?'

Everyone in the room dissolves into shrieks, and a barrage of compliments rains down on Sabrina. She positively glows under the attention, as usual. Girls leave their places to crowd around her, examining the details of her dress, her hair, her make-up – all the things I should be interested in too. I'm glued to the ottoman though. My gaze drifts back to the mirror. My lids have been coated in some pink eyeshadow that looks too bright. My eyes are rimmed with thick eyeliner, wing-tipped and all. Lips stained a colour that looks like blood.

It's not me in the mirror, but I don't really know what 'me' is any more. The only definition I can think of is 'wrong' or 'other'. When I look at my reflection, that's all I see – someone who doesn't belong. I can feel the tears rising, threatening to push over the edge and leave a visible trail.

As they all fawn over Sabrina, the photographer starts snapping some candid shots. I can't let her get evidence of this. I slip out of the room as the first tear spills.

YOU'RE SO UGLY. *Disgusting.*
YOU'LL NEVER FIT IN.
Why can't you just be normal?

I hate it. Absolutely hate being the odd one out. I wish more than anything I could get as excited about make-up and clothes as Riya and Tahereh, that I could feel as comfortable around people as everyone else seems to be.

I stumble over to the bathroom on the other side of the hallway. I can feel my chest heaving, a panic attack about to overtake me.

YOU'RE SO USELESS.
You don't fit in **WORTHLESS.**
anywhere.
No one would even notice if you were gone.

I can't push the Chaos away any more. I try to focus on my breaths, but I'm gulping and gasping for air. I try to focus on the bathroom tiles, try to count them, but the Chaos pushes the numbers out of my head.

USELESS.
WORTHLESS.
Cut. You'll feel better if you cut.

I clutch the sink basin with both hands and look up into the mirrored cabinet door. My vision is already blurring, part tears, part impending panic attack. All I can see through the haze is the garish red on my lips. I pull up my arm and wipe the lipstick off with a harsh swipe.

**You can't rub off the weirdness.
CUT. CUT. CUT. CUT. CUT.
IT'S THE ONLY WAY YOU'LL FEEL BETTER.**

I open the cabinet door with a shaky hand and rummage through the shelves looking for a razor, nail scissors, anything. My wrist is pulsing, itching.

**YOU DON'T FIT IN ANYWHERE.
No one would even notice if you were gone.
Cut. Cut. Cut. Cut. Cut. Cut.
YOU'LL FEEL BETTER.**

No. That's not true. No no no. There's one place I felt like I immediately belonged – with Cara and Olivia. From the first time we met, I've never felt out of place or like a misfit with them. I remember I promised I'd contact them if I ever felt the need to cut again.

I call Olivia first, but the ringing just goes on and on with no answer.

**SHE'S GOT BETTER THINGS TO DO
THAN LISTEN TO YOUR WHINING.
She has an actual life.**

I try Cara next, but hers doesn't even ring.

SHE'S BLOCKED YOUR NUMBER. THEY BOTH HATE YOU.

I can't take this. I can't take this. I can't take this.

57. OLIVIA

My phone *buzzes*
    PINGS
  lights up
        as it sits on the living-room table.

          'You're very **popular** today.'
              That's Mother.
           She sounds **PROUD**.
      I've never made her **PROUD** before.
             And I never will.

The phone *buzzes* again.
    buzzes
  and
    buzzes.

Mother looks at me from her seat
which is **directly** in front of me
and *something* inside me
  tells me
THIS IS IT.

This is the time.

I need to tell her.

I need to tell her
> *before* she sees the photo
> *before* she hears the **rumours**
> > the word
Slut. Slut. Slut. Slut. Slut. Slut. Slut. Slut. Slut. Slut.
Asking for it. Asking for it. Asking for it.

'Mother, I need to talk to you . . .'

> > > She puts down her book.
> > > > **Looks** at me.
> > > > *Really* looks at me.

> > > 'Is something wrong, dear?'

I look into her eyes
and I *don't* see the **preoccupation** I normally do.
She's not **searching** for *him*,
> **thinking** about *him*.
She's **looking** at <u>me</u>.

She's been **looking** at me for the past few days.
Really seeing me.
Maybe for the *first* time
ever.

I can do this.

'Mother, there's something –'

A **KNOCK** at the front door.

Mother **holds my gaze** for a *split* second
as an **apology**
before standing up and <u>leaving</u> the room.

I can do this. I can do this. I can do this. I can do this.

I get the urge
to call Mehreen and Cara,
feel a deep-rooted desire
for their **encouragement**.

But then I hear it . . .

I hear **his** voice at the door.

58. CARA

I'm starting to think Mum must have been a chef in a past life. She seems to be obsessed with feeding me. She's trying something new today; I saw an ad online for a recipe book by her fave TV chef and it arrived this morning. She gave me a hug so tight it almost squashed my intestines, before running to the shops to buy ingredients. She asked me if I wanted to come.

Asked.

She's never asked me before.

So of course I went with her.

'Do you think it's supposed to be that colour?' she asks, taking the saucepan off the stove and showing me the dark brown gloop.

'Sure,' I say. 'That's what happens when you put the chocolate in, right?'

'Chocolate?! I'm making a casserole!'

I bite my lip, but can't hold back the laughter. Mum stares for a second before she joins in.

'Oh well,' she says, slamming the pan back on the stove. She moves her hand to the knob to turn the gas off but I push her hand away.

'Don't stop,' I say. 'What did Dad used to say? "Just because things aren't going to plan, doesn't mean you should . . ." Uh . . .' I try and try to remember his words, but they just don't come to me. I'm already forgetting him.

'Doesn't mean you should shoot the sheriff,' she laughs. 'I never understood what he meant by that.'

At least Mum will always be here to remind me of him, of the things I forget. Between us we'll keep him alive.

'Exactly. So you'd better keep cooking. Don't want the sheriff to die. Plus I'm so hungry, I'd eat anything.'

Mum opens the cupboard and pulls out a giant pack of chilli Doritos. My fave.

'Only a few though,' she warns.

It's been so long since I've had Doritos. My fingers turn orange and sticky within seconds.

'So I've been thinking,' she says as she stirs, 'after the Easter holidays, how would you like . . . what do you think about . . . going back to school?'

'What? Really?!' I ask.

No more hours spent with Mum confusing the First and Second World War, no more sitting there while she looks up the answers to my questions on Wikipedia. Heaven!

Everyone always says spending time together makes people closer, but I think there's a limit, and when you push past it, it slams back in your face. I think we reached that limit when Mum decided to homeschool me.

'Is that . . . something you'd like?'

I can tell this is hard for her, so I try not to show how much I'd like it.

'Yeah, that's . . . that sounds like a good idea. I think I'm ready for that.'

She stops stirring the pot and smiles at me. 'No more baby steps then, eh?'

'No more puns intended.'

'You've come such a long way,' she says in her sappy mum voice. 'I'm really proud of you.'

'Long way? I'm only a quarter of the way through the pack,' I say, lifting up the packet.

'Oh ha ha.' Mum kicks the side of my chair softly.

I crunch some more Doritos, waiting for Mum to tell me I've had enough or that I'm going to ruin my appetite and that I need to wait for her to finish her chocolate casserole.

'I'm serious,' she says instead. 'I've seen a real change in you recently. I'm guessing . . . it has something to do with this support group?'

I think about it, and she's right. Shit started changing after I signed up to MementoMori, after I met Mehreen and Olivia. They didn't really do anything major, and yet . . . everything with Mum is different now. Even just a few days ago, I couldn't have imagined I'd be talking like this to her, that we'd be cooking together, that I'd buy her a present when it wasn't her birthday or Christmas. It's weird how such a simple thing as joining a website can lead to such a big change.

'Yeah, maybe,' I reply.

I think back to yesterday, the argument with Olivia. The crap she said to me.

'How are the girls anyway? You should invite them round for dinner sometime.'

'I don't think they'll want to come.'

'Oh no – have you had a fight?' Mum stops cooking and turns to look at me again, like I'm this broken puppy.

'Kinda,' I admit. I should probably lie, tell her everything is just peachy, but I guess it's best that she knows the girls will never see me again, or at least Olivia won't.

'What happened?'

'Olivia and I had a fight. She . . . accused me of doing something I didn't.' I'm freaked out by how easily I'm telling her the truth. I guess I'm sort of hoping, now that she's acting like a real mum, that she'll somehow be able to fix this.

'Did you tell her she was mistaken?'

'Of course I did!'

'And I'm guessing you got defensive? Used some . . . colourful language in her direction?'

'Well, obviously. She was accusing me of all kinds of shit.'

'That's your problem right there.' Mum sighs. 'You're so quick to turn to swearing. Olivia doesn't seem like a girl who'd make accusations lightly. If she was mistaken, there were better ways for you to have dealt with it, rather than getting gobby.'

Ah, there's the Mum I know. Defending a stranger over her own daughter. Maybe I should tell her exactly what Olivia was calling me. What she called Mum.

'You weren't there,' I say. 'She was . . . she was being really mean.'

Mum laughs. Actually laughs. 'You realise *you're* mean quite a lot of the time, right?'

'Am not.'

She laughs a little again. 'Friends fight, Cara. It wouldn't be a real friendship without a few fights, name-calling, hair-pulling.'

'You saying I should've pulled her hair?'

She rolls her eyes as she sprinkles some herb into her pan. 'I'm just saying that one little fight isn't the end of a friendship. I've never seen you happier than you have been since you met those two. Even before the accident. I want that to last. I want you to stay happy. So I vote you call Olivia.'

'What? Me call? What for? She was the one who –'

'It doesn't matter, Cara. If you make the first move, she'll see you really care. Sometimes you have to just suck it up and be the bigger person.'

'That sounds like adult advice,' I mutter, trying to find a good Dorito at the bottom of the pack.

'My little girl's all grown up.' She raises a hand to her chest and laughs. 'Now go call her.'

I roll my eyes, even though she can't see me, wipe my hands on my leggings and move into my bedroom.

It feels wrong, calling Olivia after everything, but I get Mum's point about making the first move if you want things to go your way. Plus, I know Mum will pester me to death if I *don't* try and fix things.

I try to put myself in Olivia's position. Having a photo like that leaked online must be horrible. Even more for someone who's so insecure about their image and reputation. Especially with all that stuff with her mum's boyfriend. Oh crap, what if he's seen it? Or, fuck . . . what if he's behind it all?

Fuck fuck fuck. I was so angry, so pissed she would even think such a thing about me, that I forgot to really think about what was happening. Fuck, what if he's come back?

I call Olivia. Her phone rings and rings and rings.

I hang up and try again and again and again.

'What?' she barks when she finally answers.

'Hi . . . Olivia. It's Cara.' I sound like an idiot. I don't even know what to say.

'Yes, I know. That's what caller display is for.'

What a bitchy comment. I feel like hanging up, but force myself to be the bigger person.

'I just . . . I wanted to apologise.'

'How is your apology going to help? Will it stop the barrage of abuse I'm receiving online?'

'Olivia, c'mon. Can we just –'

'Just what? Pretend nothing happened?' There's some rustling on her end; her voice dips and I hear a door shut.

'You're making this a bigger deal than it is,' I tell her. 'I told you, if you just ignore it, it'll soon go away.'

She laughs once. A harsh, bitter sound. 'What a delightful outlook that is. So I'll just go about my business as normal and wait for everyone to stop thinking I'm a slut then, shall I?'

'God, calm down. You're acting like this is the end of the world. This shit happens every other day at school. The amount of nudes I've had passed around to me.'

'Oh, I'm sorry. I'm overreacting, am I? I thought you were my friend!'

I groan, wanting to strangle her down the line. 'This isn't

MY fucking fault! It's not my fault this photo got taken, got leaked. It isn't my fault your life's a mess!'

Shit.

Me and my stupid big mouth.

'I'm only in this *mess* because of *you*,' she spits. 'Who leaves their laptop on with the lid open when they're not using it?'

'Stop trying to pin the blame on me! Maybe you should've been looking around while you got changed. There's a huge fucking light that comes on when the webcam is running. Any idiot could have seen it.'

'Oh, so now I'm an idiot, am I? An idiot whose life is a mess, right? Why did you call me again?'

'Fuck knows. I was trying to be the bigger person.'

'Well, please be the bigger person by *never* contacting me again.'

The line goes dead.

Bigger person my arse. Good riddance, the snooty bitch.

59. MEHREEN

There's nothing to cut with in the bathroom cabinet. No razors or anything remotely sharp. My hands are shaking, desperate for release. I dig my fingernails into my wrist but I don't even feel it, so I sink down to the floor, back against the side of the bathtub and cry. I cover my face in case someone outside can hear me and the result is just a string of strangled cries that aren't even cries, just gasps, hiccups.

I try my usual breathing exercise; breathe in for seven seconds, hold it for five, exhale for seven. Each breath is a shudder and I can't make it to seven seconds, no matter how hard I try. I start reciting the Quran under my breath, the most common verses I use when I pray. The words move from my throat to my mouth, without ever appearing in my brain, which leaves it susceptible to be overtaken by Chaos.

No one will even notice.
You're not like them. They don't care.
CUT. CUT. CUT. CUT. CUT.

The words aren't working. I'm just reciting monotonously. I don't have the right prayer. I fumble with the clasp on the stupid clutch bag I had to bring because this hideous outfit doesn't have any pockets, and pull out my phone. My fingers are still trembling, but they have a purpose now. If I can just find the right prayer, the right verse, the right thing to say to God, this'll stop. This'll all stop. *Dear God, please make it all stop.*

I open the Muslim Pro app and click over to the special category for *duas*. The short prayers, supplications, are categorised here, under various labels. I click on 'Joy and Distress'. There's a prayer to recite when sad, when startled, when you've received good news. I scroll through them, but the closest I can find is one 'for anxiety and sorrow' – words that do not come even close to describing what I'm feeling right now. I recite it anyway. Over and over and over. Desperate to lose myself in the rhythm, the words, the meaning.

EVEN GOD CAN'T MAKE YOU NORMAL.
JUST GIVE UP.
No one will even notice.
CUT. CUT. CUT. CUT. CUT. CUT. CUT. CUT.

A line pops into my head. 'God grant me the serenity to accept the things I cannot change; courage to change the things I can; and wisdom to know the difference.'

The phone is on its fifth ring before I hear a click.

'What?' Cara says sharply.

You haven't even said anything and she's mad.
That's the effect you have on people.
SHE HATES YOU.
SHE WISHES YOU WERE DEAD.

'Cara, I . . . I . . .'

'You what, Mehreen?'

'I need your help . . . I need you to . . .'

'She's been bitching about me to you, hasn't she?'

'W-what? Who?'

'Olivia. That bitch. Bet she called you right away, didn't she?'

'Cara, I don't know what y-you're . . . talking about.'

'Whatever, Mehreen. You can tell her to go to hell, all right? I'm fucking done with her.'

'Cara, please . . .'

'No. I'm done being the bigger person or whatever. Look where it's got me.'

'Grub's up!' I hear her mum call in the background.

'Listen, Mehreen. Just . . . leave it, yeah? She's not worth it. Right? And next time you call, make sure it's not during mealtimes; Mum's already pissed at me for not making up with Olivia. Can't be dealing with you too.'

She hangs up.

Just like that.

SHE CAN'T BE DEALING WITH YOU.
No one can be dealing with you.
NO ONE <u>WANTS</u> TO DEAL WITH YOU.
No one would even notice...

I try Olivia's number. There's a part of my brain telling me she'll react the same way as Cara, but Olivia's the nicest one out of all of us. She'll know how to calm me down, right? Plus I'm just so, so, so desperate right now.

The phone rings.

Please please please . . .

'Hello?' Her voice is quiet, broken, raspy.

'Olivia!' I almost shriek it in my jittery state.

'What do you need, Mehreen? I'm . . . busy.'

'Olivia, please. I just . . . I need to . . . I need to talk. I need to call an emergency support-group meeting. Just us.'

'What's wrong?' Her voice sounds normal again. Soft. Caring. She'll know how to fix this. She'll make it better.

'I just . . . It's so much. The Chaos. It's too much, Olivia.' I force myself to hold back my sobs. 'I'm at my aunt's. The wedding. People, everywhere. I just . . . I just can't.'

'Are you having a panic attack?'

'No, not . . . not quite. It's just . . . I'm so . . . overwhelmed. I can't shake this . . . I don't know how to describe it . . .'

There's a noise on her end – a woman's voice laughing in the distance.

'Well, what do you want me to do about it?' Olivia asks, her voice sharp as a dagger.

My breath hitches.

'Olivia, I just . . .'

Another voice in the background at her end. A deeper one.

'Some of us have *real* problems, Mehreen. Just suck it up and deal with it for a few hours. It's not the end of the world.'

The phone goes dead.

**IT'S NOT THE END OF THE WORLD.
SOME OF US HAVE REAL PROBLEMS.**
What do you want me to do about it?

I cradle the phone in my lap as the tears fall faster, harder than before. I press the bangles on my arm hard against my wrist and twist, hoping they'll actually dig into the skin and make the marks Mum thought she saw in the first place. But all that happens is that my arm gets covered in red and gold glitter.

**YOU SHOULD HAVE JUST ENDED IT
            WHEN YOU HAD THE CHANCE.**
No one will even notice when you're gone.
YOU'RE SUCH A BURDEN.

I pick up the phone, navigate over to the website that started this all off. I log into my account and bring up my answers to the questionnaire I answered when I first signed up.

I can't handle the pain of being alive any more.

I can't. It's true. Nothing has got any better in the past two weeks. Nothing's changed. *I* certainly haven't. What's the point in even trying?

I read through all the correspondence from the website, noting with a gasp that today . . . today is the date of termination. The date this website decided would be best to end my life. This website was my saviour once. Could it be again?

60. OLIVIA

He's back.

He's back.

It's not over.

~~It's just beginning.~~

He laughs.   Mother laughs.
As I stand

                    outside

the kitchen door
Listening to their **reunion**.

I hear her ask him

to move in again.

My phone **buzzes** in my hand.
Mehreen calling again.
I press the **reject** button
and run upstairs to the bathroom.

They're back together.

61. CARA

My phone buzzes. Mehreen again.

'No phones at the table,' Mum reminds me.

I wasn't planning on answering anyway.

I pick up the phone, put it on silent and stash it in my pocket.

I'm still too angry to speak to her.

62. MEHREEN

There's a loud banging at the door. A succession of short, sharp raps. I stumble to my feet immediately, anticipating someone bursting in without any warning, as if I hadn't locked the door, which maybe I haven't. I furiously wipe my eyes and face, only realising when I pull my hands away that I've now smeared the make-up Riya put on me. I must look like an utter mess.

The knocks come again. Urgent, obviously belonging to a youngster. I splash some water on my face and wipe off the make-up once and for all, before drying my face with a towel. The urge to cut is still flowing through me, but I'm taking this knock on the door as a sign that I'm not supposed to do it, an excuse to escape before the need consumes me.

TODAY'S THE DATE OF TERMINATION.
IF THAT'S NOT A SIGN. WHAT IS?
There's still time.
CUT. CUT. CUT. CUT. CUT. CUT. CUT. CUT. CUT.

A little boy is waiting outside the door, holding his crotch. Before I'm even out completely, he sneaks around me and into the bathroom. He closes the door, pushing me out in the process. Then I'm just standing there in the hallway. Do

I go downstairs? Go back into Sabrina's room and pretend I'm as excited as the others? Go and find a closet to hide and cry in?

'Mehreen?' a voice calls from my left.

I turn to find Mum at the top of the stairs, staring at me with a creased brow.

'Are you OK?' she asks. 'Have you been crying?'

Mum notices. She noticed! I can talk to her, right? She's my last hope.

'Mum, I . . . I . . .'

I what? What can I tell her? She'd never understand my Chaos, why I feel like this.

She tuts and looks around.

'Mehreen, please. I really don't have time for this. We're about to leave for the venue. Can you just . . . just for one day, try to be normal?'

Be normal. BE NORMAL!
WHY CAN'T YOU JUST BE NORMAL?

Mum continues staring at me. She's not expecting me to reply, but I can tell she's frazzled.

'The cars are waiting. Can you just get in one, please?'

She bustles off into a room, muttering about needing to fix her scarf. I take the chance to run down the stairs. The front door is open – everyone's bustling around grabbing trays of food, posing for the photographer and videographer. Outside, cars wait with their doors open.

343

NO ONE'S EVEN LOOKING FOR YOU.
You could just stay at the house and no one would notice you were missing from the ceremony.

I sneak out of the door – I say sneak, but really I just walk out in full view of everyone. I head around the side of the house, down the path leading away from the street.

YOU'LL NEVER BE NORMAL.
They're better off without you.

I start to run. Sandals slapping on the concrete pavement, eyes stinging from the tears until my sides are aching too much for me to carry on. I look up to find I've somehow come to Bossfort Beach, the place where MementoMori wanted me to die. My sandals are already sinking into the soft sand. A little to my left, I can see the slipway where we had our anti-suicide ritual just days ago. A few metres in front of me, I can see the waves crashing every which way. Back, then forward. Left colliding into the right. Waves build up like a tornado, then come slamming down to create an earthquake.

There's not a single person on this beach.
IT'S A SIGN.
No one will even notice. JUST DO IT.
IT'LL ALL STOP IF YOU JUST TAKE THOSE FEW STEPS.

I stand on the shore, watching the waves rushing towards me, pausing, then retreating. Teasing. Inviting. Begging. The water reaches my ankles, completely ruining my sandals.

JUST KEEP WALKING. ONE STRAIGHT LINE.
Like the Quran says,
'Far better is the house in the Hereafter.'

I take out my phone. My hands are still shaking like crazy, but I find the document I'm looking for and attach it to an email. Then I start typing out a message. I expected this to be hard, not to be able to find the right words, but somehow they flow out of my fingers, the letters appearing faster than I can type.

IT'LL BE EASY. SO EASY. YOU'RE SO CLOSE.
It'll be better. Much better.

I press send and wait.
Wait for a message to pop up saying it couldn't be delivered.
Wait for the phone to ring.
Wait for someone to turn up.
Wait for my brain to tell me this is a bad idea.

But nothing happens.

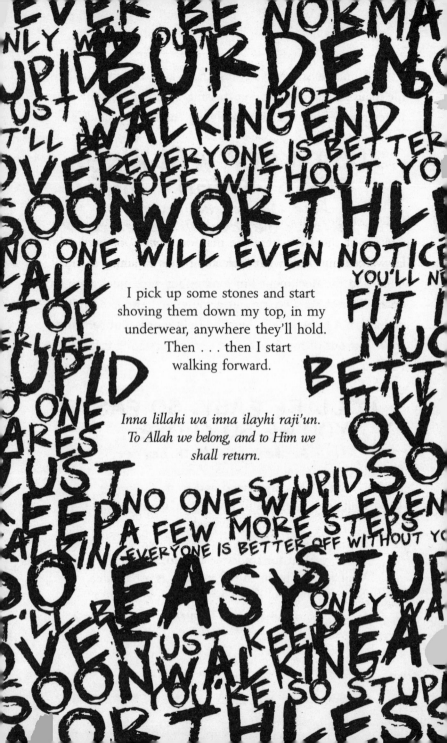

I pick up some stones and start shoving them down my top, in my underwear, anywhere they'll hold. Then . . . then I start walking forward.

Inna lillahi wa inna ilayhi raji'un.
To Allah we belong, and to Him we shall return.

63. CARA

'His casserole looks just as bad as yours,' I say to Mum, pointing at the TV, where the man on *Come Dine with Me* has walked out with what look like plates of actual shit.

She elbows me in the side. 'Rude dinner guests get points taken off, remember that. I'm grabbing a drink, do you want anything?'

Normally that question would drive me mad – I'd feel like she was trying to say that I was incapable of getting one myself, but now I realise she's just offering to be nice. She'd ask the same question even if I wasn't in the chair.

'No, thanks,' I reply. 'Your hands and food don't mix.'

She rolls her eyes before getting off the sofa.

My phone beeps with a new email.

At first I'm pretty sure it's gonna be something from MementoMori, because honestly who else even emails any more? But when I tap on the screen only Mehreen's name pops up.

From: Mehreen Miah (mehreenmiah@hotmail.co.uk)
To: Cara Saunders (SpaghettiCarbonCara@gmail.com),
Olivia Castleton (Castleton.Olivia@net.com)

Subject: Sorry

Dear Cara and Olivia,

I'm sorry. For everything. I'm grateful to have met you in the darkest moments of my life, but I'm sorry for casting a shadow over yours. With me gone, hopefully things will turn around for you, like you both deserve. I'm sorry if my presence over the past few weeks has been an inconvenience.

Cara – I hope you and your mother continue on the trajectory you're on. I know you're going to accomplish so much with your life and I'm sorry I won't be around to see it. I love that, despite everything, you've managed to keep your humour; it's something a lot of people could do with.

Olivia – You are by far the kindest soul I've ever met. Don't let life stamp that out of you. Please report your mother's boyfriend to the police – take it as my dying wish. You deserve so much more than the bad hand you've been dealt and you're definitely more than the labels attached to your experiences. You can beat this. You can get through this. I told you you were the strongest person I know, and that hasn't changed.

I'd be grateful if you could pass on my original note to my family. I think it covered everything that they need to know.

I've attached a little surprise for you – I finally finished our comic. It's rougher than I would have liked, but with time constraints it's the best I could do. Apologies it's not up to standard. I just wanted you to have a copy.

Again, I'm so sorry for everything. For all the pain I've caused you both, for all the times I was annoying.

I was stupid to think I could defeat my Chaos.

I hope life brings you both everything you deserve.

Love,
Mehreen

Fuck. Fuck fuck fuck fuck. No. No way.

This is MementoMori, right? They're the ones sending this, not Mehreen. Mehreen wouldn't. She . . . she was doing good. She IS doing good. No. I'm not falling for this shit. I've been waiting for them to play this kind of trick on me. First they sent Mehreen her note, then Olivia with her photo. It was only logical they'd do something to me. But fuck, this is sick. I've been telling the others to wait it out until it's over, but now I can't help but think about how many other people must have joined this website, how many might actually crumble under the pressure. How many people the fucktard that's running this sick website has convinced to actually kill themselves.

And this is exactly what they want. To freak us out. Mehreen and Olivia completely fell apart when they got their surprises, but I won't. I knew it was coming. Perks of being last, I guess. I close the email and put my phone back in my lap.

It *was* fake . . . right?

I pull my phone back out and reread the message. It sends chills through my body again and hurts my chest in that way that makes you automatically cry. It . . . does sorta sound like Mehreen. And it . . . knows a LOT about our lives. Sending Mehreen's note was easy enough since they had a copy, and Olivia's photo, well they just hacked my computer and took a photo – even my cousin Eric knows how to do that. But this . . . this seems super-personal.

I stop at the line about her comic. Mehreen's talked a lot about this, and I've been dying to see more. I open up the attachment and the entire thing is there, like a proper comic. The characters look just like Olivia, Mehreen and me, and they say things that only we could know . . . that we've only said in person. The style of the drawings is also consistent with Mehreen's talent.

And fuck.

This is real. It's really from Mehreen.

Fuck. Fuck. Fuck.

I pull up her number and call it. It rings and rings. And then FUCK. Another thought hits me. She called me earlier. She called me and I was a bitch to her because I thought she was calling about Olivia. But that couldn't . . . that wouldn't have pushed her over the edge, right?

Fuck. Fuck. Fuck.

Ring. Ring. Ring.

PICK THE FUCK UP, MEHREEN.

I cut the line, try again. But no luck. She sent that email almost five minutes ago now. God, she could be . . . No. No.

I try Olivia. Maybe she saw the email and got to her in time. But she doesn't answer the damn phone either. For fuck's fucking sake!

'Mum!' I shout.

She runs back into the living room immediately, the empty mug in her hand. 'What? What's wrong?' Her eyes scan my body wildly.

'We've got to get to the beach!' I'm panicking and breathless and Mum probably thinks I've gone batshit. I grab my chair and start transferring into it.

'Cara, what's wrong? What's happening?' She comes over and helps me into the chair.

'Mum, it's an emergency! We just . . . Can you please drive us to the beach? Quickly. It's really, really . . . just an emergency.'

'Cara . . . what . . . ?'

'Mum, PLEASE! I'll explain everything on the way, I promise. We just need to go, NOW.'

She rushes to grab her keys.

64. OLIVIA

NUMB.

It's something I've felt **a lot** over the past few months
but today there are new

depths to it.

So

deep,

I'm *wallowing* in it,

SUFFOCATING in it,

rather than the **numbness** being a *relief,*
a **protection.**

The phone is ***buzzing*** from the opposite side of the living
room.
Buzz. Buzz. Buzz. Buzz. Buzz. Buzz. Buzz. Buzz. Buzz. Buzz.
Pause.
Buzz. Buzz. Buzz. Buzz. Buzz. Buzz. Buzz. Buzz. Buzz. Buzz.
I don't know how long I've been sitting here.
Minutes? Hours? Days?
Ever since *he* walked into the room,

told me,

'I'm here to fix things with your mother,'
and they *disappeared* into the kitchen
to chat.

I've been following their movements,
                                eavesdropping,
                                        even though it's rude.
They're upstairs now,
I can hear feet padding in the **master** bedroom.
The *squeak* of the pipes as the shower turns on.

Numbness isn't enough
to protect my *heart*.
It starts **HAMMERING**
as another pair of feet,
a **heavier** set,
skip back downstairs
towards the living room.

Towards me.

'Miss me?'

Don't look. Don't look. Don't look. Don't look. Don't look.

He steps further into the room
and I can feel his *presence*,
his **SHADOW**
looming

behind me.

'Come on, Liv, aren't you going to welcome me home?'

LIV.   He calls me Liv.

HOME

noun

The place where one lives **permanently**,
especially as a <u>member of a family</u>
or a household.

'I saw an interesting photo online today.'

He's in **front** of me now.

My eyes SNAP up.

His gaze is **glued** to my body

and I feel so suddenly

EXPOSED.

He holds his phone in one hand

and *waggles* it.

I JUMP off the sofa.

The picture.

My picture

is

s p r e a d

across *his* screen.

He's seen it.

He's seen *me*.

He thinks I'm

asking for it.

'It's what brought me back.
Knowing you were waiting for me.
Willing as always.'

He steps closer.
So close
his breath
falls on my face,
warms my cheeks.

'Next time though,
take off another layer.'

THUMP. THUMP. THUMP.
In my chest, my ears.
My stomach *churns*.
He's never this **BRAZEN**
when we're not home *alone*.

'But Mother . . .'
I manage to squeak out
as I *twist* my body and move to the side.
Out of his gaze.
Out of his personal space.

I start to take a breath

but he **GRABS** me.
He **WRAPS** his fingers
around my forearm
and **PULLS** me close.
So close his <u>lips</u>
are in my <u>hair.</u>
He laughs.

'Don't worry, Liv,
I've got enough energy left over
for you.'

His fingers **TIGHTEN**
and then
it's happening.
His MOUTH on mine,
his free HAND
travelling
from my waist
^{up}wards.

'Relax and it'll be OK,'

he whispers.

I **LOCK** myself away in my head,
in <u>that place</u> I've learned to go.
The place where I'm not   in this body,
this vessel.

~~*This isn't happening to me.*~~

I'm floating above the scene,
watching as he

FORCES

me **down** onto the sofa.

Hands climbing,

fingers *SEARING* my skin.
I watch the tears l
                    e
                      a
                        k
                          i
                            n
                              g   out of the corners of my eyes
as I lie there,
motionless,
knowing that there's **NOTHING**
                                else that can be done.

I watch from above
as **Mother** walks in to the room
in her dressing gown,
see her mouth drop
as she shouts,

'*What* is going on in here?!'

65. OLIVIA

I used to *imagine* the way **this** would happen.
Used to.
Before the **last** bit of **HOPE** got *sucked* out of me.
I *used* to think Mother would **CHARGE** in
and *drag* him off me.

But instead . . .
she stands there,
IMMOBILE.

SILENT.

He *jumps* up and wipes his mouth.
I stay lying on the sofa,
FROZEN.

My stomach
My bra
My heart
on display.

'Baby, it's **not what it looks like.**'

He runs a hand through his hair.

'She threw herself at me!'

I stand up on *uncertain* legs,
waiting for Mother to jump in,
for her to *declare*
that she knows I would

NEVER

do such a thing.

The way she **declares**
in the dreams I *used to* have.

But she doesn't.
She just stares.

I look into her eyes
and she's **UNSURE.**
There's a part of her,
(I don't know how big a part)
that **BELIEVES** *him.*
TRUSTS *him*

more than me,
her own daughter.

'That's not true,'
I manage to say.

In my dreams
I don't say **anything**,
but then **I don't need to.**
I speak up again.
'He's lying.'
My voice *cracks*
but it's AUDIBLE
and that's so much **MORE** than I expected from myself.

'Have you seen this?'
He **shoves** his phone in Mother's face.
'She sent this to me.'
No. No. No. No. No. No. No. No. No.
I want to reach out, *snatch* the phone and

THROW it on the ground.

DIG my heel in so that the screen SM A SH ES
so that the photo

that photo

is no longer visible
to anyone.
~~But I'm frozen again.~~

I can only watch *helplessly* as Mother's eyes **WIDEN,**
flicking from the screen to **me.**

'Olivia?'
There's a c r a c k in her voice
and I <u>feed</u> off that *hesitation*

enough to pipe up,

'No! I **didn't**. I *wouldn't.*'

'You're the strongest person I know,'
Mehreen once said.

I can do this.
It's time.

'He's **lying**,'
I repeat.
'It's . . . It was **him**. He
FORCED
himself on me . . .
And this isn't . . .
the first time.'

I went through a phase of reading about
victims
confessing their **abuse,**
and so many of them spoke about

the **RELIEF** that comes

from **telling** someone,
from *confronting* their **abuser.**

But as the words *leave* my lips

there is **no** relief,
perhaps due to
Mother's **unchanged** expression.

I **wait**

    and **wait**

        and **wait**
for her to say something.

                      He's **blabbering** away,

                          but I tune him out.

    This moment is between me and Mother.

But before she can open *her* mouth,

there's a **RING** at the front door.

We all turn our heads to the noise
but nobody moves.
The sound of the doorbell echoes around the house.

BEEP   BEEP   BEEP

Outside, a car horn blares.

'OLIVIA! OPEN THE FUCKING DOOR.'

There's only **one** person in the world that could be,
and her voice screams **URGENCY**.

I reluctantly leave the room,

      open the front door to find . . .

         Cara's mother?

She stands there sheepishly, **opening** and *closing* her mouth.
Her car is parked on the driveway right in front of the house.
Cara sticks her head out of the passenger window and **shouts,**

                  'About fucking time!'

I barely open my mouth before she launches into a
ga r ble d series of sentences

*'Ohmygod why haven't you been checking your phone?
Mehreen's about to **off herself**. We need to go, **NOW**. I
realised **today's** the date we were set. I'm thinking she's at
the beach, **cause that would make sense, right?** Tell me all
this makes sense and it's not just another trick by that fucking
website. **I mean, either way we have to go, right?** NOW
NOW NOW. There's no way we <u>can't</u> go. The email was like
ten minutes ago, fuck knows what's happened since then. I've
already called an ambulance, but your house was on the way
and . . . I just . . . I need you. Please?'*

I want to ask a barrage of questions
but there's **PANIC** written all over Cara's face,
and a tenderness I've not heard before.

I need you.

The words
'ten minutes ago'
echo
echo
echo in my head.
Mehreen. Sweet, sweet Mehreen.
I remember her phone call earlier,
how **TERRIFIED** she sounded,
and how I *dismissed* her completely.

'What is going on out here?'

Mother has stepped into the hallway
and is **gawping**
at Cara,
whose head is sticking out of the window
and Cara's mother,
who stands there
speechless.

Cara,
who is

NOTHING

like the friends Mother would deem **appropriate** for me.

NOTHING

like the friends I've had my whole life.

Cara's mother begins to explain the **situation**,
but her voice *fades* in my ear
when
he appears **behind** Mother.
Their bodies **too close**.

I know that if I <u>leave</u> now,
if I **go** with Cara,
he'll work his <u>magic</u>,
fill her mind with his **LIES**.

But if I stay . . .
What will happen to Mehreen?

66. OLIVIA

It's so very **bizarre** to think that
if things had turned out *differently,*
I would be at this **very spot**
on this **very day**
ready to end things
                            for myself,
rather than to **save** <u>my friend</u>.

Mehreen.
Poor Mehreen.
I can't imagine how **desperate**
                            helpless
                            lost
                                        she must have felt
                                        in those **last moments**.

NO.

Not **last moments**.
I *have* to believe she's **OK**
that we will get to her <u>in time</u>.

                    'Where the fuck is the ambulance?'

                                      That's Cara of course.
                                   She looks out of the windows
                                                all around.

As we drive down the slipway,
it feels like we're about to
sub
    m
        e
            r
                g
                    e
                ourselves into the water too.

Mrs Saunders stops about a hundred yards from the water
and I **BURST** out of the car.
There's not a single soul on the beach.
        No lifeguards.
        No dog walkers.
        No teenagers skipping stones.
        Not a single person that would have **seen** her,
                                would have tried to **stop** her,
                                would have tried to **save** her.

I turn to look for Cara,
so we can strategise what to do,
but she's being helped into her chair by her mother
and I can't wait.
We can't afford to wait.

I scan the horizon,
the surprisingly *tame* water,
looking for any sign of **DISRUPTION**,
hoping to see Mehreen just swimming along
back to the beach.

But instead there's nothing but
calmness.
As if the **sea,**
the **world,**
the **universe,**
life itself,
is mocking me.

As if MementoMori is mocking us.
'Did you really think you could beat me?'
They did it.
They finally got her to give up . . .

But wait
over   there
a way out   into the sea
to my right
a **FLASH** of red,
a scarf **floating**
lazily
TAUNTING.
<u>Calling.</u>

Instinct kicks in.
   The swimming lessons Mother forced me to take.
   The lifeguard training I did last year.
I run
run run run run run run.
Inwardly **begging**
         Please. Please. Please.
The water is **ICE.**
The shock of it
leaves me *gasping.*

I force myself through it,
using the advice **drilled** into my head:
         Keep moving.
         Don't stop.
         Keep the end goal in sight.

         Mehreen.
         Mehreen.
         Mehreen.

      I make it to the scarf,
      take a huge breath
         and

D
I
V
E

67. CARA

When you tell someone it's an emergency, you expect them to drop everything and come running. It's been ages since I called the ambulance, told them that someone was dying right that fucking minute. The woman was a complete idiot who didn't seem to understand the word emergency, despite working for the fucking EMERGENCY SERVICES.

The water's still, has been for fucking ever. It's at times like this that being in a wheelchair is the worst. I want to jump in and go after them both so fucking badly, but I'm trapped on the slipway. I keep expecting Olivia to burst out of the water like a dolphin, with Mehreen over her shoulder or something, but it's been too long, right? Far too fucking long for either of them to survive under that . . .

What if Mehreen wasn't even here to begin with? All this is just a hunch after all. What if she's just sitting at home, watching TV, having changed her mind again, or what if she's found another method to do it or just . . . GAH, THERE'S TOO MANY WHAT IFS, it's driving me fucking crazy.

Mum's up at the top of the slipway, where it meets the road. She's walking around in circles as if that's how you make ambulances come faster. Gotta give her props though – she barely asked any questions on the way. But Mum's good in a crisis; she's the one who suggested calling the ambulance right away, rather than waiting to see if Mehreen was really here. I'm sure one day she'll get the whole truth out of me, like how the three of us really met, but right now . . . right now Olivia needs to fucking come out of that water already.

I finally hear a siren. Thank fucking fuck. It's like that moment in films where the woman falls to her knees, throwing her hands up in the air to thank Jesus or whatever. But of course that's not gonna happen here – I don't believe there's anyone looking over us. Well, I don't usually. Right now I'll believe in anyone and anything that'll keep Mehreen and Olivia safe. The ambulance drives down the slipway, right to where I'm waiting. A paramedic steps out, looking as relaxed as someone would if they were just rolling out of bed on a Sunday afternoon. I want to punch him in the gob so fucking bad. Another one comes out of the other door and Mum's already yapping away, catching her up on everything we know. God bless Mum.

The paramedics look over to the sea and the one nearest to me drops his shit on the ground, rushing towards the water. FUCKING FINALLY. I turn and spot Olivia's head and I feel my chest squeeze. She's thrashing about a bit and I'm worried she's going under again, but soon she rights herself and manages to float. I squint, peering to see if she's alone, and gasp when I see she's got Mehreen's arms over her shoulders. Paramedic Guy wades into the water and helps Olivia out. He bends over and his arse is in the way of me seeing what's happening. I move to the side a bit as he starts

371

dragging, literally dragging, Mehreen by her wrists onto the sand. Olivia walks out of the sea, gasping for breath. I want to go over and hug her, cry with her, wrap her up and never let her go, but of course my stupid chair won't go on the sand.

Paramedic Guy shouts over to Paramedic Girl, who kneels down next to Mehreen with her equipment. Mum goes over too. The guy is once again blocking my view of Mehreen's face, but I'm actually glad for it. I don't want my last image of her to be of her face all bloated and blue. I curse myself for even thinking that. She's going to be OK, she is. Of course she is. Things like this don't happen to nice people like Mehreen. She has to survive this, she just fucking has to.

Paramedic Guy starts pumping on her chest, like they do in films, and I watch Olivia, who's staring at Mehreen. Judging by her reaction, it's not looking good. I want to go over to Mum, just let her cuddle me and make all this go away. I don't want to be living this scene, this moment.

Paramedic Guy moves a bit and I can see the top of Mehreen's head, her hair spread across the sand. I move myself further back so I can't see her top half at all. Mum's got her thumbnail in her mouth, muttering something under her breath. She's standing behind Paramedic Girl, who's hooking Mehreen up to some small machine.

Please be OK, please, please, please . . .

I want to move closer to Mum or Olivia. I have a sudden need to be with people, a desire I've never had before to be touched, held. I'm suddenly missing Dad so fucking much.

I can't help but think that something like this must have happened after the crash. The paramedics pumping his chest, trying to get his heart to start again. I imagine Mehreen as Dad and start crying.

Suddenly Mum's next to me, her hand on my arm. I let out a sob, and the next second, she's got her arms around me, her head on my shoulder and squeezing so hard that I completely crumble. She doesn't stay like that for long though, even though I want it to last forever. She pulls away and looks at me – I can see how red and watery her eyes are. She barely knows Mehreen and yet she's crying this much.

'She's going to be OK,' Mum says, although her voice cracks and I know she doesn't fully believe it. 'I'm gonna go check on her, OK?'

She waits until I nod to step back onto the sand. They've got Mehreen onto a stretcher now, an oxygen mask over her mouth – that's a good sign, right? They'd still be pumping her chest if she didn't have a pulse – that's how it goes in *Grey's Anatomy* anyway. Olivia's wrapped in a silver blanket, and she's walking behind the stretcher as they bring it up towards the ambulance. I finally see Mehreen's face; it's mostly covered by the huge mask but I'm relieved to see that the rest of her still looks like her. A gross pale grey version of her, but still her. Paramedic Guy and Girl put the brakes on the stretcher by the ambulance doors.

'We're taking her to Bridgeport General. You can follow in the car, right?' Paramedic Guy looks at Mum, and she nods.

'Can I come in the ambulance?' Olivia asks.

They nod and start pressing the clip things on the stretcher to move it up.

'Wait!' I shout.

Everyone stares as I go right up to Mehreen. I look close into her face, wishing her eyes would open or at least flicker. I turn to Mum. 'Mum, can I have your scarf?'

She looks confused but doesn't question it. She takes off the thin scarf wrapped around her neck and hands it over. I wrap it around Mehreen's hair and head as best as I can, considering she's soaking wet and her hair's fanned out everywhere, hanging off the stretcher and everything. I move away when I'm done and Paramedic Girl gives me a little smile before loading Mehreen up into the back of the ambulance.

'We'll look after her, I promise,' she says to me before going to the front of the ambulance and getting in.

'That's your fucking job,' I mutter after she's safely inside.

'C'mon, sweetheart, let's go,' Mum says.

I want to ask her if she thinks Mehreen is going to be OK, if the fact that she's in the ambulance now, with a mask on, means that she's going to live. But I can't help thinking that maybe we were too late. If I had believed her message when I first read it, if I hadn't stupidly thought it was a joke, we would have been here sooner, maybe even before she went into the water.

If she dies, it's going to be all my fault.

68. CARA

'Hospital gowns suit you,' I say to Olivia as I hand her the hot chocolate I just got from the vending machine.

We've been sitting in this waiting room for ages; the paramedics gave Olivia a dry set of clothes (à la hospital gown) and she's got a proper blanket wrapped around her now. Mum's sitting a few seats away from us, on her phone. She got Mehreen's parents' number from the hospital and asked if she could call them personally, to soften the blow or something. Olivia and I haven't spoken much since we got here. She doesn't even say thanks when I give her the cup. You know shit's bad when Olivia forgets her manners.

I sit in front of her, sipping my own hot chocolate. 'I didn't think hospital food could get any worse than what they gave me when I was here, but apparently I was wrong. This tastes like toilet water.'

Olivia doesn't respond. Her head's down, her wet hair across her face as she looks into her drink. She's probably still pissed at me for earlier. I can't even remember the specifics – just that I said some shitty things to her, not that she didn't do the same, but I guess that's not the point.

'Olivia . . .' I start, without a clue what to say next.

She slowly raises her head, so that's something. Her face

is so pale she almost looks unreal, or like one of those Halloween masks. Her eyes aren't red and puffy like Mum's and mine, just . . . blank is the only way to describe it, I guess.

'You never told me you were some kind of lifeguard,' I say.

She laughs a little. 'I did lifeguard training for my Duke of Edinburgh,' she says, looking back down into her drink. 'At the time I never thought I'd actually use those skills – I just wanted some time away from home. Well, and the qualification.'

'I'll tell Mum to sign me up.'

Olivia doesn't reply, or smile or anything.

'I thought . . . When you weren't answering your phone today, I thought you'd done something too . . . That's why we came to get you. I was so scared, Olivia.'

She looks at me, but stays silent.

'Good thing I did, huh? You saved Mehreen's life.'

'We don't know that yet,' she whispers.

'Hey, that's my line. You're supposed to be the positive one.'

She laughs again. 'Goodness knows where you got that from.'

'Remember that time we went shopping?' I look to the side to make sure Mum isn't listening. 'When we had to buy clothes for our own funerals? You turned something so incredibly morbid into something . . . even *I* enjoyed.'

She smiles a bit.

'I thought it was a wind-up,' I say quietly after a few seconds. 'Mehreen's email. I thought . . . I thought it was

MementoMori again. I ignored it . . . I don't know how long for, but I ignored it. If I hadn't . . . God, Olivia, what if that's the difference?'

She puts a hand over mine. 'Don't,' she says. 'Don't think like that. It'll haunt you forever, the what-ifs. Right now we just have to focus on Mehreen. Times like this make me wish I believed in God.'

'I was thinking about that earlier. I can see how believing someone's looking over all this could make a person feel better. Didn't Mehreen once say that everything's destined to be, God has a plan, blah blah blah?'

Olivia laughs. 'Sounds about right. Does it work if we pray on her behalf?'

I nod. 'Yeah, that's a good idea.' I put my drink down on the seat next to Olivia and she does the same. I clasp my hands in my lap and look down, closing my eyes. 'God, well . . . Mehreen's God. Allah, I guess. Mehreen can't pray to you right now, so we're doing it on her behalf. That's cool, right? Anyway, can you just . . . make her better, please? I know that she might believe it's her time to die or whatever, but I'm telling you it isn't. She's barely lived. She's . . . she's changed my life . . . our lives. And just basically the world would be shit without her. So, uh, please do your voodoo and save her, yeah? Cheers.'

Olivia laughs and I look up to find that she had closed her eyes and bowed her head to pray too. 'God does voodoo?' she asks.

'Magic, miracles, voodoo, all the same shit. End result is always the same, right?'

'Let's hope so.'

We drop back into weird silence again and I start to feel the way Mehreen said she does, the need to fill it. It's also the perfect time to say what's on my mind.

'Olivia, look,' I say, 'I'm . . . I'm sorry, for . . . everything. I said some really shitty –'

'Cara, no.' She wraps her fingers around mine. 'It should be me apologising. I accused you . . . I accused you of such horrible things.' She takes a deep breath. 'I don't think I ever really believed you would do something like that. I was upset and angry and you were right there, so it was easier just to . . . to blame you.'

'I get it,' I reply. 'I guess it seemed more likely that it was me, someone you know, rather than some sick fucking website. I don't even *get* how they're doing all this. It's really scary though. It's like they *enjoy* freaking us out.'

'Like you said, this is a website run by someone who's trying to get other people to kill themselves. The sadism is inherent, I think.'

'It'll stop today though, right?' I ask desperately. 'It's finished now. Done. Mehreen . . . they got her to . . . to try, pushed her to the edge. They fucking made your life misery with that photo.'

Olivia cringes slightly.

'Did you . . . did you manage to get it off your profile?'

She shakes her head. 'It doesn't matter. It's too late now anyway. *He* saw it.'

'What?' My heart jumps.

'He told Mother . . . that I sent it to him.'

'What? That fucking prick! He's back? What happened? What did your mum say?'

She sniffs a little. 'He came back earlier today. That's why I was snippy on the phone with you earlier. He was . . . trying to get back with Mother. Well, he was successful. It was . . . It turned ugly. And now . . . everything's out in the open.'

'Wait – what do you mean *everything*?' My heart's thumping again. I want to grab and shake her until the full story tips out.

'Mother . . . found out. And then . . . I told her everything. Well, I had started to, before . . . before your mother came banging on the door.'

'Shit. Oh my God, what happened? Did she beat that prick up? Did she yell? Scream? Throw her shoe at him?'

Olivia shrugs. 'We had to leave before I had the chance to properly explain . . . She's probably over there right now, listening to his . . . lies. He's just going to twist everything and blame me again and . . . and . . . she'll believe him.'

She starts gasp-crying and I lunge forward and pull her into a hug. 'Hey, hey, it's OK,' I whisper in her ear. 'It's going to be OK, right? Everything's better out in the open.'

She nods against my shoulder, then sits upright. 'Yes, that's true. I suppose whatever happens now . . . even if Mother doesn't believe me, at least he . . . he hasn't got that hold on me any more.'

I take her hand. 'There's no way she won't believe you. She's your mum. Mums are supposed to support their kids, no questions asked. By the time we get back, she'll have kicked him out and it'll all be over.'

'I don't know,' she replies slowly. 'She gets silly around him . . . as if he's got some spell on her. She was like this with Daddy too, just so desperate to please him, keep him on side, even after he cheated on her. I genuinely don't know what's going to happen, how she'll react. Of course I'm hoping she'll be rational, but honestly, who knows? It's not like I have any solid proof. She could be over there agreeing to marry him, for all I know.'

I look up over Olivia's shoulder, where a woman has just approached the nurse's desk. I've been on high alert, waiting for Mehreen's family to burst in like they do on soaps, but the woman at the counter is white and looks nothing like Mehreen. She does look oddly familiar though. She looks up from her phone and then around the waiting room.

'Um, I'm pretty sure your mum isn't falling for his lies right now,' I tell Olivia.

'You don't know her. She's –'

'She's right behind you.'

Olivia turns around and gasps as she makes eye contact with her mother.

69. OLIVIA

'Mother, what are you doing here?'
She walks over from the desk to the waiting room,
her eyes
LOCKED
on mine.
Her face is <u>stoic</u>
         <u>impassive</u>
         <u>unreadable</u>
as always.

> *Castletons don't show emotions openly.*
> *Even when they learn their daughter is being abused.*

My heart
THUMP-thump-THUMPS
                    as she approaches.

'How did you know I was here?'
She holds her phone up.
         'I downloaded an app to track your phone.'
                  She's mere steps away.
'You've been stalking me?'

She looks *sheepish*.
'After the **incident** last August, I thought it best to
keep <u>an eye</u> on you,
just in case.'

The **incident**.
She calls my first suicide attempt,
the *only* one **she** knows about,
an *incident*.

'I wanted to talk to you about it but . . .'

but

but

but

'I was of the opinion that **discussing** it would
<u>ENCOURAGE</u>
you to try again.'

'**I did try again.**'
The words *slip* out of my mouth
and I want to ^{reach up} and **catch** them,
but Mother **gasps**
and I know that this **conversation**
is one we should've had months ago.

As if she too knows this, Mother says, '**We need to talk.**'

<u>Talk</u> about

all the
things we never said.

I give Cara one last glance as Mother and I walk to the far
end of the room.

Mother and I sit
side   by   side
on uncomfortable plastic chairs
in one **corner** of the waiting room.
My heart is still

THUMP-thump-THUMPING
and my mouth is suddenly so

very dry.

'Olivia, what you told me . . . back at home . . .'
She can't say **it**,
can't even <u>look me in the eye</u>.
He's **convinced** her I was lying,
that I **MADE** the whole thing up
for attention.
She's about to tell me that I have to
apologise
for **'THROWING MYSELF'** at him.

NO.
I won't let *him* win.

This needs to **END** now.
I summon my <u>courage</u>
and **b l u r t** it all out.

I tell her how it all started
when he drunkenly kissed me.
How he **FORCED** himself on me
while she rushed to the office to submit a building design.
How he started to become more **daring**
as it went on,

GRABBING
GROPING
ABUSING

me even while she was in the house.
I tell her how I was **terrified** of telling her,
of saying it **out loud**,
admitting it **was happening**.
How I *cry myself to sleep* almost every night,
and even then can **barely sleep**.
I tell her how I felt like it would be easier
to sit in the car and let the fumes

take   me   away.

(I don't tell her about MementoMori – I don't want to incrim-
inate the others.)

I **talk** and I **talk** and I **talk**,
forcing myself <u>NOT</u> to watch her face as my words come out,

just in case they **don't** *sink in,*
    in case he's already **hardened** her.
Of course she's going to take **his word** over mine.
Why would she not?

                'He makes me happier than I've ever been before,'
                      she used to tell me.

She wouldn't give that up.
She wouldn't let the neighbours,
      her friends,

           find out that she's been dating
              and is **in love** with
              someone like him.

When the words finally exhaust themselves,
I let out a last, *slow* breath
and stare down into my lap, letting the tears f

                  a
                    l
                    l

      And don't look up.
      Don't look up.
      DON'T LOOK UP.

Seconds pass, minutes even.
Neither of us **moves**.

I think suddenly
about Mehreen
and feel **bad** that I've taken my *focus* off her.

          'Oh, Olivia,' Mother breathes.

She **PULLS** my body to her body
<u>conjoining</u> us,
my **head** pressing against her **chest.**
      Her arms
      squeezing
    too tight
    MUCH TOO TIGHT.

                  I'm there,
                  beneath him,
             his mouth on my body,
             his hand moving south.

Mother lets go
and I **B R E A T H E**
A GASP
and I see that she's . . . crying.
Her eyes wide and red and so very **sad.**
        'I'm so sorry,' she sobs.
'I'm sorry I brought that . . . that monster into our home,
into our lives.

I'm sorry . . . I didn't see this happening, that I left you
alone with him.'

<u>She . . .</u>
<u>She . . .</u>
<u>She believes me . . .</u>
<u>She's on my side.</u>

We hug again,
but this time I draw **her** to *me*,
PUSHING away the thoughts of him
and replacing them with the **LOVE**
<u>surging</u> out of my **mother**.

She whispers, 'I'm sorry,' into my hair over and over.
I want to tell her
that it's **OK**
that I **love** her
that I can't believe she **chose me**.
But all that comes out is
'Mummy,'
a name I haven't called her in years.

I end the hug as the images in my head start
overpowering this moment again.
Mother places her hands on either side of my face and wipes
my tears
away
with her thumbs.

'It's going to be OK,' she says. **Firm**. <u>Determined</u>. **RESOLUTE**.
Like the Mother I know.
Her **resolve** helps me PUSH AWAY the torture in my mind,
and bring <u>myself</u> back into the moment.
The moment where
Mother
is on
my side.

'We're going to sort this, OK? I've already contacted the authorities.
I made him think . . . I pretended to take his word. It's better if he doesn't see it coming.
We are going to deal with this, sweetheart. I promise. I'm going to . . . I'm going to make this right. He'll get what's coming to him.'

Make this right.
Nothing will ever make it fully right.

<u>He'll get what's coming to him.</u>
Is there any punishment apt for this crime?

'Sweetheart . . . I'm so proud of you.'

Mother is . . . proud of me?

*'I know it must have taken so much courage
to speak out . . .'*

You're the strongest person I know.

'I promise. We. Will. Get. Through. This.'

<u>I **WILL** get through this.</u>

70. MEHREEN

I've always been the type of person who can tell they're awake before they're *actually* awake. My eyes will be closed, my body still, but I'll hear what's going on around me, know I'm *about* to wake up, if that makes sense.

I have that right now. My eyes are closed and I can't move, but I can hear a murmur of voices, a tannoy announcement calling a doctor to Resus, and the hum of a machine next to me. I hone my listening and identify the two voices. Cara and Olivia.

My eyes open slowly, as if my lids weigh a ton. The room gradually comes into focus: the stark white ceiling, the blue paper curtain in place of a door. I realise I'm in an A&E cubicle. Suddenly everything comes crashing back to me. How I ended up at the beach, how I started walking in, how I couldn't find it in me to stop. My eyes scan every inch of the cubicle, my brain realising that . . . I'm still alive.

I find Olivia and Cara sitting to my right, whispering to each other.

'Is that a hospital gown?' I ask, noticing Olivia is in an outfit identical to mine. 'What happened?' My voice comes out as a croak and turns into a cough as I try to clear my throat. I push myself up on my hands and try to push myself up into a sitting position, but dear God, my body aches so much.

'Take it easy,' Olivia says, rushing to help me sit up. 'Keep your blanket on – you need to stay warm.'

Cara takes the remote for the bed and presses a button so that the mattress tips up to support my seated position. I practically fall back onto it.

Olivia tucks my blanket around me then passes me a cup of water. 'Should we call someone?' She looks to Cara. 'We should probably get a nurse.'

'No, please,' I say, raising the cup to my lips. 'I just . . . Can we give it a sec?'

'Of course.' Olivia sits on the bed and intertwines her fingers with mine. I notice the plastic tube taped to my hand, though it's not attached to anything.

'How're you feeling?' Cara asks. She's super-fiddly, her fingers picking at the bottom of her T-shirt. I get another flash from earlier. Her voice on the phone when I was calling for help, the anger that radiated off her.

'What happened?' I ask. 'I mean . . . how did you find me?'

'Oh, that was Cara's brilliant thinking,' Olivia pipes up. 'She realised today was the Date of Termination and that, with your logical brain, you would have . . . followed those instructions.'

'And then Baywatch over here just ran up and jumped in. Didn't even take her cardigan off or anything. Which is why she's in the gown. She dived under the water and pulled your sorry arse out lickety split,' Cara expands.

'Lickety split?' Olivia cocks an eyebrow at Cara.

'Oh, you know what I mean.' She rolls her eyes, then smiles at Olivia.

I look back and forth between them.

Look how friendly they are.
They've bonded without you.
I BET OLIVIA REGRETS SAVING YOUR LIFE.

The Chaos is back.

Of course it is. Why did I ever think I could get rid of it? Stupid me. It's at a level where I can push it away by focusing on something else though. I force myself to ignore it, look at Olivia instead.

'I take it you guys made up? Last I remember, you were at each other's throats.'

'Yeah,' Cara replies. 'Funny how your best friend trying to commit suicide brings people together.'

I duck my head at the mention of that word.

'Seriously, Mehreen, what happened? Did something . . . trigger this?' Olivia asks, lowering her voice when someone walks past our cubicle.

I fiddle with the blanket, pulling it tighter around my chest, hoping they'll move the conversation on, but they're still waiting.

'I can't explain it,' I sigh. 'Everything just got too much. We were supposed to be going to a function for my cousin's wedding, and it was just . . . horrible, being around them all. I'm so unlike literally everyone in my family. It's hard *not* to feel like there's something wrong with me when I'm around them. It was just a really bad Chaos day. It seemed like fate that today was . . . the date we were given.'

'I'm so sorry I was short with you on the phone,' Olivia says. 'I had . . . an issue at home and was preoccupied. Can you ever forgive me?'

I sit up a bit more, moving so fast my head spins a little. 'God, no, don't apologise. This was *not* your fault, OK? This would have happened regardless. Besides, I'm not your responsibility.'

'We still feel bad,' Cara says. 'We could've talked you out of it.'

'Maybe not. It . . . it got so overwhelming that I literally couldn't see any other way out. What I was thinking and doing made so much sense at the time that I don't think anyone or anything could have stopped me. Honestly, please stop feeling guilty.'

'You . . . regret it though, right?' Cara asks tentatively. 'Like, you're not sitting there wishing it had worked?'

I nod right away. 'Yeah, of course.'

From the way her face relaxes, I can tell she buys it. Truth is, I don't know whether I regret it or not. The Chaos is still there, and now that I've actually attempted it, it feels like things are going to get even worse. Doctors don't take suicide attempts lightly. They're going to want me to . . . talk about it. And they're going to bring my parents into it.

Oh God, my parents.

As if on cue, I hear a scuffle of feet outside my cubicle. The curtain is yanked aside and there are Mum and Dad, their faces aghast and pale.

71. MEHREEN

'Mehreen!' Mum half cries, half gasps as she runs over to me.

My body tenses at the sight of her, but I relax when she throws herself onto the bed and pulls me to her. I can feel her chest heaving, shaking, hear her sniffles and feel her tears on my hair.

'Oh, Mehreen, Mehreen,' she says over and over as she kisses me all over my head.

I can't remember the last time she showed me this much affection, and it feels bizarre. So bizarre that it causes me to start crying too.

'Mum,' I breathe as she pulls away and holds me at arm's length, just staring at me.

Her eyes are redder than I've ever seen, her mascara smeared all down her face. Her lips are quivering as she looks over my face, my body, for any signs of damage. During her silent inquisition, I look over her shoulder at Dad. When we make eye contact, he launches himself down next to me too and . . . wraps his arms around me. Dad has never been the touchy-feely type, and I honestly can't remember the last time he hugged me. I tentatively thread my arms around him and hold him close, taking in the smell of smoke that always surrounds him. Like Mum, he's crying into my hair and it makes my chest ache to think that my actions have caused Dad, the most together person I know, to cry like this.

'Oh, *priyo*,' he says, arms wrapped tightly around me, my head resting just under his chin. 'We were so worried.'

Priyo. *Sweetheart*. He hasn't called me that since I was seven.

He loosens his grip slightly and I miss the warmth of his embrace so much that I pull him close again. I don't want this moment to end. I don't want him to look at me, to think about what I've done. He makes a little sound – a laugh, or a gasp, or a hiccup. But regardless, he pulls me so tight that it's almost painful, but I feel safer than I've ever felt before. He's still murmuring, 'Priyo . . .' and then he . . . kisses me on the head.

I break down completely. Crying, wailing, shuddering.

I feel Mum's arms tighten too, and then we're all just sitting there in a big blubbering mess. The feeling of completeness lasts both forever and not nearly long enough. Eventually they both slowly pull away, but they sit on either side of me. Mum keeps her hand in mine, while Dad uses his to wipe his tears.

'Mehreen, baby, what happened?' Mum asks, breaking the near silence, the peace. 'On the phone, they said . . . they said you nearly drowned?'

I look to the side of the cubicle, where Olivia and Cara are by the sink and various bins. I can see they've both started crying and Olivia smiles at me encouragingly as Cara wipes her eyes.

'We'll be in the waiting room,' Olivia mouths, pointing. She pulls the curtain closed as they leave.

And then I'm alone with my parents, trying to think up a way to explain what happened. Where do I even start? Should I pretend it was an accident? That I was just paddling and the current got too strong? I don't know what Olivia and Cara have told their mothers and the doctors, what they will eventually tell my parents. My head's a jumbled mess as I just sit there trying to form a sentence.

Thankfully a doctor walks in and detracts the attention from me. He fake-knocks before entering. My parents turn to face him as he comes to stand at the end of my bed. I'm surrounded by adults on every side of me and a wall behind, and it starts to seem a bit claustrophobic.

'Ah, good to see you're awake, Mehreen,' the doctor says, looking at me. 'I'm Dr Singh. How're you feeling?'

I nod a little. 'Yeah, fine.' My voice comes out as a rasp though and Dad passes me the cup of water from the little table.

'Grand,' he says with a smile. 'Well, your blood results are normal. We'll be taking you along for a chest X-ray soon, and I'll get a nurse to do your obs again now that you're awake. Although they were fine earlier. Thankfully the paramedics managed to warm you up enough to avoid hypothermia, but do make sure to keep yourself wrapped up. Are you having any trouble breathing?'

I shake my head.

'Wonderful.' He writes something on his notes. 'We're going to be moving you to the Intensive Care Unit soon, and will monitor you for a few days, just to make sure there's no lasting damage. But everything seems fine so far, so that's good. We'll also need you to see someone from our Mental Health Liaison team, considering the circumstances.'

Dad whips his head around to face Dr Singh. 'What do you mean, "considering the circumstances"?'

Oh crap. It's all about to blow up.

Dr Singh looks at me and I try and beg him with my eyes not to do this. 'We can talk about this in private if you'd like, Mr Miah.'

'No, no, just tell us.'

'Well, your daughter nearly drowned. We found stones in her clothing, so we have cause to believe –' he looks back at me, almost apologetically – 'that this was a deliberate attempt to take her life. And as such, we need to declare her mentally sound before discharging her.'

Dad whips his head back round to look at me and I catch a quick glimpse of his shattered face before I drop my eyes to look at the neat rows of holes in the blue blanket that's covering me. I want to lift it over my head and hide beneath it. Close my eyes and just sleep for eternity.

'A deliberate attempt?' Mum says, turning to stare at me too. 'Mehreen . . . is this . . . is that right?'

I can't look up at her. Don't want to see how crushed she is too. See how my stupid actions have ruined their lives. But I also know that it's time for the truth, that I can't white-lie, alternative-truth my way out of this.

I nod and then completely dissolve into tears again.

'I'm sorry,' I sob over and over as my sobs turn into gasps.

I feel a pair of arms wrap around me and Mum hugs me once again, so tight it comforts me a little. I feel my sobs dying down.

'It's OK, baby,' Mum whispers into my ear.

The curtain gets pulled aside again and I look up to find a blonde woman standing in the doorway. She's in a deep blue outfit – I can't tell whether it's a nurse's uniform or a doctor's.

'Is this a bad time?' she asks, looking over at Dr Singh. She's got a friendly face and a perma-smile.

Mum loosens her grip and straightens up to face the lady, but keeps one arm wrapped around me.

'Ah, that was quick!' Dr Singh says. 'Mehreen, this is Dr Atkinson, from the Mental Health Liaison team. Are you ready to talk to her?'

I want to say no. I want to tell them all to go away and leave me alone, to let me just sleep. But there's something inside me that's flaring up. Not Chaos. It's the overwhelming sense that this conversation is inevitable. Necessary even. I know that if I fob her off like I so desperately want to, if I bury this, it'll just resurface soon, worse than ever. I could easily convince everyone that this was a one-off, a spontaneous decision, but the Chaos would just lead me back there. Back to the website, back to the beach, back to the thoughts that won't go away. I need to get rid of it once and for all, need to say all the things I've never said. There's no way this is going to go away on its own.

'Would you like to talk to me in private?' Dr Atkinson asks. 'I can ask your parents to step outside?'

I shake my head. 'No, it's OK. I'm ready to talk.' I sit up straight in bed, crossing my legs under the blanket.

I can do this. I can. I need to do this.

'Right, well, I'll leave you to it,' Dr Singh says. 'I'll be back a bit later.' He gives me a smile and Mum and Dad a nod before leaving.

Dr Atkinson drags a chair over to my right and gestures for Dad to sit on it. He does. She tries to do the same with Mum, but I hold on to her hand, begging her to stay close to me. She obliges and Dr Atkinson takes the chair instead. Mum tightens her arm around me.

'Right, Mehreen. You can call me Lesley. I just need to ask you a few questions to make sure we get you the help you need, OK?'

She doesn't say it in a condescending tone and for that I'm grateful. I nod, trying to conjure up the answers to the questions I know she's about to ask.

'So, can you tell me about what happened? What led you to go to the beach today?'

I think about how to put it, but everything's muddled in my head. 'I . . . I can't explain it,' I admit.

'OK, let's go a bit smaller. What happened this morning?'

I look to Mum, hesitantly. 'It's OK, sweetie. Just be honest, OK? We're not going to . . . It's going to be OK.' She kisses me on the head.

I look back to Lesley. She's giving me a warm smile, but I can't look her in the eye. Instead I focus on the little bunny enamel pin attached to her breast pocket. 'It's my cousin's mehndi today. That's . . . like a pre-wedding ceremony we have.'

Lesley nods encouragingly.

'So I spent the morning getting ready. We went over to my aunt's house at around midday.'

'And how were you feeling? Were you excited for the ceremony?'

I want to look over to Mum again, because I know she's not going to like my answer, but I resist. I need to just get through the questions. I need to pretend my parents aren't there listening, but I also need them to hear me.

'I . . . uh . . . no. I don't . . . I don't enjoy weddings. Or social gatherings as a whole. Especially with my family. They make me . . . anxious.'

Lesley writes something on her pad.

She thinks you're crazy.
THEY'RE GOING TO LOCK YOU UP.
COMMIT YOU TO THE PSYCH WARD.

I close my eyes and clench my fists, trying to push the Chaos away. I know Lesley's about to ask another question, but I rush in to speak first.

'I get these . . . thoughts, when I'm in situations I'm not comfortable with, or when I'm around . . . the unknown. It's like a voice in my head telling me that I'm doing everything wrong, that everyone's thinking bad things about me, that everything's going to end badly. But not like an actual voice, just how my thoughts manifest, I guess. But a lot of the time I can't control them. So when one bad thing enters my head, not only can I not get it out, but it's like it attracts more and more bad things, until it gets too overwhelming. I don't know if I'm making any sense.'

'You're doing great.' Lesley smiles. 'Go on.'

'When I'm at family events, I feel like it's worse. There's this expectation in my head . . . in my parents' heads, in all my relatives' heads, of who I should be, what I should be like. I often feel like I don't fit in anywhere, around most people, but with my family the differences are magnified. I feel like everyone expects me to be like my cousins. Someone who *likes* to get dressed up, who's sociable and knows how to hold a conversation. Someone who doesn't get antsy around people, rather enjoys their company. Someone who's . . . normal.'

'What's your definition of normal, Mehreen?'

I shrug. 'Someone who's . . . like everyone else, I guess.'

'And you think that's something to aspire to?' She looks at me intently. There's a part of me that thinks she's being sarcastic, making fun of me, but her expression says otherwise.

I shrug. 'Well, yeah. It's better than sticking out for the wrong reasons.'

Lesley pauses for a few seconds, but doesn't question me like I know she wants to. I know Mum and Dad are bursting to butt in too, but they've been surprisingly quiet so far. Maybe they don't understand what I'm saying.

Eventually Lesley gently asks, 'So you were anxious about the ceremony. Did you consider not going? Or telling someone about how you were feeling?'

'God, no,' I reply immediately. 'What would I even say? "Sorry I can't go because I'm feeling too anxious"?'

'Yes,' Lesley says, leaning forward in her chair. 'You can say exactly that. Anxiety isn't something to be ashamed of, Mehreen. People will understand. Your parents will understand.'

'Why didn't you say?' Mum asks quietly. 'I know you don't like these things, but I thought . . . I thought it was just a teenager thing. I had no idea you felt like this.'

'Me neither,' Dad adds, his voice still pretty croaky. 'Mehreen, of course you're not abnormal. There's no definition of what normal is, and anyway we'd rather have you the way you are. We *love* you the way you are.'

I start sobbing again. 'I know that . . . deep down, I do. It's just sometimes . . . sometimes the Chaos is so strong, so convincing. It just takes one little thing and then it's like there's a storm in my head. Thoughts swirling round and round, blocking out my ability to think anything else.'

'The Chaos?' Lesley asks.

'That's what I call it. It feels like that to me, just chaos in my head. I keep looking for an off button. I thought . . . I thought what I did today was the only way to find that off button.'

'Well, it's good that you've managed to identify it. That's the first step. You seem aware of your triggers too. Was there anything specific that made today special? Made it worse than normal?'

I can't tell her about Cara and Olivia; the doctors would be all over them, interrogating them too. They might even call the police on us. But there's no way I can lie either. I look back at Lesley and take a deep breath. This needs to come out. 'Doing this . . . it's been on my mind for a while. I . . . I . . . I signed up to a website. One that plans your suicide for you. It gave me a list of tasks to do . . . to prepare for my . . . for the end. It gave me a date and place of death. That was . . . today, at the beach. I'd changed my mind a few days ago, but nothing really got better. And then today I was so overwhelmed, and it just seemed so apt that it was the date I'd been set. It just . . . It seemed like a sign.'

Mum lets out a little gasp again. 'Oh Mehreen, I wish you'd told us how you were feeling.'

I shake my head. 'I didn't . . . I didn't know how to bring it up. I didn't think you'd understand.'

'Oh, darling.' Mum wraps me in a huge hug and starts crying again.

I hug her back and let my sobs take over.

Lesley straightens up, as if getting ready to leave. 'You've done a great job of explaining all this, Mehreen. I know it must be confusing when you have such powerful thoughts and feelings that you don't know how to deal with. I'm going to refer you to the mental health services through your GP. I'll make sure to tell them it's urgent. But as far as the incident today goes, your physical health seems great. I just have one last question.' She takes a breath, fiddles with her pen.

'The hospital has a duty of care to you. We can't let you leave if you say you still want to harm or kill yourself. So considering everything we've talked about, and having had time to think about things . . . do you regret what you did today?'

I look to Mum, who has black tears streaming down her

403

face. Then to Dad, whose eyes are red and puffier than I've ever seen. They're here. I remember the way they came rushing in. Olivia and Cara too – they cared enough to figure out where I was. Olivia could have died trying to save me. Despite what my brain says, there *are* people who care about me. People who would miss me. I look up and spot Imran peeking through the curtain, rubbing the back of his neck. Imran's here? Not only that, I swear he looks concerned. He finally makes eye contact with me and . . . he smiles. He does a weird, awkward wave, before stepping into the cubicle and standing behind Dad's chair.

All these people. Here for me. All these people, upset about what's happened today. All these people that would miss me. If I'd been successful today, I never would have known how much they care. It only hits me now, how much I would have missed if I had died. Finishing school, going to university, learning to drive, figuring out what to do with my life.

'Mehreen?' Lesley prompts. I've been quiet for too long, imagining all the things I can do now, realising how much lighter I feel having told people who want to help about how bad I'm feeling.

'Yes,' I say, resolutely. 'One hundred per cent, I regret it.'

Mum tightens her grip around my waist and pulls me towards her.

'What happens now?' I ask Lesley.

'We're going to get you some help, Mehreen. We're going to make sure this doesn't happen again.'

72. CARA

'"Ubiquitous" is so *not* a word,' I say, looking down at the phone screen. 'There's way too many u's.'

Olivia laughs. 'I told you I'm the master of Scrabble.'

'Cos you're a cheat!'

'I'm pretty sure you can't cheat on an app,' Mehreen says, pulling her blanket tighter around her. It's weird to see the cannula on her hand – it reminds me of all the time I spent in hospital after the accident.

'Why can't we play a normal-person game?' I groan.

'You're the one who let me choose!' Mehreen laughs.

'I was trying to make you feel better!'

'Seeing you get this het up about a word is definitely making me feel better.' She rearranges her pillows and presses a button on the side of the bed to raise the head of the mattress up a bit more.

I roll my eyes and move my tiles on the screen to make the word 'fart'. I laugh as I pass the phone to Mehreen. We've been playing Scrabble for nearly ten minutes now, they brought her up to the ward about an hour ago. Her parents will be back from praying soon, and then Olivia and I will have to go back home. I don't like the idea of that, of leaving Mehreen alone here in the hospital.

'Are you though?' I ask her. 'Feeling . . . better, I mean.'

She looks down at the blanket over her lap and starts poking her fingers through the little holes. I feel bad for making her uncomfortable, but it's like the elephant in the room. I can't stand people not talking about the obvious things. The number of times strangers have wanted to ask about the chair but thought it would be too awkward and so settled for stupid small talk instead is unbelievable. I'd be a hypocrite if I did the same.

'Yeah, I am,' she says quietly. 'I'm glad they made me talk to Lesley. I think saying it out loud really helped.'

'That was your intention with the support-group idea, wasn't it?' Olivia asks.

Mehreen nods. 'Yeah. I remember when we first met up, just being around you two, y'know, people who really understood and listened, that really helped.'

'But . . . not enough?' I ask. 'I mean, obviously.'

Mehreen shakes her head. 'I was telling Lesley about this earlier. Not the pact and everything, of course. But like how things did genuinely seem like they were getting better for a while after I met you. She told me that that can happen, the good periods, but unless I get some proper help, it's not going to last. She recommended I go to see someone, learn some techniques to manage my anxiety and get some talking therapy for my depression.'

I look at her and can't stop myself from smiling. It's good to hear her talking about the future, about wanting to get better.

'I'm so glad she helped,' Olivia says.

'Yeah,' Mehreen replies. 'It was great that she managed to get my parents and me to actually talk about everything, y'know? I don't think that would ever have happened without some outside intervention, but it's such a relief to have said it.'

'I know what you mean,' Olivia says. 'Mother and I sat and had a long talk about . . . everything. It was very uncomfortable, but as you say, necessary.'

'I can't believe she finally knows,' I say, stealing a grape off Mehreen's table and popping it in my mouth.

'I can't believe she believed me,' Olivia says.

'Weird how family can surprise you, right?' Mehreen asks, passing the phone over to Olivia for her turn. 'I would never have expected my family to be as . . . understanding as they were.'

'I dunno. My mum's always been the same ditsy bint who doesn't know how to change a light bulb,' I say, taking another few grapes.

Mehreen and Olivia laugh.

'Mother has set up a meeting with a crisis worker for later,' Olivia says. 'She thinks it's best to act on everything quickly, before . . . he . . . realises Mother isn't on his side.'

'Are you going to be OK?' I ask. 'Do you want me to come with?'

Olivia shakes her head. 'No. Thank you, I'll have Mother with me. I am really nervous though. I'm sure they're going to ask me all sorts of prying questions . . . intimate questions . . . and I . . . it'll be hard. But, if Mehreen can talk so openly about her problems, then I can do the same.'

Mehreen reaches for Olivia's hand.

'Get a room,' I say, taking some more grapes. The pack's half empty now.

'You're just jealous,' Olivia says. After a second, she stands up and sits on the edge of Mehreen's bed, right in front of me. She reaches for my hand, while holding Mehreen's with the other.

I stare at her. 'What, do you want us to start singing "Kumbaya" or something?'

She rolls her eyes. It's super-annoying when she does that. 'Just do it, silly. This is a symbolic gesture for an important moment in our friendship.'

'God, you and your fucking symbolism,' I grumble, but I lean forward and take her hand while reaching across for Mehreen's.

We hold hands in a triangle – Mehreen sitting cross-legged in bed with Olivia next to her and me sitting in front of them. They're leaning over so I don't have to stretch much.

'Are you going to make another soppy speech?' I ask, looking around to make sure no one else witnesses this weird-ness.

'I thought I'd leave that up to you actually,' Olivia says.

'Me?'

'Yes, come on, you *always* have something to say. Say something meaningful, considering what's happened today.'

'I don't *do* meaningful.'

'C'mon, Cara,' Mehreen says. 'Just once. I want to see your soft side.'

God, how can I say no to that? There's so much I want

to say to her; the soppy phrases form in my head, but I'm way too embarrassed to actually *say* any of them, especially on the spot like this. Soppy stuff is generally what you put in get-well cards.

'I'm glad you're not dead,' I blurt.

Stupid stupid stupid. I look up at Mehreen, thinking she's going to be looking at me like I'm fucking crazy, but instead she's got a small smile on her face.

'Thanks,' she says quietly. 'I am too.'

'Me three,' Olivia chips in.

We all squeeze each other's hands.

'I've gotta admit,' I continue, 'when Olivia dragged you out, and you were just like . . . limp and whatever, it was like . . . like . . . being punched in the gut. I know we haven't known each other long, but you two . . . are the best people in my life and I feel so fucking terrible that you felt that shitty, Mehreen.'

Mehreen looks sad and I feel bad.

'What I'm trying to say is that you two have helped me through one of the worst times in my life, and if you had actually died today, I don't know what I would have done. God, I told you I'm no good at the soppy shit.'

Mehreen squeezes my hand, but she's smiling. 'That was great.'

'I'm just saying, that I . . . y'know, appreciate you guys. And I'm glad our little support group didn't get broken up. Also, I'm so glad you're getting the help you need now, Mehreen. Although, of course, we're always here for you too, right, Olivia?'

'Always,' Olivia replies.

They both lean over and we do an awkward three-person hug. Just as we break apart, with both Mehreen and Olivia crying again, there's a knock at the door. I turn to find Mehreen's mum standing there.

Behind her are the police.

73. MEHREEN

There are two policemen standing with Mum, well, one policeman and one policewoman. A wave of fear runs through me, but then the officers turn their attention to Olivia. Of course. She did say she had a meeting about her mother's boyfriend.

'Um, these officers wanted to ask you a few questions,' Mum says to me as she walks around to the side of my bed.

'Me?' I ask. Oh crap, are they going to arrest me for trying to drown myself?

'Evening,' the male officer says, taking his hat off. 'I'm Sergeant Adeyemi and this is Constable Mardem. We wanted to ask a few questions.' He turns his gaze to Cara and Olivia. 'Do you girls mind popping out for a second?'

'No!' I almost shout. 'I want them to stay, please.' I need them here. Need the confidence they bring out in me.

The officers both look at each other before turning to Mum for confirmation; she nods.

'OK then,' Sergeant Adeyemi says, turning back to me. 'Your doctors have informed us that the incident today was connected to a website? One that tries to incite you to commit suicide?'

I feel Cara and Olivia turning to look at me. I forgot to

411

mention to them that I'd spoken out about the website. God, they must think I've ratted them out. I try and telepathically tell them I would never do that.

I turn my gaze to Mum, and she sits on the bed next to me and takes my hand. 'It's OK,' she says with an encouraging smile. 'Just tell them the truth.'

I nod and look at the officers. 'It's called MementoMori. com.'

They share a look before stepping closer. Constable Mardem takes out a notebook. 'Just as we thought,' she says. 'You're sadly not the only one in the area who's been using this website. There was a case a few days ago actually –'

'The people at the train station?' Olivia asks.

Constable Mardem looks at her and nods. 'Unfortunately so.'

Wow. It's weird to think someone else in our town was using MementoMori. What if it had been someone I know? Is that how people at school are going to feel when they find out about me? God, they're going to find out, aren't they?

'Damn shame it is,' Sergeant Adeyemi says, looking straight at me. 'But luckily you survived.'

I look down and fiddle with the blanket that's starting to fray by this point. I can see the judgement in his eyes: *Stupid teenagers and their stupid suicide attempts getting in the way of my day.*

'We need you to tell us everything, so we can catch the people behind this website. Can you do that?'

I nod. Somehow telling the truth about all this doesn't seem as daunting any more. Well, most of the truth. There's no way I'm bringing Cara and Olivia into this. 'I signed up about two weeks ago. I first came across it about a month before though, and had just been constantly browsing it, trying to pluck up the courage to actually apply.' I look over to Mum to find she's got tears in her eyes. She smiles for me to carry on. I take a big breath. 'Suicide is . . . it's a big sin in our religion, but I started feeling like it was my only way out. So I thought that if there was someone else instructing me, helping me along the way, then I wouldn't feel like it was . . . my fault, my responsibility, y'know?'

Constable Mardem nods again. 'From what we understand, the website capitalises on the fact that people are more likely to go through with it as a group; who were your partners?'

'No one,' I say, quickly and resolutely. 'I did it all alone.'

Sergeant Adeyemi's gaze snaps to me and I feel transparent, as if he can see all my thoughts. This. This is why I don't lie. I can hear Cara and Olivia whispering behind me and I wish I'd told them to leave the room before this all started. Although I don't know that I'd be this courageous if they weren't here.

'Listen, Mehreen,' Sergeant Adeyemi says. 'You're not in any trouble here. We just want to catch the people behind this website and the only way we'll do that is with your full cooperation. If you –'

'It was us,' Olivia butts in. 'We were her suicide partners. Right, Cara?'

I hear Mum gasp beside me.

Olivia looks over to Cara and I half expect her to call

413

bullshit, but she doesn't; she nods steadily, as if it's the easiest thing in the world for her to admit it.

'No, guys, it's –' I try to stop them both but Olivia holds her hand up to me.

'If it'll help the investigation, help catch the sadists behind the website, then I think it's better to be completely honest.'

'Right, OK,' Sergeant Adeyemi says, scratching his nose. 'Are you both happy to answer some questions?'

Olivia and Cara nod.

Between the three of us, we tell the officers everything: the tasks we were given, how they seemed innocent enough at the beginning but then got more and more dangerous. I tell them about the condolences card that got delivered to my house, and how someone had typed my suicide note out inside it. Olivia quietly tells them about the photograph and how Cara's laptop was probably hacked as well as her Instagram. Cara mentions the relentless emails, even after blocking them, and how they meddled with our phones – deleting all of her apps, the phone call with no one on the other end, the blaring noises Olivia experienced. We make connections we hadn't before, like a text message Cara received from my phone telling her not to contact me, which I *definitely* did not send. Mum stays surprisingly silent throughout, which I'm grateful for. I tell the officers how the pressure of it all started to make me feel like it wasn't going to end unless I went through with it, how the date seemed symbolic. They both ask questions, but don't judge us – at least it doesn't seem like they do.

'They kept mentioning their terms and conditions,' I say when we've gone through everything. 'And how if we didn't comply, they'd have to take "further action". We couldn't find any information on the website as to what that actually meant.'

Constable Mardem nods. 'It's quite clever actually. They take advantage of the fact that people, especially those desperate enough to be considering suicide, don't usually read the fine print. But in their actual terms and conditions, it states that failure to follow their instructions, or even trying to back out of the pact, will "result in retribution". Nice and vague.' She rolls her eyes.

'We've been tracking this website for a while now,' Sergeant Adeyemi says. 'We've got a lot closer since the incident at the train station. The parents of the victims kindly allowed us access to their laptops and phones. We'd like you three to do the same, if that's OK? Not right now, but soon.'

Olivia, Cara and I share a look before agreeing.

'Can they . . . ? Can they still get to us?' I ask. Even though everything's out in the open now, it's hard to believe that MementoMori will just stop.

'Once we have all your devices, we should be able to remove all their malware. And hopefully we'll manage to catch the administrator and take down the website soon. You should be fine.'

I breathe a sigh of relief. Fine is such an overused word, but somehow now it brings me a bit of relief.

'Anything else you girls can think of?' Sergeant Adeyemi asks.

We all shake our heads.

'Great. Thank you all so much for your help.' Constable Mardem puts her notepad away.

'Do you know who's running it then?' Cara asks. 'Like, any clue at all?'

'We've tracked the IP address to somewhere in Idaho. We're working with officers over there to investigate further. Hopefully the evidence we gather from you will help us catch whoever's behind this,' Sergeant Adeyemi explains.

'From what we gather,' Constable Mardem continues, 'it always goes roughly like you've described. When someone signs up to the website, they download a zip file which contains hidden hacking software. Either they follow the set tasks and finish by ending it all, or they don't, and their lives are made hell. It seems like the sole reason they ask for photographic evidence is so they can exploit it – as you've unfortunately experienced first hand.' She shakes her head a little. 'The twisted person running the site seems to be playing some sick game. Manipulating people's lives, making them dance for their amusement. They don't even appear to gain anything from it, other than the kick they get from exploiting vulnerable people's desperation and misery.'

'Have there . . . ? Have there been many cases?' Mum asks tentatively. 'How many have you linked the website to?'

The officers share a look. 'Around a dozen victims that we know of. Most of them are in the US though,' Constable Mardem says.

'Can you not just shut down the website?' Cara asks. 'I

mean, really, how hard is it? You must have some nerdy tech guys?'

Sergeant Adeyemi sighs. 'We have shut down many sites. Unfortunately they keep popping up, new ones every month, and some of them, like this MementoMori, are run by people who know what they're doing. Nerdy tech bad guys, if you like. There's layers of encryption and intelligent computing going on here that takes a while for our team to crack.'

'This one is different though,' Constable Mardem says. 'The assignment of tasks is something I haven't seen before. Almost like you're being made to play a game. It seems counter-productive. Impulsivity is usually a factor of most suicide attempts. That impulsiveness is taken away by the allocation of these tasks and by the lengthened timescale. What with the demands placed on their completion, I'm surprised people don't get turned off.'

I can't seem to stop myself from piping up. 'I actually really liked that aspect of it at the beginning. I liked that these tasks felt designed to help us prepare for what was going to happen. It was kind of a way of helping out those we left behind too. It made me feel a bit more at ease with my decision.'

Constable Mardem seems to digest this. 'Hmm, I get that, I guess.'

'Right, well,' Sergeant Adeyemi prepares to leave, 'thank you, girls, once again. We'll be in touch soon.'

Mum gets up too, to show them out – as if they were guests in our home or something.

'Oh, and Olivia,' Constable Mardem adds. 'I'll get on to

our . . . nerdy tech guys . . . to get a rush on removing any trace of that photo. After we've completed our analytics of course.'

'Thank you,' Olivia says quietly. 'I appreciate that.'

The officers nod and smile as they leave the room. Mum walks out with them, and I can hear her asking Sergeant Adeyemi something.

'Guys, I'm sorry,' I whisper, as soon as I'm sure the officers and Mum are out of earshot. 'I didn't want to bring you into it. I was going to pretend it was me alone.'

'It's fine,' Cara says. 'Didn't think we'd last long without it all coming out anyway. Honestly, Mehreen, don't stress.'

'I'm rather glad everything is out in the open,' Olivia says. 'It seems. . .'

'Symbolic?' Cara asks sarcastically.

Olivia laughs. 'I was going to say cleansing.'

'You don't mind?' I ask. 'I honestly didn't mean to land you in it.'

'Nah,' Cara says. 'Let's just hope all this coming clean means they'll catch the fucker behind all this.'

'It sounded as if they're close,' I say, looking to make sure Mum's still occupied. I spy Constable Mardem handing her a business card. 'That's going to be so weird. Do you think we'll have to testify?'

Cara grimaces as she looks at me with wide eyes. She jerks her head towards Olivia and I bite my lip.

'Crap, sorry,' I say right away. 'Olivia, I didn't think –'

'It's OK,' Olivia says, with a slight smile. She checks her watch. 'And on that note, I need to go and meet Mother.

We've got our appointment soon.' She gets up and gives me a huge hug. I accept the warmth and comfort of her embrace, pulling her tight against me.

'Thank you,' I whisper in her ear. 'For . . . you know . . . saving my life.'

Olivia chuckles. 'You saved mine too.'

Tears pool in my eyes and I feel the urge to have another soppy breakdown where I thank them both for everything today and since the day I met them. But then I realise that we've got plenty of time to cover that, now that none of us are going anywhere any time soon.

Olivia hugs Cara too, and I notice that Cara barely even winces or rolls her eyes this time, rather pulls her closer.

'What time are visiting hours here tomorrow?' Olivia asks.

'I think they said twelve till six,' I reply.

'Great, I'll come sometime in the afternoon. Keep your phone on – I'll text you.'

'Um,' I say. 'My phone is kind of at the bottom of the sea . . .'

'Oh, right, yes,' she replies, looking mildly embarrassed.

'God, Olivia,' Cara says, 'I can't believe you didn't think to pick that up on your way back to shore.'

We all dissolve into laughter.

74. OLIVIA

Mother sits in the waiting room
next to **Cara** and **Mehreen's** mothers.
I stop ~~short~~ in my tracks,
worried they're all **sharing stories**,
revealing <u>our secrets</u>.
But then they all

       BURST OUT

             in laughter, and I relax.

Mother's **smile**

      d

       r

        o

         p

          s

           a little

              when she sees me.

As if being happy around this

              poor

              abused

              girl

              is a crime.

She stands up and excuses herself,
plastering a smile back on as she approaches me
pretending she's happy,
that I haven't completely
SH ATT ER ED
her existence.

But then she **surprises** me
with a hug.
A hug so **warm** it takes me back in time
to when I was a child,
before Daddy **left**
and Mother became an **empty** cold *shell*.
A hug **brief** enough
for me to **enjoy** it.

She passes me a bag containing a fresh set of clothes,
smiles as I enter the bathroom to change.

We walk into the lift together,
drop down to the ground floor.
Mother doesn't say anything
but she holds my hand.
Tight. Tight. Tight.
Like she did when I was a child crossing the road.

There are two ladies *waiting* for **me**
in an otherwise empty *sterile* room.
They're not wearing the same uniform

as the officers that were in Mehreen's room,
but they tell me they are with the
Child Protection Services,
who work with the police.

They're here to protect me.

I sit down at the table,
with Mother by my side,
my hand still in hers.
The women introduce themselves as
Angie and Emery.
They have *kind* smiles
and offer me a drink of water.
They *ask for my permission* to record our conversation
and I oblige.

I squeeze Mother's hand
then let it go.

> I need to do this **on my own**.
> I need to be **confident**.
> <u>I</u> need to do this.
> I <u>can</u> do this.

I expect Angie and Emery to treat me as *breakable*,
to walk on eggshells,
but they make me feel **comfortable**.

They make me believe that <u>everything will be OK</u>.
They're not **judging** me.

They explain the *procedure* to me,
the **steps** ~~we're~~ I'm going to have to take
over the next few days

        weeks

        months

        maybe even **years**, they say.

They repeatedly tell me I have **CONTROL** of this situation,
that things will move at my pace.

And if I say **stop**
they will <u>listen</u>.

Tears well up in my eyes.
My mind *flashes* with an image of him
of all the times I said no.
Those times I could actually **speak**.
Of how he'd <u>grin</u>
and shut me up.

                             'No one will believe you.'

I must have **tuned out** of the conversation
because Mother places her hand on my knee and
squeezes.
I FLINCH
automatically,

stuck in the memory.

> She removes it and whispers.
> *'It's OK, sweetheart, take your time.'*

I **force** myself *out of* the memories,
into the present.
Focus on the *patterns* in the wooden table
the little dent to the right
where I stick my thumbnail in.

I take a few breaths,
bring myself **back** to the moment
and find Angie, Emery and Mother all looking at me,
waiting for me
to tell a story,
the story I'm going to have to tell
over

and

OVER,

going into details I've **repressed** in my mind,
details that I can't **bear** to say out loud,
details I'll **NEVER** be able to <u>forget</u>, regardless of what happens.

> 'It's OK, he can't hurt you any more.'
> That's Angie.

I want to tell her that the memories hurt the most,

ask her if there's a way to **erase** every trace of him
from my mind.

'He's in police custody.'

I look at Mother,
expecting her to be sad
that she's
lost
the man **she**
loves.
But she smiles at me.

> *'My little plan worked.*
> *He was waiting for me to come home,*
> *but was greeted by the police instead.'*

I grab her hand again.
I *can* do this **alone**,
but I don't *have* to.

Mother is here.
Mother believes me.
Angie and Emery believe me.
People are on my side.
And he . . .
he is rotting in jail,
as he should be.

It's going to be **OK**.
Everything is going to be **OK**.

*'It started just a few months after
I turned fifteen . . .'*

EPILOGUE

MEHREEN

The beach is packed today. The summer holidays only started three days ago, but it feels like we're well into them. An inflatable ball flies across my path as I walk across the soft sand towards the slipway; I kick it back to the little boy. It's hot, but not too hot; I can tell that by the time midday comes I'll be fanning myself with my scarf again, but the breeze coming from the sea now is a delight.

I spot Olivia walking from the opposite direction and wave at her. Cara is already waiting. She's staring at the people walking on the slipway near her. An elderly couple pause in front of her; I expect her to shout at them to stop blocking her view, or even just glare, but she just smiles and soon they pass.

'Morning!' Olivia says when we meet at the top of the slipway. She puts her arms around me and pulls me into a hug. A tighter one than usual.

'Hey,' I say back as her hair tickles my nose.

'How *are* you?' she asks when she pulls away. She's wearing the same expression Mum has been for the past three months, as if I'm going to relapse any second.

'I'm *fine*,' I say, rolling my eyes. I hook my arm in hers

and we begin walking down towards Cara. 'More than fine. I'm great.'

'How is it that *you've* become the late ones?' Cara asks when we're within earshot.

I laugh. 'You're obviously just into us more than we are to you.'

Olivia wraps Cara in a hug before she can reply. It's weird to see Cara returning the hug earnestly, even weirder to feel how tightly she hugs back when I give her one.

'How you doing?' Cara asks me when I pull back from the hug. She's wearing the same breaking-glass look as Olivia. A look that neither of them has had in a long time.

'I'm *fine*. God, I'm getting a sense of how you must have felt after your accident now, Cara. It isn't half annoying.'

It's usually at a point like this that the Chaos would spark up, infiltrate my mind, overpower it. But not today. Today, I know that Cara would never think I was getting at her, or equating my experience to hers.

Cara laughs. At my joke, not at me.

'It must be strange though . . .' Olivia says slowly. 'Is this the first time you've been here since . . . ?'

'Since I tried to kill myself?' I ask, turning to her with a smile.

She blushes.

'It's fine, honestly. I chose it for you. I know how much you like your symbolism.'

She smiles. 'As if you don't like it too.'

I laugh. 'It seemed fitting. The first time we've been together without someone's parent looking over our shoulders, makes sense to come here, right?'

I look around the beach, at the giggling children, half-built sandcastles, beach towels and umbrellas. I look across at the spot from where just three months ago, I walked and walked until the water dragged me down. I don't know what I expected to feel when I returned to the scene – sadness? Fear? Relief? I can't really define exactly what I *do* feel right now.

'Don't start,' Olivia says. 'I had to beg Mother for almost an hour straight to agree to let me come today. I would have considered not telling her, or lying about my whereabouts, if it weren't for my therapist's "whole honesty" policy.'

Cara snorts. 'Yours has that going on too? Mine calls it "truth or nothing". As if naming it like a game makes it better.'

'So, *did* you tell your mum you were coming to meet us?' I ask.

Cara averts her eyes. 'Maybe . . .'

Olivia and I burst out laughing.

'To be fair, Mum doesn't have a problem with me seeing you. Not as much as your parents anyway. She likes you.'

'My mum likes you two too,' I say. 'She's basically indebted to you, Olivia. She worries about *everything*, not just who I'm with. She forced me to postpone my GCSEs for crying out loud, despite me telling her everything was fine.'

'I think this is just how they show they care,' explains Olivia.

'By being overprotective mares?' Cara asks.

'C'mon, think about it,' I say. 'This doesn't even compare

to how she was after your accident, right? So technically, she's got better.'

Cara shrugs. 'Guess so. Anyway, can we just get on with it? I've only got half an hour before Mum comes to pick me up.'

We head over to the Sundowner Cafe, chatting and laughing as we go. It's always great when we meet up, but it's like we've been on edge the last three months, not being able to talk freely because we were always at someone's house with one of our mothers hovering.

'Right, Cara, you wanna start?' I ask once the waitress has delivered our drinks.

Cara clears her throat. 'God grant me the serenity to accept the things I cannot change; courage to change the things I can; and wisdom to know the difference.'

Olivia and I mock clap. 'You managed to say it without a hint of sarcasm!' I say.

Cara shrugs. 'It's grown on me.' She straightens in her seat. 'So . . . updates. Mum's been a lot better since the anniversary. She told me to say thanks again for the cake, by the way, Olivia. We went to meet Owen Gentry the other day. It was really, really weird, but I'm sort of glad we did it. Closure and whatever. Turns out he wasn't doing it to get a shorter sentence, like Mum thought. He's genuinely really sad and sorry about what happened. I sort of . . . sort of felt bad for him.'

'Are you going to see him again?' Olivia asks.

Cara shrugs again, then shakes her head. 'Probably not. It's not like I hate the guy; he made a mistake and he's paying for it. But every time I think about him, it's like losing Dad all over again, and things are just starting to get better, you know?'

I nod. 'Speaking of . . .' I say, looking at Olivia hesitantly. 'Any update on your case?'

Olivia puts her coffee down and dabs her mouth with a napkin. 'We're still working towards the hearing later this month. The social worker has interviewed me over a dozen times now. I've asked her if there's any way of recording my testimony or doing it over a video feed so that I won't have to actually be in the same room. She's looking into that. Oh, that reminds me, are you two still happy to give evidence? It'll just be a few questions about that time you met him.'

'Of course,' I say straight away. 'Whatever you need.'

'Sure thing,' Cara replies. 'Just let me into that courtroom – I'll run that fucker over with my chair.'

Olivia laughs – something I never imagined her doing in relation to this topic. 'Thanks,' she says.

'How's your mum doing?' I ask, after taking a sip of my juice.

'She seems OK. I did find her crying in the bathroom the other day though. I suggested she find a therapist too and she seemed to be open to the idea, so that's good.'

'Whatever you do, don't go to family therapy,' Cara adds. 'I had to beg Mum to stop our sessions. I always felt like I was holding back and then she kept saying things I didn't even know she was feeling, and it was just weird.'

Olivia laughs. 'Too late. My social worker has already suggested it to Mother, and there's no chance of her going against official advice.'

'Uh-oh,' Cara says. 'Don't say I didn't warn you.'

'So, Mehreen, your turn. How are things?'

I fiddle with the pins on my scarf before answering. 'Yeah, things are . . . things are actually pretty good. I think the doctor finally got my medication right; I haven't had a panic attack in a while, my Chaos is under control. I'm starting to feel . . . Well, I was going to say normal, but I've realised that's not even a real concept.'

'Your new therapist working out for you?' Cara asks.

I nod. 'Yeah, I like her. I think it helps that she's Asian. We have the same frames of reference and she understands how horrible social gatherings can get.'

'Racist much?' Cara cracks. 'I totally understand how horrible social gatherings are.'

'That's only because you hate *everyone*,' Olivia laughs.

'Except us, of course,' I add. 'Cara loves us.'

'Not ashamed to admit it,' Cara says before downing the rest of her Coke. 'You guys are like my sisters. My suicide sisters.' She grins.

I see the woman at the next table in front raise her eyes and stare at us. There's a familiar tickle of fear in my chest.

'Keep it down,' I mutter light-heartedly, before smiling over at the woman. She smiles back before continuing her meal.

Cara's phone beeps and she groans dramatically. 'C'mon then, off we go,' she says. 'Mum's waiting to whisk me off for a session of "and how does that make you feel?"' She starts moving away from the table and out of the cafe. Olivia and I follow.

The sun blasts my skin as we walk out, filling me with warmth from head to toe. Olivia hooks her arm through mine again as we walk back up the slipway. 'So, next meeting?' I ask as we leave the beach behind us.

'My place on Friday?' Olivia asks. 'Maria's testing out a new treacle-tart recipe she's been raving about.'

'Tarts? I'm in,' Cara says.

I laugh. 'Me too.'

We hug and say our goodbyes. When they're both gone, I walk back down to the beach, carrying my sandals in my hand. I weave through the children and sunbathers right to the water's edge. I roll my leggings up to my ankles and step forward into the water, smiling at the freshness against my hot skin. The water rushes towards me and retreats. Teasing. Inviting. Begging. I stand in it and raise my face to the sky and say a little prayer of thanks to God.

Allah,
I never imagined I'd be standing here, feeling as content as I do right now. That's all down to you and the people you've brought into my life. I've realised that things will be hard. There will be many tests and hardships in life. But I've also learned that I can survive it. I have survived it, and I will continue to survive it. Thank you. Alhamdulillah for everything.

RESOURCES

If you are affected by any of the issues raised in this book, please consider reaching out to one of the organisations below.

Samaritans

Confidential emotional support for anyone in emotional distress, struggling to cope or at risk of suicide. Lines open 24/7.

Call free on 116 123 or visit www.samaritans.org

Childline

A private and confidential service for young people up to age 19. Counsellors available to talk about anything.

Call free on 0800 1111
or talk online at www.childline.org.uk

YoungMinds

Mental-health support for young people, including a free 24/7 crisis text-messaging service.

For urgent help, text 'YM' to 85258
or visit www.youngminds.org.uk

NSPCC

The UK's leading charity helping children who have experienced abuse, including sexual abuse.

www.nspcc.org.uk

The Survivors Trust

Offering support, advice and information to those affected by sexual abuse.

Free confidential helpline: 0808 801 0818
or visit www.thesurvivorstrust.org

Harmless

Resources and advice for those who self harm.

www.harmless.org.uk

Hope Again

Offers help to young bereaved people.

Call free on 0870 808 1677 or visit www.hopeagain.org.uk

ACKNOWLEDGEMENTS

All The Things We Never Said is a book that's been in my head in some shape or form for years. It took two master's degrees and a whole host of people to drag it out of my brain and onto the page. I feel so blessed to have such an amazing support group of my own.

My wonderful agent, Hellie Ogden. Thank you for your enthusiasm and encouragement. I still treasure the fan mail you sent me after we first met. Your belief in me is just the best thing (next to your adorable face).

Emma Matthewson – the kindest, most brilliant editor a writer could wish for. Thank you for being such a sweetheart and making the process so fun. Your passion and general kindness have warmed my cold, dead heart.

Big-up all the team at Hot Key Books, especially Talya Baker – everyone told me copy-edits would be the hardest part of the process, but your comments were an absolute delight. Thank you for all your help, and for putting up with my never-ending pestering! To Alexandra Allden for the beautiful cover, Clare Kelly, my wonderful publicist, Roisin O'Shea in marketing and Melissa Hyder for her eagle-eyed proofreading. Shout-out to everyone at Palimpsest for their patience with typesetting such an oddly formatted book.

Emily Walters – thank you for being my Mehreen, Cara and Olivia – I wish everyone could have a best friend like you (although I'm not willing to share). Thank you for not resenting me, even though I now owe you all the leaves in the world. Thank you for always being there – even when it's 4 a.m. and I just want to tell you that I'm feeling sad, and for always being proud of me, even if all I've done is managed to brush my hair. I don't know what life would be like without you.

To CJ Skuse, for being the best personal tutor evah and showing me that there *is* a place for darkness within YA lit. Thank you for giving me the confidence to be the kind of writer I want to be, and convincing me not to ditch this book halfway through. (Also, sorry for the five billion emails!)

Enrolling in the Bath Spa MA in Writing for Young People is one of the best decisions I ever made. Thanks to all my classmates for their insightful feedback - in particular Nizrana Farook for letting me bounce ideas off her and providing the calm, rational thoughts that I sorely lack. Thanks also to Rachel Huxley for letting me vent when necessary, and bringing me back from the brink on MANY occasions. Big-up to Hana Tooke for listening to me whine on a daily basis (even when I interrupt her naps), and recovering my manuscript when I somehow corrupted the document. Shout-out also to the Aubergines groupchat for always being a source of amusement and encouragement.

Aisha Bushby, for being the cutest bean. I cannot put into words what a joy you are to have in my life. I just want to smush your cheeks. Thank you for your constant support, encouragement and for being my biggest fan. I'm so thankful we were thrown together by the Changebook gods. It's been such a blessing to have you by my side. All the blue heart emojis.

Lucy Powrie, who is the best cheerleader, and always has cute guinea pig photos to hand. (Also the best Internet stalker I know.) It's been so wonderful sharing this journey with you. The UKYA scene is so lucky to have you (despite your love for classics – bleugh).

Enormous thanks to Megan Quibell, ambassador for Inclusive Minds, and Jane Martin for their insightful sensitivity reads. Your notes were invaluable and have made such a difference to the book. Cara and I tip our hats to you. Also thank you to Paul Curtis for his Paramedic Guy expertise. Any mistakes left within the text are entirely my own.

Shout-out to Juwairiyya and Sofia for their early reads and feedback, Lesley-Anne for just being adorable, Katya Balen for all the lols and jelly babies and Sarah Ann Juckes for being my twin and one of the few people who doesn't recoil at how dark my brain is.

And lastly to my family. I know most of you don't *get* this writer business, but thank you for celebrating my victories and letting me get on with it. I may never be able to verbalise it, but I truly appreciate all of your love and support. And since my nieces and nephews will get a thrill from seeing their names here, let me list them – Anjum, Falaq, Umayr, Zaiba, Zikra, Saira, Safiyyah, Idrees.

ABOUT THE AUTHOR

YASMIN RAHMAN is a British Muslim born and raised in Hertfordshire. ALL THE THINGS WE NEVER SAID is her first novel. As a child, she wanted to be a postwoman, but decided to settle for being an author. She has an MA in Creative Writing from the University of Hertfordshire and an MA in Writing for Young People from Bath Spa University, both with Distinction. Her short story 'Fortune Favours the Bold' was published in the Stripes anthology *A Change is Gonna Come* in 2017, with the *Bookseller* awarding the contributors a YA Book Prize Special Achievement Award 2018 for commitment to making YA publishing more inclusive. When she's not writing, Yasmin makes bookish fan art; her designs are sold worldwide on behalf of John Green.

HOT
KEY
BOOKS

Thank you for choosing a Hot Key book.

If you want to know more about our authors
and what we publish, you can find us online.

You can start at our website

www.hotkeybooks.com

And you can also find us on:

We hope to see you soon!